PENGUIN BOOKS

BLACK ROSE

Buddhadeva Bose (1908–74) was one of the most versatile Indian writers of the twentieth century, with an oeuvre spanning poetry, novels, short stories, plays, works for children, translations and literary criticism. He brought a unique, modern sensibility to Bengali literature, which identified him as the only possible successor to Rabindranath Tagore. Winner of the Sahitya Akademi award in 1967 and the Padma Bhushan in 1970, Bose has left behind a literary legacy that is being continuously rediscovered for its astonishing experiments with subject, form, voice and language.

Arunava Sinha translates classic, modern and contemporary Bengali fiction and non-fiction from Bangladesh and India into English. He also translates fiction from English into Bengali. Over ninety-five of his translations have been published so far in India, the UK and the USA. He teaches creative writing at Ashoka University, where he is also the co-director of the Ashoka Centre for Translation, and is the books editor at Scroll.in.

BUDDHADEVA BOSE

Black Rose

Translated from the Bengali
by Arunava Sinha

PENGUIN BOOKS
An imprint of Penguin Random House

PENGUIN BOOKS

Penguin Books is an imprint of the Penguin Random House group of companies whose addresses can be found at global.penguinrandomhouse.com

Published by Penguin Random House India Pvt. Ltd
4th Floor, Capital Tower 1, MG Road,
Gurugram 122 002, Haryana, India

First published as *Golap Keno Kalo* in Bengali by Ananda Publishers, Kolkata 1967
First published in English in Harper Perennial by HarperCollins Publishers India 2013
This edition published in Penguin Books by Penguin Random House India 2025

10 9 8 7 6 5 4 3 2 1

The publisher gratefully acknowledges permission to reproduce copyright material. Every effort has been made to trace and contact copyright holders. If there are any inadvertent omissions we apologize to those concerned and will undertake to include suitable acknowledgements in all future editions.

ISBN 9780143469889

Typeset in 11/14 Bodoni MT at SÜRYA
Printed at Gopsons Papers Pvt. Ltd., Noida

www.penguin.co.in

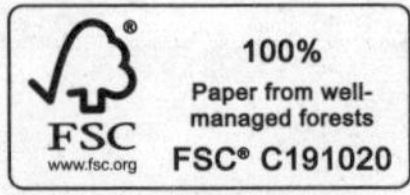

BLACK ROSE

One

Welcome. Did you take a tour of my garden? The roses haven't bloomed yet, it's barely May. I have seven shades of roses: two of yellow, two of pink, two of red, and one white, of course. Each of them grows to the size of my fist. The rose is my favourite flower. Do you know why? Because though it was imported, it's ours now. From Iran it spread across the world: the Mughals brought it to India. The original name, gulaab, is half Persian, half Sanskrit. You could call it a symbol of international union. I believe in internationalism.

Oh no, you're not disturbing me at all, I have nothing to do—take a seat, stay as long as you like. People often come to see this house, this garden of mine, it's a tourist attraction in Ootacamund now. Did you see the Japanese garden on that side? There's a winding lake, the cherry trees are budding, a few spells of rain and the blossoms will appear. Lots of people take a walk there at sunset. I don't stop anyone, how much can I take in alone with these two eyes of mine anyway? Beauty is for mass enjoyment, isn't it? And I still crave the appreciation of other people. But no matter what people say, there's nothing extraordinary about it, there are thousands of gardens like this in the world. I haven't been able to add an eighth colour to the seven, have I? You know, I had this fancy once—I wanted to create a rose of a different colour. Blue or purple or black—why not black, after all? I had lots of books sent to me from Japan, from Holland. I couldn't sleep for nights in excitement; trembling, as though I was about to get a key to a hidden chamber. Why are there no black flowers in the world? Flowers, fruits, grain—whatever springs from the earth is limited in colour to the seven shades of the rainbow, but why? White, which is a mixture of all colours, is still available as a colour for flowers, but black, where the colours have disappeared—why don't we see black flowers? Don't they exist, or is it just that we haven't found them yet? Wouldn't the first person to make a black rose bloom be considered greater than even God? What if it were me? Don't be afraid, I haven't gone mad, even while I dreamt of a blue rose I knew it wasn't to be. You could call it a game with myself, a way to pass the time, something interesting to do, that's all.

Excuse me for speaking in English with you. Yes, of course I'm Bengali. From Dacca, in fact. But I've been living outside Bengal for a long time, I haven't used the language in ages. I don't read Bengali books either. If I lapse into English now and then, assume it's for convenience, out of habit. As a matter of fact, I don't talk much these days. Don't have to, either, except once a week with my steward. I live by myself, don't go anywhere; I'm a widower, both my sons live abroad.

Pardon me? Oh, yes, the name of my house. Bonheur.

It's a French word, meaning joy, happiness. The name was chosen by Nellie—Nalini, my wife. We used to discuss the location of our final residence. At first we had decided to continue living in Malabar Hill, close to Nellie's father's house. He was the one who gave Nellie the house. At one point we were inclined towards the Riviera, but on a vacation to Ootacamund, Nellie fell in love with this place. The designs for the garden, the plans for the house—everything was hers. The house was built, it was named Bonheur. But within two years she wasted away to death, struck by a mysterious disease. She left me memories, her unlimited wealth, and her dowry. Her father was Gujarati, her mother, Kashmiri—she was what people call gorgeous. Her goodness was incomparable too. I was very fortunate to have a wife like her. Would you care for some tea? Nilgiri, or Darjeeling?

Tell me about Calcutta, about Bengal. They're very unhappy, very troubled there, aren't they? I read about it in the papers sometimes. But then, where do you find people living happily in India? Nobody knows just what they want, all they do is stir up trouble on any pretext: internal conflicts, hunger strikes at the drop of a hat, trains being burnt, riots, killing. On top of that, throw out English, bring back the Middle Ages, build a monolithic Hindi kingdom. What do you think? Will India be fragmented into many bits all over again? And then will some other superpower occupy our country again? And the British, whom we got rid of with so much fanfare, must be laughing themselves silly on the other side of the ocean. We're now using the same weapons we wielded against them, to attack and wound one another—one another, meaning ourselves. It's a joke, isn't it?

You know, I too had believed that all it would take to turn India into a heaven on earth was to drive out the British. I was reading for my MA in Dacca at the time. Oh, you too, really? When was that? But I was there at the same time! Do you know Bakshibazaar? The orphanage? What! I lived near the orphanage too. Very ordinary middle-class Bengali-Hindu family—born and brought up in it, but there are many things I hate about them: far too constricted, too poor, too claustrophobic. It isn't just economic poverty, their minds are like cesspools. When I read English literature, history, I wonder whether these extraordinary feats were really achieved by the same people who were nothing but plunderers in our country. Was it because they were a formidable nation, or because of some fatal flaw in ourselves? You know, I wanted to be 'like them'—independent, reckless, powerful. I wanted to free myself from the shackles of our family-bound lives, where even joys and sorrows are measured, where not even hope can extend very far. And I even found a way out—when I met Mitu Bardhan, when I became acquainted with Arthur Jones. Here's your tea.

Did you ever run into Arthur Jones? No? Many people in Dacca knew him. The fellow was a fresh ICS officer. Spoke Bengali, mingled with Bengalis, took part in debates at the university, even visited locals at their homes. A music lover. I met him at Mitu Bardhan's house. Have you heard of her? That's remarkable, that you still possess Amita Bardhan's records. Very well, let me tell you something, I've been all over the world, clinging to all these old memories means nothing at all. Just like gout, just like leprosy, just like paralysis, memory is also an illness; it debilitates. Take India—we are still basking in the glory of the Upanishads, of Kalidasa, of Tansen. But after that? Aren't all our achievements thanks to the British?

Do excuse me for not joining you with a cup of tea, I'm having gin. A little for you . . .? All right, to each his own, can't argue with that. It's the same with women—pardon me, I meant wives. Oh, the prohibition—alcohol isn't a blue rose, after all, it's not beyond reach when you want it. And if breaking the law is illegal, following it is illegal too. That is my opinion as a legal expert. We picketed schools and colleges once upon a time, set post-offices on fire, now we block trains whenever we like: each of these amounts to interfering with people's independence, depriving them of their rights. Alcohol is a minor issue in comparison, minor and harmless—peaceful, private, personal—no one is being harmed, no one else cares. You're on your way to take your BA exams, I don't let you go; you're taking a train to see a dying relative for the last time, I gather a mob and block the train; whereas here, without coming between you and your wishes or your movement, I get a little pleasure out of having a drink in my own home . . . Can there be any doubt about which of these is illegal and which isn't? Whether it's alcohol or acrostics or kissing in films—all these cases will eventually be thrown out by the high court. Pardon me? Oh, I was in a government job. Seasoned criminal: an ICS from the British era. Ranajit Dutta, ICS, Barrister-at-Law. Currently retired, settled here . . . Well then . . . Cheers! Is your tea all right?

I had never met a real live Englishman before Arthur Jones. Of course, I'd never seen a dead Englishman either—although they were dying left, right and centre from terrorists' bullets. To me, Englishmen were people I'd read about in books, seen in films. And, sometimes, figures I had seen dimly in Calcutta. The Chowringhee-Park Street area, a mere slice of an enormous metropolis, an illuminated island replete with pleasures, indulgences, wealth; beyond our reach. Tall, hearty men with flaming red necks, dolled-up women on their arm: unfamiliar, distant, majestic. Like different creatures, not human beings but something else, as though they didn't breathe the same air as the rest of us. This on the one hand, and on the other, the books I read which said just the opposite. I was young, unable to reconcile the two. In my head I had created an incredibly fine and talented England, whose flag was not the Union Jack but Shakespeare. Whose ships didn't take away tea, jute, cotton and gold from India, but delivered Shelley's poetry and Dickens's novels to every port. Shelley was a vegetarian, Keats was only five feet tall, but how glorious they both were to look at, and how much pain their poetry held. They felt so very much a part of my life, was it even possible that they were Englishmen too? The same nationality as those people who strutted around on Chowringhee as though even the stars in their sky bent to their wills? Whose Firpo's restaurant didn't let in anyone wearing a dhoti? The mere sight of whom in the tea gardens of Assam meant that the babus (perhaps my own uncles) had to get off their cycles? I felt the urge to explain to those bovine idiots, the tea and jute bosses that I knew their country far better than they did, since I had occasional conversations with Shelley and Keats . . . Conversations? Well, maybe not, there are no exchanges, it's all one-way. An idea, an ideal, in other words, a toy I've made for myself. Shelley and Keats, perhaps as dim, as unreal, as the John Bulls on Chowringhee. But it was only after meeting Arthur Jones that I realized that Englishmen are human beings too, just like us.

I see you find this amusing. When were you born? What a coincidence, that's *my* year of birth too. Don't you remember what it was like back then? Have you forgotten it all? Let me tell you, when I was growing up, the British lion hadn't become toothless yet. And also take into account the atmosphere at home, everyone a government servant, low or middle-level—my father, his brothers, other members of the family—almost everyone. That was their Holy Grail, the objective, beginning and outcome of their lives: a government job. No retrenchment, annual increments, a pension after retirement, and what a pleasure to work under the British! They carefully avoided any other kind of job or business or profession that had the slightest degree of uncertainty attached to it, that needed a little extra intelligence or initiative—loathsome! It makes my stomach turn. I've seen many of the women in my family get married; I've been present at the 'display of the prospective bride' on several occasions. Caste, sect, genealogy and horoscope; so much in cash and so much in gold; pedigrees and mongrels; this village or that; are the Ghoshes of Varakar higher or lower in standing than the Mitras . . . I had no choice but to listen to all this as a child. Even my elder sister, with an IA degree, a talented student of Eden College, had to appear in near-bridal finery before a group of unknown men and women, my mother laid out plate after plate after plate heaped with food for them, my father behaved in the most obsequious manner possible. Execrable!

I had a personal problem too. Ever since I had passed my BA exams, everyone kept telling me 'take the ICS, take the ICS'. Since scoring high marks in exams was one of my shortcomings, there was nothing else my family could talk of. Imagine, some of them were scribes, some postmasters, some clerks; apparently, the mere thought that one of their own could become the administrator for an entire district—that he might even become a high court judge some day—gave them 'the strength of an elephant', made them feel like they could 'conquer mountains and rivers and seas.' As though the job were a stairway to heaven, where the last rung wasn't even visible to them. I put on an all-right-since-everybody-insists air, although I knew perfectly well that the two things I would never go in for were a government job and an arranged marriage. What happened, then? Fate, I tell you, fate; man proposes, someone somewhere disposes.

When did you watch a film for the first time? What a pity you don't remember, I do. I was very young then, the war with the Germans was on, the First World War. There was a free show at Coronation Park. First some random images of cannons, tanks and warships, Marshal Fosse, Lord Kitchener's moustache . . . and then, suddenly, those horrifying scenes. Children being tossed in the air and impaled on bayonets, young girls in chains being whipped—all the Germans' doings, of course. I trembled in fear, but still couldn't think of Germans as ogres, because I'd seen at home that the grown-ups couldn't stop smiling whenever there was talk of the Germans. They were ready to throw parties when the Emden kept sinking British warships. 'They'll go to hell now.' 'The British won't know what hit them.' 'No more fun and games, my friend.' But they said all this in whispers, leaning back on their bolsters on their bedsteads. But out in the streets? In broad daylight, in the open, if they so much as caught a glimpse, even from a distance, of an Englishman or an equivalent Indian, or a person of fair skin or in a high government post, their spines bent, their faces paled, they forgot where they were going and dashed into the nearest lane. When the war raged, when every family cursed the British, even then I saw in many houses photographs of Government House in Delhi, of King George V of England, sceptre in hand, surrounded by his wife and a gaggle of children. My grandmother's prayer-room had a picture of Queen Victoria too. You're laughing? I'm not making it up, believe me. Among the images of Radha and Krishna entwined with an Om, of Shiva with a snake round his neck, of Ramakrishna Paramahansa, of Chaitanya Mahaprabhu, of Lakshmi, was a photograph in 'three-colour half-tone' of that fat, dead woman who reigned over a distant cold island, who had been referred to by a Frenchman as 'the old hag with the yellow teeth'. In my grandmother's opinion, the days of the empress were the golden age, the ideal world. During the Non-Cooperation Movement I had managed to get rid of the photo of Government House in Delhi, but my grandmother clung to the empress affectionately—'Oh, please don't take her away, she is a goddess come to earth!' However, to satisfy both public opinion and me, she added a photograph of Gandhi next to that of Victoria. She was happy if her pantheon gained more gods, but she was unwilling to lose a single one.

Let me tell you an amusing story. I saluted the governor once. It was in Dacca, on Nababpur Road. I was in primary school. The governor was visiting Dacca. After getting off the steamer at Sadarghat, he was on his way to Government House in Ramna; I stood among the crowd of people gathered by the road. Escorted by a convoy of thick-whiskered Pathan soldiers on horseback and white sergeants on motorcycles, an enormous black car approached. A ruddy face in profile, sharp nose, puffy cheeks, a grey moustache—a face no different from hundreds of other nondescript faces—flashed past me. Amidst that crowd, under that sun, a momentary glimpse of that profile blinded me as it were. As the car passed, I suddenly stood to attention and saluted. Why did I? No one else did, no one had told me to; it came to me spontaneously. Back home, I told my parents jubilantly what I had done, they merely laughed.

Pardon me? Yes, I know what you mean when you say it was just childishness; it didn't prove anything, wasn't even worth considering. But you know, when I started frequenting Mitu Bardhan's house—where I met one or two other significant people too—when I started thinking about things afresh, started seeing things differently from the way I had earlier, this insignificant event came back to me. At times I felt our lives were nothing but one humiliation after another. We swallowed humiliation with our food, sipped humiliation with our drinks. Had I saluted the governor because I was an innocent child? Or was I particularly evil, a sinner, which made such base behaviour possible? Or did we all—young and old, educated and uneducated—offer salutes forever, in our heads if not with our hands? Why else was *Kim* one of the textbooks in our university curriculum—written by Kipling, to whom Bengalis were 'bunderlog' and all that you could find between Peshawar and Rangoon were animals, their keepers and British Tommies. Many such thoughts assailed me at the time—I felt pain, for more than one reason I felt pain. At times I even felt that those who assassinated Englishmen were avenging this humiliation. A fitting revenge. You can't have forgotten all the things happening in the country at the time. First in Chittagong, then in Dacca itself: at Mitford Hospital, then in the heart of Calcutta, at Writers' Building. Tell me, for those people whose hearts can only flutter, can do nothing but flutter, isn't it natural for war-drums to start beating in their breasts when they see one of those formidable Englishmen slump to the ground—not in battle with the Germans, but from a bullet fired by a mere Bengali?

Two

What do you think of Ootacamund? Isn't it beautiful? So green and sprawling. These are the reasons Nellie liked it so much; as did I. Or maybe Nellie came to like it because I did. I don't care for Darjeeling: it's too claustrophobic. The mountains are so close at hand, they look like they'll smother you, and that Kanchenjunga of yours is like a sleepless chief justice . . . I've been a judge myself for twenty years, you see. I know how a criminal feels in the presence of the judge. But Ootacamund isn't claustrophobic, you can breathe . . . just like England. But the countryside is being destroyed there as well . . . When were you there last? Oh, all right, you haven't been. But yes, it's just as you've heard, just as you've read. To some extent, at least. At first glance it looks like a scene from a Wordsworth poem: lambs grazing on the green hillsides, daffodils blooming too. But where will you find such sunshine in England? Just look outside, such a glare that you feel warm if you take a walk in the afternoon, but it is so cool as soon as you come indoors. It's the same weather all year round, neither hot nor cold. No torrential downpours either, never gets too sultry. The ideal climate in my opinion. I fear the heat like the devil, the cold is intolerable too. It's the cold that scared me off the thought of living in England. Besides, whatever other faults we may have in this country, servants and maids are always available. How do you live without them?

You must have noticed that the town is like a blend of East and West. Flowers from different countries, fruits too. Like Goethe writing *Shakuntala*, or Schopenhauer, the Upanishads. Bananas and strawberries together. Gooseberries and apples. Can you imagine, banana trees at an altitude of 7,000 feet? Besides, there are other advantages too. With no factories anywhere, there's no polluting smoke, no processions of striking workers. Since there aren't many merchant offices either, there aren't too many petty clerks. No Tibet or Pakistan nearby to attract refugees in droves. A handful of English families have bought houses and stayed on, a few rich people from Madras, Mysore or Bangalore come and go. It is a quiet, civilized place. Yes, I know they have an anti-Brahmin movement in Madras. But then, this world's no heaven. Besides, what do I care? Let Bengalis be hounded out of Assam, let the Punjab be split, let them purge Sanskrit words from Tamil, let them allow people to starve to death so that they can save monkeys, rats, cows and other ancestors of ours—what difference does it make to me? I'm fine. I'm happy. From my veranda it doesn't feel as though India is bursting at the seams with people. It doesn't seem that China is lurking north of the Himalayas. I cannot even recollect the turmoil over Kashmir and NEFA. I no longer remember the headlines from Delhi or the hullabaloo in Calcutta. If you leave out a few redundant things such as the radio and newspapers, it doesn't even feel as though I'm in India. And let's say the Chinese do invade India, it's going to take them some time to get to the distant south, won't it? By then I may not remain in India, or even in the world. Isn't this place a wise choice?

Must you leave now? Do stay a while. Stay as long as you like. You're on holiday, surely you're not in a hurry. I have nothing important to do, I never do. I don't go anywhere, don't do anything. I spend my time by myself. If you like the veranda, why don't you turn your chair a little? The view in that direction is quite nice. Rolling greens, blue hills in the distance, the sun, the light, the sky—the glass windows block out the sound of the trees, the sound of the wind—the world appears filled with nothing but peace and brightness. And the flowers in my garden—they grin like idiots too, they're delighted just to have been born, they have no complaints. Do you know what I wish I could do sometimes? I wish I could go into the garden with a stick, destroy the garden with blows from it, uproot the plants, stamp the flowers out of existence beneath my feet. What an interesting game that would be, wouldn't it?

Tell me, do you think India really will split—is splitting already—that in another fifty years we will once again be converted to Andhra-Bengal-Gujarat-Karnataka? Why do you say that's impossible? After all, what we had always thought of as India no longer exists, two distinct parts become another nation—what had seemed impossible became reality, so what prevents more of the same? Nothing at all, besides an idea named India. What people refer to as a 'country' is in fact nothing but an idea, a mystery, the imagination of poets; what might be termed a certain mystique, which survives only on people's faith. Take that tiny little place Great Britain, there too people have had to assume, have had to believe, that England, Scotland and Wales actually make up one country. Just like Tagore and others also led us to believe that this 'seashore of the superman' is named India. Of course, that was backed by the power of the English, their warships, their armament. Not only that, the British had also believed in the imaginary concept of the 'British Empire' at one time—how else could India and Burma and Ceylon have been thought of collectively as a single state? The day they stopped believing this was the day their downfall began. As for them, good riddance to bad rubbish; but what I wonder is, hasn't the idea on whose base the Union Jack flew, on which Tagore wrote his poem, also faded from our minds?

No, I was never part of the swadeshi brigade. Despite spending my entire childhood in Dacca, I never joined any of the leaders of the freedom movement, nor did I become a disciple of Mahatma Gandhi and switch to homespun clothes. I wanted to be self-reliant, to achieve something on my own, to do something significant. I wanted to be known for who I was, not for being part of a particular group, or for occupying a particular position. But how? What would I have to do to get there? What did I want to do in life? Sometimes I thought of becoming well known as a writer, sometimes I thought of getting a job of some kind on a ship and setting out to sea—to see the world, to know the world. I'd read Conrad—sometimes, in my bed before going to sleep, I could smell distant ports. All childish fancies, of course. In my heart, waves of hope alternated with the certainty that I would achieve nothing, that I would be good for nothing.

You can't have forgotten the state of the country at the time, can you? The waves of economic recession around the world had washed up on these distant shores too; there was panic and despair everywhere over retrenchment and unemployment. The occasional Hindu-Muslim riots in Dacca, and on top of that the Salt March, shootings and détenus. Jobs and girls—these were the principal topics of conversation among young men of my age. Like ants they lapped up every crumb of information about girls from their class, girls from their neighbourhood—all those maidens whom they could at least cast their eyes upon. The best students became restive at the smell of a teacher's post with a monthly salary of seventy-five rupees. Some of them wrote reams and reams of poetry addressed to the sixteen-year-old object of their affections. Some wished they could become détenus so that they got their monthly allowance! Some dressed up on Sunday evenings to visit the Brahmo Samaj and meditate on the formless Brahma with their eyes shut, all the while peeping beneath their lashes at the 'sisters' gathered there and listening in rapt wonder with tilted heads at the sacred music emanating, in female voices, from behind the red room-dividers. Some, although close to twenty-one, had their haircuts on dates specified by their fathers and returned home before the sun set. Yet others took on the responsibility of protecting the morality of their peers, thrashing anyone they suspected of trying to consort with young women.

I beg your pardon . . . did you say something? Yes, of course there was more to life—plenty of pleasures too. There is never a lack of pleasures at that age, is there? It's only in those few years that we enjoy the compassion of nature. It's just those few years when the world seems a friend, when the idiot seems talented, when the fraud seems a saint. You can see, can't you, what an illusion pleasure weaves. But yes, only temporarily. You're right, everything in life is temporary. A succession of moments, like fireflies, an incoherent exhausting play, where one scene has no bearing on the next. Or is there one we cannot grasp? Have you ever read Bergson? *Matter and Memory*? There you are, that's where I beg to differ from you. I don't collect the trash from the past; I agree with Henry Ford: 'History is bunk'.

Oh yes, there were good things too. Conversations at tea shops, unwarranted laughter, wandering around the riverside, munching peanuts on the grass, candyfloss. And Valentino, Wilma Banke, Pola Negri—Hollywood's temptresses: images, nothing but images. But sometimes I wished for another world. A wide, generous, liberal world where prospective brides would no longer have to be put on display, where arranged marriages and dowry would not exist, where young men wouldn't discuss their female classmates' appearances with greasy words, where young couples could walk hand-in-hand on the banks of this same river. A lot of other things would change:

nobody would consult astrologers or seek some kind of miraculous intervention from holy men or pursue jobs desperately. Some of us would go off on expeditions to the Sahara, some of us would discover gold mines, some would become millionaire mushroom farmers, some would pilot a plane solo from Calcutta to Tokyo—women as well as men. I used to think there was some magic, an undiscovered formula of chemistry—I was the one who would come up with it, I was the one who would light up people's lives. As you can see, I was unhappy, the unhappiness that is the luxury of youth, agonizing because I thought I was capable of much more, but I couldn't grow, there wasn't enough light, enough air. But even in that humdrum existence, variety appeared in the form of Fotik-mama's return from England after five years. And as soon as she heard, my mother had Kajol move into our house. Kajol-mami was Fotik-mama's wife.

My mother had lost her mother before she was married; her only brother Fotik was about five at the time. After his daughter's marriage, her father—the village postmaster—obtained a second wife for himself. As soon as she had settled down in her new household, my mother brought her brother over to live with her. He was fifteen years younger, motherless, a turbulent teenager, an expert at wrestling and bodybuilding and swimming and snake-trapping, but not particularly interested in studies—my mother loved him to distraction, much more than usual for a Bengali woman, by virtue of his being motherless. Fotik-mama ensured nobody could accuse Bengali young men of not being strong or healthy, several prizes at the college sports were practically reserved for him, but he couldn't get through his BSc exams despite two attempts. Instead of trying a third time, he suddenly went off to England. Not all that suddenly, actually, it was he who made up his mind about going. My mother busied herself in trying to meet this demand. She couldn't afford it, of course, but there *was* another way. The tried-and-tested strategy: the father-in-law's money. My mother and grandfather were unanimous on this point: he could go if he wanted to, but he must get married beforehand, or else he'd probably bring back some brazen foreign woman. Money begets money, peace begets peace. My father objected mildly—'Let him graduate here, after that . . .' But he was a gentle soul and my mother shut him up with a few choice words. 'Wait and see, when he comes back from England, he'll come back a real man.' England! Just think of the magical power of that word. The embers of India would apparently burst into flames as soon as they were exposed to England's air. And marriage, the ultimate pill! The wife no one he knows, lives six thousand miles away, but her attraction for him will apparently keep the husband on the straight and narrow. Hats off to Mother India!

After two months of effort, a suitable father-in-law was obtained for Fotik. He ran a lorry-transportation business in Jalpaiguri, owned shares in tea-estates; in short he was loaded. And his daughter? After a detailed discussion about her features, the length of her hair, her bone structure, her complexion—somewhat dark or rather dark?—the women's conference of our family announced that she was acceptable. Her father spent money unstintingly—apparently it was a small price to pay for snagging a high-caste son-in-law like Fotik-mama. A month after his wedding, Fotik-mama boarded the ship from Bombay and the newly wed bride went back to her parents' house in Jalpaiguri.

He was supposed to have been gone two years, to study in some polytechnic or the other in Glasgow, but he was there for five years, I don't know exactly what he did there. Once we heard he had got a job in Germany, another time it was America. Balancing the sheets on her knees, my mother wrote four-page-long letters sometimes, but the replies came much later, in the form of one or two lines: Don't worry, I am well. I'll come back as soon as I can.' There was a long separation, a long period of waiting, and when he did return, the scene of his reunion with my mother was truly heart-rending.

My mother held her brother to her breast, tears rolling down her cheeks, my uncle sobbed too, kissing his sister on the cheeks, putting his head on her shoulder. (I was a little surprised to see a strong, able-bodied young man sobbing in that fashion, but I learnt later that these were not just tears of joy, there was another reason.) After his exchanges with his sister had ended, he glanced at the rest of us. He greeted my father; 'Ranju, how tall you've grown, let me see how strong you are,' he said, squeezing my biceps so hard that an 'ouch!' escaped my lips; 'Minu, you're a proper lady now!' he exclaimed, picking her up by the waist and hoisting her into the air. 'Fotik hasn't changed at all,' said my mother with a broad smile. Suddenly he said, 'Who's this girl, didi?' My sister went into peals of laughter. Blushing, Kajol-mami suddenly bowed her head, and my mother said, 'Really! That's

Kajol, your wife. Go on now, Fotik, take a nap—Kajol, will you see if he needs anything? What do you want for dinner, Fotik? Something special?' 'Anything, didi, whatever you make, I came back only so I could eat your meals.' 'See how greedy he is.' My mother smiled at Kajol. 'You'll have to start cooking now.' She made the bed for the two of them with noticeable ceremony, but mama spent half the night on ma's bed chatting with her.

Fotik-mama's homecoming became rather an event. My grandfather arrived, my sister and brother-in-law turned up from Mymensingh, there was a crowd of relatives, and Minu went around telling everyone that mama 'looked exactly like an Englishman, his suitcase gave off a British smell whenever you opened it'. I was quite excited by his arrival too, for he was the only one in my circle of relatives who had broken through the barrier of government service, he was the only one who had experienced what might be called an adventure—he had even been to America, and now he was saying he wouldn't take a job but go into business instead. I asked him in minute detail about whether he'd been to Paris, to Venice, which Shakespearean plays he had seen while in England, but I wasn't satisfied with the answers he provided: 'Yes, there are many theatres in London', 'Paris really is very beautiful', 'It was raining heavily in Rome!' and similar responses. They were nothing like the kind of things I wanted to hear, wanted to know. When I heard that he had lived in Frankfurt, I couldn't help asking, 'Then you must have seen Goethe's house?' Immediately, my mother said, 'Never mind all that about your books, Ranju, Fotik's an engineer, what does he know about them!' Engineer! As soon as I heard the word, other seeds sprouted in my brain; I placed mama in that class of people which ran trains underground and spanned the opposite banks of wide rivers with bridges, whose expertise had apparently even brought speech into films. I felt inadequate at being so ignorant about all this, the fact I wasn't even fit enough to ask him anything. After spending a month or so with us, Fotik-mama went off to Calcutta because his business venture required him to live there; I assumed it had something to do with setting up bridges across rivers. He came to Dacca sometimes for a few days, then went back again. About a year passed this way. 'Take Kajol with you this time, Fotik,' this plea of my mother's was met with, 'It's not convenient yet, didi, these are hard times, let's wait a little longer.' When my father expressed his anxiety at Fotik's inability to make much headway in a country where doors opened automatically to people who had been to England, my mother reassured him smilingly, 'Don't worry. Don't you remember what Trigunananda had said after reading his palm? Fotik will earn pots of money.'

My parents considered me a child, I had no right to say anything concerning family matters, and I didn't want to either, but I felt an unexpressed dissatisfaction growing within me as Fotik-mama refused to take Kajol-mami back with him each time he came. I used to picture in my mind the couple's neat, tranquil household in Calcutta. I had identified a small pink one-storeyed house on Heysham Road in Bhowanipur for them, I had seen the house in the morning sun while passing by, a To-Let sign hanging from the door. I'd felt that the people who came to live in that house would be very happy. I had wanted to see a happy couple in it, older than me but not old. I would visit them from time to time, join in their happiness, and perhaps get a glimpse of the mysteries of conjugal life. After Fotik-mama's return, I wove just such a tale around him and Kajol-mami. But I could see no inclination on mama's part to fulfil this natural and extremely logical expectation of mine; why, I had no idea. I felt my mother should have insisted more strongly, but I could see why she did not. She felt that insisting might make him think she didn't want to bear the burden of supporting his wife any more. Besides, she had to ensure Kajol was 'suitably prepared' for her husband. My mother had taken on that responsibility, because in her opinion Kajol's father had money but no 'class', with dozens of children his household was in a 'mess'— 'Can't you see he hasn't even bothered to get his daughter to pass her matric exams—couldn't he have used this five-year period to "prepare" his daughter by having her study at a convent school in Kurseong?' No, these things never even occurred to him. So my mother closed in on Kajol like a sympathetic critic; buying her pastel-shade saris as dictated by current fashion, explaining what kind of jewellery to wear with each, doing her hair in new ways every day, teaching her to cook, getting her to arrange her things neatly in her room, taking her out to call on people or to watch plays at our university. She tried to make Kajol sparkle in the way she spoke and conducted herself, even accusing me of not trying to teach her English, or at the very least some conversation skills. But Kajol didn't seem interested in any of this, wasn't able to concentrate on any of this, five years of indolence in her own home seemed to have snapped her connection with reality. With no activities besides eating and sleeping, she had become fatter, possibly lost her sharpness. Her expression was drowsy, as though she'd just woken up; her smile couldn't go beyond her lips to include the rest of her face; her large eyes were as still as a pond. She walked slowly, she talked slowly. She did everything my mother asked her to do: dressed up, went out, did the housework, but she could never shake off that unfocussed, drowsy, detached demeanour. One day my mother got to know Kajol wasn't keeping well; she had headaches, couldn't sleep at night. Worried, she summoned the doctor.

Three

I hope you don't mind, but I'm going to take another gin. What about you? Not this time either? A drop of Cinzano? Oh, it's not all that late in the morning – it's barely twelve. And so what if it is? There's nothing to do anyway. You're here on holiday, and I . . . I don't do anything, don't go anywhere, live by myself. But why do you have to get back to the hotel? I know, why don't you have lunch with me? Please? No, it's no problem at all. I have every convenience: a dozen servants for just the one person, this house, the garden, the roses, the German Shepherds. And Nellie's estate . . . You'll stay for lunch then? Thanks. Thanks a lot. I really will be glad to have your company. You were in Dacca, you're my age, your responses reveal that you are a connoisseur of the good things of life, you're compassionate too. Let's chat. Relax, make yourself comfortable. Let me draw the curtains a little, the sun's getting quite strong. All right, let me offer you something else—try it, just a sip. If you don't like it, let it be. Anise—it's an aniseed liqueur. Oh, I have people to supply these things to me. There's something else I need too, every night. I'm afraid at night, you know. I have a pair of German Shepherds as pets: they look like tigers and roar like lions. They're locked in their cages all day in darkness, they eat one meal a day and I let them loose at night. No thief or robber or murderer dares target me. Still, dogs are animals after all, and their world and mine aren't the same. I feel lonely at night, you know, very lonely. I need a human being then, a companion—a female companion. To sleep with my head on her shoulder, to sleep with my face on her breasts. A warm body rising and falling as she breathes, alive, her touch dispelling my fears. Fortunately, there are women in this world. Fortunately, not all of them are lumps of inhibition . . . You seem startled. It's not all that serious, I don't force anyone. They come willingly, go back with their purses full of money. Clean transactions, no complications. Just like we spend money on medicine when we fall ill, something like that . . . Some people need sleeping pills every night—this is my version. I can't do without it. I see you're surprised, I see you're wondering, at this age . . . I can see you haven't overcome all your old inhibitions either. Abstinence is all very well in youth, life swarms so strongly over you that missing a turn here or there makes no difference; but when the sun is on the decline, when the long, very long nights weigh down on you like rocks, how do you breathe, tell me, without a body by your side—offering life, offering a touch, offering the tenderness of a living human being? Besides, it's a long-standing habit—why should I give it up suddenly either? Many habits desert us on their own, but are there any as faithful as the ones that stay with us loyally till the end, ignoring the dying state of our bodies?

Oh, don't make me laugh—a second marriage! Look, let me tell you something clearly. I think this is best, this relationship based on cash, there are no repercussions, no commitments to be carried through. If our life is indeed a succession of moments, a row of fireflies, incoherent and meaningless, does it make any sense using our todays to paint our tomorrows in colourful hues, or in black ones, for that matter? Ah, I see you disagree. Are you an idealist? A romantic? But tell me, isn't what we call a conjugal relationship also based on money? Let your money be mine, let my body be yours: this is the real mantra of marriage. They stand on this bedrock—our domestic goddesses, harbingers of fortune. Sometimes there are variations too: let your money be mine, let my money be mine. As in my case. Do you suppose I could have come within the vicinity of Ratandas Dalal's daughter had I not been an ICS officer? He was a big businessman, everyone in Bombay knew of him. Yes, of course I fell in love. But then it was possible to fall in love with Nalini Dalal of Malabar Hill. I had mentally constructed an idea of what people refer to as love. I succeeded in convincing her too that she had fallen in love with me within only a few days of being acquainted with each other. Is there anything we cannot do if we really want to? Our wants, our brains, potent weapons, all. Since marriage was inevitable, why not marry Nellie? I could see she was beautiful, had a gentle temperament, she couldn't be completely devoid of good qualities. At least my home would be prettified, I would look well-dressed at parties. And then there was Ratandas's money. Where would I find anything better? How many heiresses *were* there in the country anyway?

Nevertheless, I had no time for elaborate courtship, I would have to start work very soon. Very exhausting, this courtship business: visit here, go out there, twinkling smiles, small talk, get up, sit straight, eat peanuts off the bowl in your lap without chewing noisily—all pretence, a waste of time. She was the bird in the hand, to grab while I could. And as soon as I decided to marry her, the gentle breeze of romance began to waft into my heart. Nellie was easy prey.

But there was one area where I'd miscalculated. The more days that passed after our wedding, the more I realized Nellie really did love me. She developed this air of 'you're my element, you're my world'. I found it funny, then a faint irritation grew within me like a persistent itch. Anything I said enraptured her, she agreed with me on everything, she did the house up to please me; to make me happy, she did herself up, got the cook to make new dishes every day. And even with her looks and her riches, she appeared naïve, hapless, helpless—she wanted to entwine herself around me, as though she wouldn't survive a day without me.

People have such strange quirks. Take Nellie—she'd been to school in Switzerland, met thousands of people since her childhood, not a single one of Bombay's crème de la crème was omitted from the guest list of her father's parties, she was up-to-date on the latest fashion trends and could speak several languages, but her mind, her thinking was still at the level of a child's. She was as naïve as a village girl; because she didn't know much, she believed everything easily. I learnt later that many of our wealthy families are this way, the more ostentatious they appear, the more old-fashioned they are. Ratandas's

Malabar Hill house had an automatic lift, telephones in every room, but his daughter had been brought up without any exposure to modern thinking. When I heard that although Nellie knew French she had never read a story of Maupassant's, never leafed through the books of Anatole France, I was a little surprised at first. But then I realized she had never developed the habit of travelling around the world of books. She still remembered lines from Lamartine's poems read in school and she had not forgotten Daudet's stories, but she didn't know that these were merely introductions, only the first steps on a vast, rich continent; possibly no one at that Roman Catholic school set up for rich men's daughters had ever told her either. Nor anyone at home. We lived in a small town and Nellie had oodles of time in hand, which she spent tinkling on the piano, drawing with pastels, and leafing through a plethora of women's magazines. She had fashion, housekeeping and gardening magazines and recipe books sent to her from London, from Paris, from New York. She had been taught by her mother that this was the ideal life for a happy, wealthy, married woman. On the one hand was this glitter of fashion: extensive bathroom equipment, innumerable pots and tins on the dressing table; on the other was her naïveté, which could almost be called a lack of education, a blind faith in me by virtue of being her husband—as though she really had given up her entire heart to me, clinging to me with all her faint but turbulent childish willpower. Her love made me feel claustrophobic. I recalled my days in Dacca, where, in case I was late returning home, my mother would wait for me by the window with a lantern without having eaten, my grandmother would get out of bed and pray near the door, my father wouldn't sleep either. And it wasn't just for me—this extreme concern was also on display for both my sisters, my brother-in-law, Fotik-mama and Kajol-mami. My mother seemed to have stretched out a thousand arms in a thousand different directions to protect all of us; more than from illness, old age or poverty, she seemed to feel pain from the absence of a loved one—the pain that was, by the natural rule of existence, more inevitable than illness, less curable than poverty. Ever since then I had been a rebel against love, but how could I make Nellie understand that? Not that this meant I had never wanted to love. I had, but I couldn't. Hence my rebellion.

It's not what you think, I didn't fall in love with Kajol. Or perhaps I did. At some point, on some day, on some night—but that was a meteor flung out of another burning mass of love. Or maybe I paid back to her my debt to another? I cannot say for sure. I'm no longer the person I was thirty-five years ago, so how can I tell? Assume that the 'I' I'm talking about is not really me, but someone else—a young man, born in the same year as you, who lived in the same city, in the same neighbourhood, at the same time. But I can see there's a great deal that you don't remember—should I remind you? You've seen Kajol, haven't you? Her lovely lips, through which not many words passed; her large eyes, where beneath the lifeless surface lay water and fire, don't you remember all this either? How silly of me to make such a mistake, for a moment I felt you knew everything, you'd seen everyone, that you only wanted to hear it all from me once more. No, what my mother was elated about had not happened: Fotik-mama had not left a baby in Kajol's womb as a symbol of his love for his wife, the doctor's diagnosis was nervous tension. He prescribed several medicines, but both my parents were believers in homoeopathy, they considered allopathic medicine too strong: it ended up doing more harm than good, or simply caused a new disease while curing the old one, and was very expensive too. After much discussion they called Anadi Bardhan for a visit. Anadi Bardhan was some kind of cousin of my father's—at least, that's what I'd been told. They had apparently known each other in the village they lived in as children. When it came to unravelling the mysteries of family connections, you could call my father Einstein junior; he could frequently tell from a stranger's name and a smattering of their background that they were so-and-so's cousin's husband's younger brother, or so-and-so's father's brother-in-law's niece. Where these things were concerned, his memory was as sharp as his enthusiasm was boundless; he never forgot a name, or that Mr A's son had married Mr B's daughter, or where different people lived, what they did for a living, how many children they had, what their grandfather had died of . . . His brain was an enormous storehouse of such information. And yet I'd heard he had failed in history on the first attempt in his entrance exams, barely scraping through the second time. He even felt a slight tenderness towards people he had never even seen, or only seen without talking to them, or had talked to at most for five minutes at some wedding or other, simply because they were slightly, distantly, vaguely related to him.

But there were at least four or five degrees of separation between him and Anadi Bardhan, besides other differences. Anadi-babu was not a government employee like my father, he was a renowned doctor, the only homoeopath in Dacca with an MB degree, a very busy man. A demonstration of his abilities lay in his horse-drawn yellow-and-green carriage—drawn by just a single horse, but a sprightly thoroughbred, not listless like the creatures that drew the city's carriages for hire. The yellow-and-green carriage behind the enormous black horse did elicit some respect, but my father said, 'Anadi should be driving around in a four-horse brougham—see what a downturn in fortunes can do to you! Imagine a member of the biggest family of Oleganj forced into being a homoeopath!' He had been witness to their lifestyle when he was a child; it was extremely lavish, apparently. On Mitu's birthday, all the wives of the married ones among the twenty-one sons of the eleven wives of the seven sons of Gupi Bardhan were invited. By then, Fotik-mama had also arrived in response to my mother's pleading letter—this visit was after a gap of five months. He wasn't in the habit of writing letters very frequently, his precise activities were unclear to us, though he had already been back in the country for almost a year. At first we heard he had set up an iron factory in Howrah, a little later we were told he was busy trying to sell shares in a bulb-manufacturing company. I, who had thought Fotik-mama would build a bridge over the Padma so that people could take a train from Dacca and arrive in Calcutta eight hours later, was getting quite depressed. I even saw creases of worry appear on my father's forehead whenever Fotik's name was mentioned. But the moment she set eyes on her brother, my mother jumped for a different reason—'What's wrong with you, Fotik, why do you look like that?' While his British sheen had been shed by then, no one else could make out just where his muscle-bound, demonic physique had been dented. Laughing, Fotik-mama said, 'You just like to think of everyone as sick, didi. Kajol looks nice and plump too. There's nothing wrong with me either.' But by then all thoughts of Kajol's illness had vanished from my mother's mind (actually, she probably got better after taking the medicine prescribed by Anadi-babu); all she could talk about was Fotik's losing weight, Fotik wasn't well. This time, of course, the doctor wasn't summoned; my mother performed the diagnosis herself and the prescription was hers too. How on earth could he not fall ill if he was going to eat whatever his servant cooked for him? Did you even get fresh milk in Calcutta; was the fish any good at all? Therefore, my father bought enormous quantities of provisions every day (perhaps he had to borrow money), my mother cooked at an even more furious pace, and said from time to time, 'This steamed fish is Kajol's. Kajol's made the chicken roast today. Try that chutney, Fotik, Kajol's made it.' Sometimes, in private, she said, 'Fotik, why don't you take Kajol back with you this time. Don't worry, I'll go with you, I'll set up everything for you. What kind of flat do you have? Two rooms are perfect, what do you need more for? On the fourth floor! Must be very bright and airy then. See how well Kajol is cooking these days, all you need is a servant or a maid, and you'll be fine.' 'Oh, enough, didi!' After his seven-course luncheon, Fotik-mama sank into slumber. Thus the days went by.

Four

Tell me, is it true that you no longer get carp in Bengal—West Bengal, that is? Nor catfish? Even the hilsa is only available in your dreams now, I hear . . . don't make me laugh! It's not a bad thing, we were so pampered all this while, there's no harm getting a taste of reality. I'm sure you remember the fuss over food in Dacca—even in middle-class homes—such a waste of time, such elaborate arrangements. The old men in their shanties in some refugee colony somewhere now, probably have tears springing to their eyes when they remember the quantity of food wasted at even informal dinners they had hosted back then. Take the feast for Fotik-mama, it was literally a ceremony to 'repair his health'. It began with a bitter concoction of gourd and *mourola* fish, then crisply fried *potol* and another fish, the *kachki*, followed by the entry of the jet-black carp, resplendent on its bed of deep-red oil, reclining against a pillow of cauliflower—each one so large it almost spilled out of the bowl. On another occasion, it would be just hilsa all the way: fried, steamed with mustard, smoked and served wrapped in leaves, curried with tender pumpkin, the fish-head and tail served in a light sauce with lime juice and chillies. On yet other occasions, it would be a dal made with the head of the *rui*, prawns cooked in coconut milk, large portions of the *chital* or the huge *pabda* served with the fragrance of coriander and *bori*, along with the meaty catfish made with sliced potato in an onion-and-garlic curry. There was a steady supply of creamy *doi*, of exquisite sweets like the *pranohara* and *amriti*. With the morning tea my mother laid out piles of eggs, toast with butter and three kinds of jam, alongside sweets like rosogolla and *malpoa*; on other days there would be circular pieces of eggplant, deep-fried and served with puffed up *luchi*, along with raisin-studded *mohonbhog*; on yet other days there would be flaky biscuits from the neighbourhood bakery—its top layer brown, light, crisp, but soft and sweet underneath—accompanied by the placid *paantua* and, simply as an afterthought, peanuts soaked in sugar syrup.

Then there was my grandmother's vegetarian cooking—a different world, I tell you, its inhabitants were very deferential, living with dull names like *chhenchki ghonto shaak shukto*, even worthless things like pumpkin seeds or the skin of the gourd enjoyed pride of place in it. But the cuisine that emerged from those unpublicized creations was beyond even the imagination of Paris's finest chefs. Just as painters bring out innumerable shades by mixing the seven colours of the rainbow in different ways, so too did my mother and grandmother. They created an incredible variety for the tongue from just three or four primary tastes and flavours, working in their studios with ordinary equipment, without the backing of big money. How did they do it? Do you really think it was love? The legendary maternal heart of the Bengali woman? I'm sorry, but I can't agree with you. It was labour, mindless labour—the same way in which the Egyptian pyramids were constructed well before the Machine Age. You could call it the slave system. You can fully understand that it was convenient in many ways for men to ensure that women remained slaves. It makes my head reel now to think of it. How do I say this—I've travelled to many countries, enjoyed different kinds of comforts, but nowhere have I seen meals becoming such elaborate affairs. What a waste of money, what tyranny. All that's a thing of the past now—good riddance, too . . . But *is* it all wholly in the past? Do you know whether anyone in Bengal still knows how to make *kochubaata* with mustard, coriander and coconut? Dal with flower-stalks? Diced, fried neem leaves with fritters? Do they make mustard at home any more? Is this art, this special contribution of the Bengali—or rather, of the Bengali woman—to the world's civilization lost forever? . . . Me? No, I've been away a long time, a very long time. Once I managed to get out, I didn't go back.

Well, it's not as though I never went back, but not to live. I chose not to, didn't want to, either. Please don't mind, but my heart isn't in wondrous Bengal any more. I did my duty, of course; bought my father a house in Dumdum after the Partition, sent money every month, visited my parents and elder sister from time to time. I paid for my younger sister to read economics in London, she's now married to the First Secretary at one of our embassies. I have certainly done what's known as supporting one's family. But all those years ago, the day I boarded the ship, the *City of Calcutta*, at Chandpal Ghat, I bid adieu mentally to Bengal. Wasn't it a good decision? What you might call wise? You can see the state Calcutta is in. The city seems to be dying, sinking into the Bay of Bengal. No, that's too poetic—it's sinking into its own garbage, its drains; the large underground pipes will burst one day and flood Calcutta. For my posting I chose the Central Province—Madhya Pradesh, it was still quite trouble-free at the time. For my wife I chose a Gujarati. The people I consorted with were Tamils, Marathis, Punjabis, Englishmen—all 'brother officers', or military top brass—all those people on whose shoulders the motherland has propped herself up. So you can see how interregional, how international my life was! Travelling abroad on furlough every three years to Rome or Venice or Paris or Geneva—I have to admit it wasn't a bad kind of job. You're laughing? Yes, you must have recalled my loathing for government service, you must even have wondered how I abandoned my verbiage to walk into the cage. You know what, I get a distinct pleasure in doing precisely what I loathe . . . a weird, warped sort of enjoyment, as though I'm playing a joke on myself, a farce where I'm both audience and actor. To me, my job was what you might call hilarious, in more senses than one.

At times, of course, the hilarity seemed a little excessive; in some cases things became very uncomfortable for government hotshots. Open fire on innocent people, then wait in trepidation for the bullets to be fired back at you;

write a warrant for Jawaharlal Nehru's arrest—all kinds of nasty assignments. But then, I never involved myself in such troublesome tasks. I chose the judicial line. In safe Madhya Pradesh. There weren't too many land-related cases there either. Life passed at a slow and steady pace. Only once was I in a bit of a spot with a fellow accused of murder. He had apparently delivered a blow to his wife's head with a stick. And the wife simply died of that single blow. He ran away into the jungle out of fear, the police found him there and put him behind bars. A tiny fellow, illiterate, a daily labourer, came and stood in the dock every day, looking around helplessly, his answers to the prosecutor's questioning making no sense whatsoever. He appeared not even to understand what was going on—why he had been arrested, why he was being brought to this impressive two-storeyed building every day, why there were so many guards, so much noise—none of it seemed to make any sense to him. He couldn't remember his lawyer's advice, didn't realize his life was at stake, didn't even claim the bamboo stick wasn't his, burst into loud tears on seeing his wife's blood-soaked sari. Surely he hadn't wanted to kill her, had only wanted to teach her a lesson (as we all do sometimes)—being an uneducated barbarian, he hadn't found a more civilized way of doing it. Or it could even have been the case that his wife had a bad heart, wasn't that possible? But this was British law, it was clearly a case of 'culpable homicide amounting to murder', there was 100 per cent proof—nobody could escape in such a situation, unless of course the killer was Michael O'Dyer or perhaps an intimidating white man from a tea estate. I could see that the jury was certain to find him guilty, and then . . . what would I do? Would the man hang eventually, and did I have to be the one to pronounce the death penalty? No, no, no. Never. I would never be able to do that. I seemed to feel the noose around my own neck: no air, the sun went out, darkness everywhere . . . save me! You see how compassionate my conscience is, how tender my heart. Do you know what happened? I fell ill. One of my ears seemed to stop functioning. I wasn't able to hear properly. My fingers shook when trying to light a cigarette. I could feel my back aching all the time. I was forced to take leave on grounds of health. I recovered only after a trip to Kashmir. Murder is wrong, but so is murdering the murderer. I am neutral. I am peaceful. Whether the pretext is the law or war, murder can never be good, that's what I feel. I love what's good, I want to be good.

But you know what the trouble is? Not everyone agrees on what's 'good'. For instance, Bulbul said the same thing can be good or bad, depending on the circumstances. Or that's what she'd been taught, what she'd been indoctrinated with. And to Anadi-babu, 'good' was that final, ultimate outcome that human civilization has been trying to arrive at for centuries. Did you know Anadi-babu—Anadi Bardhan, Mitu's father, the homoeopath in hand-spun clothes? Didn't you ever meet him? He was a strange man, you know—very unusual. People used to call him whimsical, eccentric, but I found him alive, enthusiastic—and his enthusiasm was unexpectedly multidirectional; I was yet to find anyone who spoke as eloquently as he did. Rousseau, Tolstoy, Thoreau, Tagore, Gandhi—an incredible cocktail seemed to have been concocted in his brain; he concerned himself with questions such as: what is freedom? What does health mean? He used to say freedom means self-reliance (and not merely driving the British out of India), and that self-reliance is actually a moral quality—for humans, at any rate. Wild animals may seem self-reliant, but in fact they live in the shelter of nature, they are nature's slaves. Humans are sent to the earth as helpless creatures, as they are the only ones with free will, which they can exercise to mould themselves as they wish. But most men are cowards and weaklings; so, despite being largely free of the tyranny of nature, they have had other kinds of tyranny imposed upon themselves—the government, the scriptures, the penal code etcetera. Humans must acquire the strength and the courage to enable them to realize that self-reliance is their natural state of being, so that they consider reliance on governments, national or foreign, for any and every thing, demeaning to their self-esteem. When all individuals learn to fend for themselves, when they don't have to live under an overarching authority, everyone will realize the simple truth that their interests are interlinked, that it is in order to protect their own interests that they mustn't cause harm to others. Anadi-babu believed that only in this condition could human beings be 'good', be 'happy'. The 'good' are also 'happy'—so there will be no conflict between people in Anadi-babu's ideal world ('If everyone's happy why should there be disputes any more?'), the inclination to persecute one another will die gradually—not because of religious instructions, but because of disuse, just as human beings had shed their tails and lost the sharpness of their nails. Maybe human beings will take a long time to get to that stage—up to millions of years—but if they do not want to be destroyed this is what their future has to be.

Another of Anadi-babu's notions was that human beings are free of disease in their natural state; what we refer to as 'illnesses' are nothing but 'imbalances', some deficiency in equilibrium—anxiety, melancholy, starvation, overeating . . . the outcome of some such condition. The body strives constantly to keep us healthy, but the effort cannot be entirely successful unless the mind cooperates too. (Willpower is in its essence excellent health: as examples of this formula, he cited George Bernard Shaw and Mahatma Gandhi, and added, that the aged Goethe had remained alive through sheer willpower till he had completed the second *Faust*, and the aged Tolstoy—whose sexual appetite had never diminished, and whose health was as solid as a rock—how peacefully and beautifully he had died of his own free will, in the fierce cold, leaning back on a railway platform bench.) Actually it is our mind that drives our body, but because doctors still consider the body a living physical entity, which falls ill whenever attacked by germs, many hidden secrets of health have not yet been discovered. Anadi-babu compared the so-called 'treatment' with the government too; since human beings are cowards, they depend on doctors where their bodies are concerned, just as they depend on governments where their lives are concerned—but they do have the ability to rid themselves of their susceptibility to sickness, and activating this ability is the job of the true 'doctor'.

I see you're laughing. Does it sound very old-fashioned? Incoherent, meaningless? Naïve? But then, you have to remember the times. And, of course, the state of the country, the atmosphere. Take our university professors: if you asked them a question the answer was: 'Read such-and-such chapter of such-and-such book.' Each of them occupied their own pigeonholes: arts, science, politics, philosophy, literature . . . different names, different pigeonholes, and each of them seemed to have been created specifically to provide opportunities for teachers to teach and students to acquire degrees. It was Anadi-babu who first led me to suspect that these different subjects are actually interlinked, and that they are part of our life, connected to our daily realities. I didn't follow his logic every time, sometimes the different pieces seemed mutually contradictory—but at least his thinking hadn't frozen, he was animate, his mind fidgeted restlessly. He seemed to me somewhat like an oasis in the desert—so did Bokul Villa, his two-storeyed home on Lamirnie Street, and its inhabitants. Their behaviour wasn't like anyone else's we knew—it was more like what my father referred to as 'Calcuttan' and my grandmother as 'playing at being British'. The house included a 'drawing-room' furnished with sofas and settees, electric lights, even ceiling-fans that whirred. There was a constant stream of people—patients, relatives of patients, and those thirsty for the nectar of music. The wind was always allowed to blow in; the world outside was acknowledged and accepted. I liked the fact that Anadi-babu didn't refer to any 'family connections' between us, he accepted me for my own sake, and conversed as though I was his age, his peer.

But Anadi-babu did not explicitly talk about homoeopathy or his daughter's music very often. He didn't because both of those were self-evident to him, not requiring proof. It's not as though you never heard him talk about how he had cured someone's stomach ailments after all other doctors had thrown up their hands, or how just one dose of his medicine had given someone else instant relief from cholera, or which famous people of Calcutta had been entranced by Mitu's singing, or which eminent musicians from Lucknow and Pondicherry corresponded with her—but his expression and voice both remained impersonal during these announcements, as though he were only offering information like 'another round-table conference is coming up in London' or 'Bradman scored three successive centuries'. Of course, some people made fun of him behind his back even for this, but I never felt he wanted to 'blow his own trumpet'. His objective was to magnify the glory of the subtle art of the organic medicine that he served and of the music that he loved. That he occasionally invited large numbers of people home to listen to his daughter sing, welcoming them with lavish spreads, that he requested real music lovers to visit often, was not out of some blind fatherly love or desire for publicity—what he actually sought was to experience the joy of listening to his daughter sing in the company of others, to share this pure joy with others. The desire to share with others whatever is good and enjoyable, and is available easily to oneself—be it money, be it learning, be it an art—is known as fellow-feeling, and this quality of Anadi-babu's was clear even to his patients. He gave medicines to many people free of cost, waiving his fees—or taking only half—from patients in poor families; when people recovered under his care, when they took pleasure in listening to Mitu sing, he did not consider them personal achievements on his own part or his daughter's—they were only the triumph of the genius Hahnemann, or of the unending appeal of the ragas. At least, that's what I thought, for I could see nothing negative in Anadi-babu's personality, maybe because I didn't want to. That he was Mitu Bardhan's father was also reason enough for me to love him.

In grooming his daughter as a singer, Anadi-babu was compelled to face a certain degree of humiliation. Right from the beginning, many people were unable to accept the fact that a girl from a genteel family—born to the Oleganj Bardhans, no less—would practise her music with Muslim ustads as ladies of the night did, play the harmonium, and sing in time to the tabla before a crowd of people. Bokul Villa was pelted with stones, crude and obscene anonymous letters were received; Shamshuddin, a student at our university, was beaten up mercilessly one evening on his way back from Bokul Villa. Some slander about Mitu Bardhan did the rounds, Anadi-babu was forced to entertain unsolicited advice from well-wishers—but none of these made the slightest impact on the Gandhian homoeopath, the music continued in full swing. Gradually the entire city came to accept her as a singer, her fame made her a household name, many of Dacca's important citizens professed pride after a record of her songs was brought out in Calcutta. She began to receive invitations to sing at various events—at our university, at the reception for Subhash Bose at Northbrook Hall, the annual swadeshi fair was never inaugurated without her singing on the occasion. The nineteen-year-old girl was invited to the upper-class homes of professors in the Ramna neighbourhood, to the house of the Chowdhurys in Haldia. And sometimes in the evening, when Mitu practised with her teacher and her tabla-player, three or four young men stood outside the walls surrounding Bokul Villa—the melody wafted across the large courtyard, borne on a cultured voice, on waves of notes the way flocks of birds fly in circles, the way fountains brim over. Some called her Papia, after the songbird, for her singing; others named her 'Golden Voice', in English. When a young man took courage in his hands to venture into the compound, Anadi-babu called out to him in pleasure, saying, 'Oh, come in, don't remain outside, what's wrong with listening to music?' Thus did a group grow around Mitu and Anadi-babu, and a recent addition to it was Arthur Jones—on whom I set eyes for the first time on the evening of Mitu's birthday.

Five

I was dumbstruck when I first saw Jones—because of his green eyes. Absolutely green, not even like cat's eyes, but like an emerald. I thought it abnormal, unnatural, I couldn't believe a human could really have eyes like those; it made me feel uneasy to even look at him. But in no other respect did he seem to be a descendant of John Bull; of medium height, his hair blackish-brown, his complexion far from ruddy, he did not substitute intelligible speech with a series of guttural groans. The drawing-room was full of people. Anadi-babu made me sit next to Jones, who started conversing with me, smiling with his thin lips—gradually his green eyes became tolerable, he seemed handsome, he was unctuously polite, his disposition almost shy. His manner of speaking softly, gently, appealed to me, and his pronunciation of certain English words made me curious. When he heard I was a student of literature he asked whether there was a biography of Bankimchandra Chatterjee in English, what I thought of Saratchandra Chatterjee's stories, what my opinion was of Tagore's plays. He asked a couple of questions about nuances in the Bengali language too. For instance, how was 'Tell him this' different from 'Say this to him'? I was a little surprised at the question (for as the water to the fish, so is our mother-tongue to us, we don't notice its peculiarities); I had to think a little before answering. 'The difference is probably in the tone—the first is an instruction, the second a request.' He asked more questions about the use of certain adjectives unique to the Bengali language, and in the process of answering—which was by no means easy—I discovered the astonishing ability of our language to register as sounds and reside as images.

I asked him whether he had learnt Bengali while still in England. 'A little, for the sake of the job, but that was insignificant. I wish to learn it properly now, but your language is very difficult.'

'No more than English is for us.'

'You people have a talent for languages, we don't. We're reviled the world over for this.'

I didn't care much for this response, I felt he was evading the real issue. 'But we're compelled from childhood to learn English,' I said, 'you would have too if Bengali had been compulsory for you.'

'That's true.' Jones smiled a little. 'And that's a problem too, for most of you speak English here, so we can get by quite well without having to learn the local language. I know . . . we ourselves are responsible for this.' Looking at me, he continued immediately, 'But on the whole it's a matter of shame that although thousands of Englishmen are spending their lives in India, their knowledge of the language is limited to a few words of Hindustani. But is it true that the first book of Bengali prose was written by an English missionary?'

'Not exactly,' I answered, 'a book written by a Bengali was also published in the same year, moreover, what "babu English" is to you, "missionary Bengali" is to us.'

'I'm sure Indian English is much better than that,' Jones protested at once. It sounded insincere.

I brought up Kipling. Did Jones like him? Did I? The question was redundant, for could an Indian ever be fond of Kipling? I said this a little self-consciously.

There seemed to be a trace of amusement in Jones's eyes. 'Kipling cannot exactly be termed an India-hater, he's not a bad writer either—but far too sentimental.'

'Not an India-hater!' I said in agitation. 'Do you remember that "Gunga Din" poem? The saintly water-carrier who was labelled a "better man" before dying only because he offered water to a British Tommy? "For all 'is dirty hide,'e was white, clear white inside!" Who else has insulted India this way!'

'That's what I'm referring to as sentimental. But please remember too that the narrator is a crude, uneducated character.'

'But don't you see the hatred for India? "Ship me somewhere East of Suez where the best is like the worst . . ."'

'As soon as I stopped Jones continued, '"Where there aren't no Ten Commandments an' a man can raise a thirst!" Do you feel this is an expression of hatred for India?'

'Of course!' My voice rose without my being aware of it.

'How much more emphatically can you announce that India is a land of barbarians!'

After a brief silence, Jones said, 'You're probably right . . .'

I couldn't tell whether he was being sincere or polite.

'But you see, there's a certain nostalgia at work, a sort of romantic image of this country, of Asia, which was actually in existence for four hundred years—or even longer, right from the time of Marco Polo—in Europe, and the last of that has been captured in Kipling's poetry. A stale romanticism, none of that heavenly flavour to it any more, you could say it's become rancid, even, but that was the medium through which Kipling has taken India into English homes. It was his writings that attracted me to India when I was a child.'

'Surely you have discovered now how distorted Kipling's images are,' I said forcefully.

'Yes, distorted in many respects, but still . . . this sunlight, this sky . . .'

'For sure!' I didn't allow Jones to finish, 'the sunlight, the sky, the flora, the fauna . . . all good. Didn't a bishop write while in Calcutta "Where every prospect pleases and only man is vile"?'

Arthur Jones reddened a little, then spoke softly, 'Yes, if I'd been born an Indian I'd have also found Kipling intolerable. But there's another side to it too. Picture the cold, the smoke, the fog, the snow of London—now consider a bank clerk, a factory labourer, uneducated, provincial, has no idea of the world—can you imagine how startled he would be if he were to see the sky here in India? You have to admit that Kipling has done a good job of bringing these marvellous sights to life. You can blame him for distorting reality in his attempt to turn India into a subject of dreams but still—you may laugh at this—that dream did shake us.'

I had many more arguments to offer, but I was caught short at Jones's last statement. It was a novel idea that India could be a dream for England's 'uneducated and provincial'. I too had harboured dreams of England, knitted together pieces of literature to create a magical London—to me the Thames meant lines from Spenser, Fleet Street meant G.K. Chesterton, Hampstead meant Keats, Chelsea meant Rossetti . . . at times I'd even felt that I had made England so much my own that if only I could get there somehow I would become 'one of them'. But Jones made me realize that this England of mine was as unreal as Kipling's India. I dreamt unrelentingly of what was but a tiny fraction of England, which made no difference whatsoever to bank clerks, to factory labourers, to millions of other people—all those people who came to our country as soldiers were astonished at the brightness, the sky, this sky full of glittering stars—who dreamt of our coconut trees when they returned to their cold and snow. They knew nothing about our lives—stained, impoverished, claustrophobic—just as I could not think of a British Tommy as anything but a British Tommy, could not imagine a wife, children, a home for him, there wasn't an inch of space for him in the England of my creation. I was not yet wise enough to know that all dreams are built on partial truth (that's where history differs from poetry); ancient Greece, ancient India, Ujjaini, Rome, Renaissance Florence—they were all like that; the dreams were not futile; their value was realized in the flowers that bloomed from them, the fruit that sprung from them. But England's India dream was spurious—empire, greed and the madness of wanting to convert us all to Christianity—which was why the egg hatched to give birth to—not Goethe's Italy or Chateaubriand's America—but only a fairy-tale *Jungle Book*, nothing but rhymes for a bunch of army barracks, the smell of khaki oozing from the beats of its parades, the whiff of sandpaper in the secretariat, the antics of maintaining a certain rural English air in a distant land full of bizarre people and even more bizarre gods and goddesses.

Since Kipling had been one of my favourite poets in childhood, I still remembered many of his lines, which was why my animosity for him was even greater; I felt I could atone for the foolishness of my ignorant childhood if I could prove to Jones on the spot that Kipling was nothing but a minor poet, little more than a blot on the landscape of English literature. I was about to ask a question I had formulated when I suddenly noticed Fotik-mama beckoning to me from his position near the window, signalling even more clearly when our eyes met. Saying, 'Excuse me, I'll be back in a moment,' I went up to him. Fotik-mama put his arm around my shoulder and drew me away. In a low voice, he said, 'This is your chance, Ranju, get Jones to teach you all the tricks.'

'Tricks for what?' I asked in astonishment.

'You're about to take your ICS exam, that fellow passed his recently, he can give you lots of useful tips.'

'Who said I'm taking the ICS exams?'

'Even if you aren't, keeping in touch with Jones is a good idea—it can prove useful.' Suddenly he abandoned me to race towards Anadi-babu, beginning some kind of financial conversation with him—I heard words and phrases like 'shy capital', 'shares' and '6 per cent'.

It hadn't even occurred to me all this while that Jones was an ICS officer in flesh and blood, the additional magistrate of Dacca—in other words, one of those people we consider 'hotshots', whom we never trust, but whom we look to for favours whenever the opportunity arises. But then, I met him in circumstances where these things didn't occur to you. Fotik-mama suddenly disturbed the friendship that Jones and I had managed to strike up only a few minutes earlier. Looking around, it seemed to me that many of the guests were not very comfortable with Jones being present (although they were glorying in it too)—as though they couldn't forget that he was unconnected, irrelevant, alien to the gathering. A combination of the power of the British Raj, the remoteness of the English language, some fear, some respect and some suspicion kept him at a distance of a thousand miles. Surely Jones himself also realized that he had no place among us, nor would he have one so long as the British ruled us; why then, instead of going to his countrymen's Dacca Club, instead of spending his time playing tennis and golf and dancing, did he come here? Only because of his fondness for music?

'Ah, Ranju!' I heard a low voice behind me; I couldn't feel delighted at the sight of its owner. It was Amulya—like me, a student of the university, but beyond that we had nothing in common. With a smile creasing his well-nourished cheeks, he said, 'I had no idea you were Mr

Jones's friend, you're a prince! My god, how you were firing those English sentences at him.'

I felt rather embarrassed, but I was familiar with his ways. I said coldly, as though nothing he said had registered with me, 'How are you? All well?'

'How indeed!' Amulya said with a grimace. 'I'm studying economics at my father's behest, but the teachers' advice is enigmatic, like all illusions are. Or like the pathetic cries of the lamb being led to the slaughter. If only I could get a job, Ranju, I wouldn't have to tolerate Nagen Chatterjee's bleating any more! But where are the jobs? Nowhere, but still we want them. We're like Rama after Sita's banishment, wailing, "Oh Sita, oh Sita." Sita is like a job, you see—they're one and the same—no matter how much of a rascal and a wastrel you are, get a job and you get a girl!'

'You're instinctively poetic, I notice,' I said.

'Oh that's nothing. I'm not a poet like you, all I can do is write some rhymes, I even set them to tune sometimes. Do you want to hear?' Amulya hummed softly:

When the tarts from north of town went walking on a
summer night
The lads from number twenty-four grew hot and
bothered at the sight
Twelve brothers, who's the dad? As boys go they were
very bad
Winking at the tarts . . .

'Never mind. We'll do the full thing later.' He seemed to roll the remaining lines around on his tongue, tasting them and swallowing them, then said, 'My real calling is probably music, you know, I'm even taking lessons from

Khan Sahib, but my voice isn't gravelly enough. I'll never be able to master classical music, or give those subtle touches that Mitu gives to her singing, I can never manage those. What do you think of her singing?'

'Good.'

'By jove . . . is that all you can say! Superb . . . wonderful . . . divine . . .' Amulya reeled off a succession of adjectives. 'I used to listen to her sing from the road, you know. Then one day I took my courage in both hands and entered the house. Mitu's teaching me Navroze's songs now . . . that Dildar Navroze of yours.' (I couldn't quite make out how Dildar Navroze was 'mine'.) 'I'm wondering if I should switch to light classical music instead. But the real question, of course, is how to earn my bread. Ah, there's Ustadji . . . I have to talk to him.' Amulya drew me further away with a jerk on my arm, and taking me to the distant corner of the room he whispered, 'Will you do me a favour, Ranju? Will you get me a recommendation from Jones? A single paragraph from an Englishman will open many doors. You know how I choke on even a single word of English—if you could tell him on my behalf. You will, won't you? And listen . . .' Now Amulya tightened his grip on my wrist, looking at me strangely. 'Be careful what you say to Jones, he looks harmless, but in fact he's a spy! Don't forget. Someone might well blow him up with a bomb, if I can get hold of a recommendation before that . . . all right now, we'll talk later.' Releasing me, Amulya raced off to the door to welcome Ustad Ibrahim Khan. The room stirred. Anadi-babu went around telling everyone, 'Please, this way . . . everyone . . . Ustadji . . . Jones . . . Ranju, all by yourself? . . . come along now for tea.'

Our lunch is almost ready, it seems; the messenger is here. This is Gayatri Gregory, my housekeeper. What kind of wine would you like? Tell me your preference. All right, if you aren't in the habit, try some Chablis, pure grape-juice, won't do you any harm. All right, Gayatri, we'll be there in a minute . . . Yes, Gayatri Gregory is a lovely name, isn't it? The person isn't unlovely either. Konkani woman, orthodox high-caste Roman Catholic. Two religions came together in her name. A strange land, our India. Gayatri is a widow, they couldn't find another husband for her of compatible caste as well as religion. She's happy here. She takes care of me, I take care of all her needs. There's the lunch bell. This way.

Six

This painting? It's Nellie's work of art—I am speaking of my wife . . . I'm not the sort of person who expects praise just because you're a guest in my home. You may speak freely with me. You must be wondering, when I look like a man of passably good taste, why I have a painting such as this on my dining-room wall. Well, the truth is that after Nellie died I felt a little sad for her, so I picked one out of the numerous paintings and framed it for this wall, as a keepsake. The rest are lying around somewhere, rolling in dust and more dust . . . No, not Ootacamund, this is a scene in Jabbalpore. Thanks to all the jungles, waterfalls and what have you, Nellie was possessed by the goddess of art. All day long she would paint, and visitors would praise her work. But that didn't satisfy her, she kept asking me for my opinion. I was silent for a long time, considering it nothing but harmless entertainment, but when I saw Nellie almost beginning to believe in her abilities as a painter, I was compelled to say, 'These scenes are already available outside, why do you need to paint them again?'

'What do you mean?'

'I mean that in your painting the hill's nothing but a hill, the waterfall's nothing but a waterfall, you haven't added anything to them.'

She stared at me blankly, not even following what I was saying . . . hah! She gave up the pastels for the piano, performing acrobatics every day with the music-sheets open, picking up tunes from an Anglo-Indian girl from time to time—she even wanted to play for me. At least paintings are silent, all you need to do is turn your eyes away, but the ears have no self-defence—the tinkling piano drove me insane. No mistakes in the tune, but no feelings either—intolerable. One day I told Nellie in that Anglo-Indian girl's presence, 'Too much noise here, I'd better go upstairs and read.' Finally the mewling of the cats stopped.

Why do you look at me that way? Are you suggesting my behaviour did not befit a good husband? That I should have encouraged Nellie? But I am an unfortunate soul—I'm not devoid of feelings, you know, never have been. At least I had the sense to see that Nellie had no talent—not for painting, not for music, not for anything. And it's right, it's good to help someone realize their shortcomings, even if the person in question happens to share a bed with you. Or rather, *for* that reason, for that very reason. That is your responsibility towards your wife, towards yourself, towards society. Do you suppose it took me more than half a minute to conclude that Nalini Dalal wasn't another Mitu Bardhan? And why did she have to be, I wanted no such thing, I don't have such idle fancies. But Nellie thought all her acquired qualities would make me love her even more. How childish! She never did grow up, spent all her life as a little girl. Besides, qualities are not everything, you need fortune on your side too. Take Mitu: one fine morning, for no rhyme or reason, she was suddenly dispatched to the detention camp at Hijli. So much for her music, so much for her admirers.

But the future didn't cast a shadow on that particular evening, that September evening at Bokul Villa on Lamirnie Street, Wari, Dacca. The sky was many-hued with the sunset, but in my heart it was the virgin dawn that was tiptoeing in. I had gained entry to a new world, where being part of the family was not the only route to inclusion, where one wasn't considered distant simply because one wasn't the aunt's brother-in-law's son, where there wasn't always a wall between men and women—a fine but insurmountable wall. Behind the drawing-room was a wide, open veranda, where small tables had been laid out for tea. When I followed everyone else in there, what Amulya had said was still ringing in my ears, I had a bitter taste in my mouth. Suddenly I found myself face to face with Mitu. She was the first to speak, 'Here you are.' She stopped at once, for we didn't know each other well enough for her to talk to me in such a familiar tone, we were only meeting for the third time, after all. 'Come to this table here in the corner, I was . . .' Maybe she wanted to say, 'looking for you', but after a moment's pause she changed it to, 'I was waiting to tell you something.'

'What is it?'

'I'm happy you gave me a book, *Mohua*, but why did you send it with Kajol-mami?'

The eloquence I had displayed with Jones half an hour earlier deserted me completely; I remembered how much time I had wasted, how much I had worried, before honouring this invitation. The outcome of all that fretting was paltry, nothing more than the book. Anadi-babu never charged us fees—possibly to reciprocate, my mother had bought a silk sari for Mitu, Kajol had bought a Waterman fountain pen, and I thought I should get her something too, since I had an income of my own from my scholarship. But despite scouring every large shop from Islampur to Nababpur, I found nothing that was worthy of her. Moreover, it had to be something impersonal, not too direct, not too invasive, something that expressed, not a desire for 'intimacy' but just natural courtesy. For this precise reason, anything delicate had to be dropped: for instance, French perfume in an octagonal bottle, brimming over with a colourless liquid that gave off a yellowish-green glow, in every drop of which was hidden a fountain of dreams; or imported heliotrope notepaper in a box, woven like a fine mat, gold-coloured thread glittering at the edges, flashes of hibiscus-red hidden within the envelopes—the first sight of which made you want to write letters even though you didn't have anyone to write to.

Therefore I had no choice but to buy a book, as usual, the eternal poetry of Tagore. But another thought assailed me after that: how would I give Mitu the book? What would I say? 'A small gift for you . . .' 'This book of poems . . .' 'I've brought you a . . .' No! All of them sounded silly, and was it something that had to be announced with so much ceremony in any case? Maybe Mitu already had the book, maybe it wasn't even proper for me to give her a gift of my own. At the last minute I told Kajol-mami, 'Give this to her along with your pen.'

I see you're laughing. I don't know if you'll believe me, but I used to be shy back then—particularly about women, I still am. No, not because of my age or because of the times, not because of the conservative atmosphere of Dacca either—that's my nature. I'm torn apart by apprehension, by doubt; that's why there's no felicity in my behaviour with the world . . . Surprised? . . . But here's what happened, with effort I overcame these weaknesses, with willpower, almost with physical force, I uprooted all those weeds that didn't allow the plant to grow. I realized that without a mask firmly set on my face I would never be an achiever. My job, my marriage, Nellie's dowry, this house, this garden, everything you see . . . all of this is my mask.

But that evening I had no cover, no skin, my defensive walls hadn't been erected yet, I was helplessly exposed to all the rain, wind and sunshine in the world. Making me sit at the same table as Kajol-mami, Mitu went off. Beyond the veranda was a garden, surrounded by a wall—not a landscaped garden but one with old mango and jackfruit trees, some saplings, grass that had grown under the rains. There were clouds in the western sky—red, golden, pink, yellow—and here and there amid those clouds could be seen a cool soft deep blue; I watched the clouds and the sky, but every now and then, between the sky and my eyes, like a strange creature from the bottom of the ocean, a young woman's figure floated up, drifting from one table to another; a green sari, a yellow blouse, as though matching the colours of the garden and the sky, as airy as the breeze slipping in through the gaps among the leaves. 'Doesn't Mitu look lovely?' I heard Kajol-mami say suddenly. My eyes turned towards her, I saw a faint smile at the corner of her lips. In a soft, dreamy voice, Kajol continued, 'I gave your present to Mitu. She examined the book at once, and said, "How strange, he hasn't written anything in it." She's right—why didn't you?'

I probably blushed a little, changing the subject quickly to hide my embarrassment, I said, 'I like this little garden.' Then, to keep the conversation going, I continued, 'I believe there's a terrace attached to Fotik-mama's flat in Calcutta. You can have a garden there with plants in pots.'

'Do you think I'm an expert gardener?'

'No, it's not that, and besides, I don't think it'll be very convenient for you on the fourth floor. I've identified a different house for you and Fotik-mama, you know.'

'For us? What do you mean?'

I told her about the one-storeyed house on Heysham Road with the To-Let sign, which had caught my eye one day as I was walking past in the brilliant ten o'clock sunshine. I expected Kajol to laugh at my childishness, but not a line appeared on her face. And then I said just what I shouldn't have to Kajol, what I had not said to either Fotik-mama or my own mother, what I had only thought about over and over again. 'Why do you suppose Fotik-mama doesn't take you to live with him?

It would be lovely if you lived in Calcutta, now and then I could . . .' Before I could finish, a spark lit up in Kajol-mami's eyes, a deep colour spread across her face. And at that moment I discovered Kajol.

At that time the females of the world were divided into two sets for me: 'girls' and 'women'. The 'girls' were those who were close to my age (usually younger by two to five years), and the 'women' belonged to my mother's group—a different community altogether. 'Girls' were worthy of my attention (I might even marry one some day) but I had no relationship with the others (apart from the care-giving they owed me). Because of this notion I could not tell their age accurately from their appearance; if they were married I pushed them beyond the circle of my curiosity, and as for those addressed as some form of aunt or the other, I didn't even glance at them, and even if I did, I saw not the real person but a symbol with the title of the corresponding aunt. Besides, I had seen Kajol all this while only at home, within the familiar walls of our Bakshibazaar home—where she was Fotik-mama's wife, my mother's faithful shadow, where she seemed to have no existence beyond my uncle and mother. Although she had been part of our family for a year, I didn't remember ever talking to her alone, just the two of us. I didn't even value the fact that she washed my clothes for me, or retrieved the books or sandals I lost because of my carelessness, I took for granted that all of these were her responsibility, that this was how she would spend her days till Fotik-mama took her to Calcutta. The most important thing was that it would be convenient for me once she set up home in Calcutta—this was Kajol's potential and her identity. I had come to know her as a caring, helpful member of the family—someone who never forgot that I took one spoon of sugar with my tea, someone who passed around snacks and biscuits she had made, someone who reminded me (because I liked to read a book with my tea) that the snacks were growing cold or that the cake this evening was from my favourite bakery—in short, someone who contributed in countless ways to my comfort but didn't have a place in my life.

But at that moment, when the colours of the clouds were deepening before disappearing and the evening breeze seemed to be swaying before my eyes like round yellow-green grapes, there on that veranda of Bokul Villa I thought of her as Kajol, sans the 'mami', and that's when I realized she wasn't all that much older than me, and that in her face were set a pair of liquid, black, intense eyes which, opening wide under the puffy lids, tearing apart the veil of drowsiness, threw a dart of lightning at me.

As the tea and snacks were served at the tables, a wave of excitement rose, a whispered murmur was heard in many voices—'Bibhabati—Bibhabati Dutta.' I saw an attractive lady in a handloom sari standing near the door, Mitu's parents had stepped up to welcome her, most eyes were turned towards her. She greeted everyone in general, then told Mitu, 'I can't stay very long, I'm afraid listening to you sing is not in my stars tonight either, but I wanted to at least meet you on this happy day.'

Mitu blushed in pleasure, Anadi-babu said, 'Please join us at this table. I was having an argument with Mr Jones here over the spinning-wheel, I'd love to know what you think.'

'I hope you won't take offence, but I'd rather spend a little time with Mitu—I'll have to leave soon.' A younger girl was accompanying her. Mitu brought both of them to our table and introduced us. 'This is my friend Bulbul Chowdhury, we used to be in school together. And I'm sure you know this gentleman, Bulbul.'

'I can't say I know him, but I know who he is,' said Bulbul, nodding slightly towards me.

'And this is our Kajol-mami.'

I was reminded once again that Mitu seemed to be forgetting how recent our acquaintance with her was.

'Please take a seat, Bibha-di. You too, Bulbul. Ranajit, you know Bibha-di, don't you?'

Getting to my feet, I said, 'I'd better go and sit over there.'

The girl named Bulbul spoke up at once, 'Why? I hope this table isn't reserved for women! Mitu, why don't you draw up a chair and join us.'

That was how I ended up having my tea in the company of four women that evening.

Bibhabati Dutta: the name bounced around in my mind, unidentified, coming to rest about five minutes later when I heard the words 'women's school' and 'swadeshi fair'. I was surprised that I hadn't realized at once that this was the well-known Bibhabati Dutta, much more famous than Mitu Bardhan in Dacca, almost a legend in herself. I didn't realize it because I was engaged in finding my way around unknown territory, which I had entered recently as a guest but where I could conceivably become a resident. Another reason: Bibhabati's appearance didn't match her fame, at least not to my eyes. She was one of the first women to get an MA degree from Dacca University; she hadn't married, she had dedicated her life to the girls' school, the swadeshi fair and the magazine *Muktadhara*, all of which she had founded. She was probably the only woman in Dacca who had emerged entirely from the women's half of the home, and had avoided public criticism despite remaining unmarried even at an age approaching thirty—even in a city like Dacca, where spreading scandal about women was one of the favourite vices of people, nobody had so much as hinted at a veiled accusation against Bibhabati. So I had assumed there would be a certain remoteness about her personality—I had pictured her as someone with unkempt hair, sharp eyes, lean of build, almost skeletal—in short, an 'intellectual'. But I was compelled to dismiss this image, replacing it with one whose appearance was feminine, her face cast in a rounded mould, slightly heavy of build—someone who, sitting next to Kajol, looked like a sister of Kajol's who had by chance inherited an ancestor's fairness of complexion. She was dressed in a white handloom sari and blouse, but that was enough to make her well-dressed—as though the natural grace of her features could adjust to any form of dressing up or the lack of it. Although in my imagination being thirty was the equivalent of being ancient, I discerned in Bibhabati all the signs that I had hitherto thought were limited to girls of my age. The dividing line between 'girls' and 'women', which had wavered a short while ago thanks to Kajol, was now smashed into pieces.

Seven

Pardon me? . . . No, I'm not a big eater, I'll help myself to as much as I need. Please don't worry about me. I find it fatiguing to chew; I prefer a liquid diet. Yes, starting in the morning. Drunk? I'll tell you, if only getting drunk were so easy, what could come between human beings and happiness? I don't, I can't, I simply can't. It only lasts a couple of minutes, a bubble, a spark that flares and dies. Sometimes you feel a certain energy, you shed your fears, you feel you'll sleep well. But no, as soon as I think I'm going to fall asleep, sleep deserts me. I need to look for other sleeping pills, have to get hold of them from anywhere and everywhere, and if all else fails Gayatri Gregory is always within reach. But then, it's not that bad a life, is it? It goes on satisfactorily. I keep to myself, don't interfere in others' lives, nobody can claim I've done them any harm. I can probably claim a little valour too—actually, I don't enjoy any of this, not the alcohol, not the women, not the roses, but I pretend, I pretend to myself that I do. Can anyone live without pretence?

Is everything all right with the lunch? Did you enjoy the crab soup? The crabs are from Kanyakumari, there aren't too many connoisseurs of crabs in this area, of course—formidable vegetarians, all these people. They've made Spanish rice with chicken, I see, at least they had the good sense to make some rice. I'd have been happy to give you a Bengali fish curry and rice, but you can't expect these Goan cooks to produce a good one. Just like you can't get real whiskey without the water and the winter of Scotland, for real Bengali cooking you need the humid atmosphere of Bengal, its soil, its water, its women. It's like magic really, black magic almost, you'll never be able to capture it in a cookbook, there's a mysterious X-factor in it, what we call the ace up your sleeve; leave that out and it'll never work. Anything but authentic cuisine is anathema to me, I don't set foot in the India Club at London even though I'm dying for Indian food, when an Englishman refers to 'curry' my blood begins to boil. Just look at the tyranny of the British with a word they've picked up from Tamil—*Shukto*? Curry! *Chochhori*? Curry! *Murighonto*? Curry! Lord!

But you know, Nellie had a tragic faith in her cookbooks. She didn't really have to fret over the cooking, the routine stuff that the cooks produced was perfectly edible, but Nellie inevitably courted disaster. She wrote out new recipes for the cook every day from her books, but beneath the bombastic French names for the different dishes you couldn't really tell the tastes and flavours apart. Still I didn't object—if this was what caught Nellie's fancy, why should I object? But the problem was that Nellie wanted praise from me—as she had for her paintings, for her music—as though these qualities had no value of their own, as though their fulfilment lay only in the praise lavished upon them by that one special person. I was amused, but I was also annoyed when Nellie asked at the dinner table whether the food was delicious or not, looking at me like a new writer staring at the editor's face after offering a manuscript. Eventually I couldn't help saying, 'They talk of borrowed plumes—that's what cooking out of a book is like.'

It wasn't easy to translate this Bengali idiom into English, of course. It took almost five minutes of effort to make Nellie appreciate the wit. No, I didn't teach her Bengali, nor did I try to learn Gujarati. Why bother? What was the point of learning all those rustic languages—what attraction did they hold? We had English, the lingua franca, it was good enough for us. It's only because of the English language that you can still get a sense of an entity named India, that a Brahmin from Uttar Pradesh can converse with a Tamil Chettiar, that a Bengali can marry a Gujarati. And it's not just the language. The real mantra of union is what my grandmother used to refer to as 'playing at being British'. After all, just look at the conflicts there can be—Brahmin versus Sudra, vegetarian versus meat-eater, untouchable or not, permitted food or not . . . Don't you think only those who have become half-British themselves in their thinking and their actions can rise above all this? I encouraged Nellie to learn German instead, to brush up on her rusty Italian—those languages come in useful when travelling, there are even a couple of books worth reading, in case one wants to. Besides, I never wanted to turn Nellie into a 'Bengali'; I had cut Bengal off from my consciousness. I'm Indian, I'm international, I'm a citizen of the world.

Nellie had created yet another problem for me by assuming I was an expert in matters of fashion too. 'Tell me if this outfit suits me. This sari, this blouse, this jewellery? Silver-grey with this pink? Midnight-black with this sunflower? Emerald-green with this Indian-red?' She had the names of the different shades down perfectly—probably the outcome of her training in art, adept or inept, although I could see for myself what she was dressed in, and it was my perspective that she wanted to know. 'Very nice! You look beautiful.' Or, sometimes, simply to please her: 'Wouldn't a blouse in a lighter shade go better?' 'Pearls with this, I think.' I went so far along this road, I tell you, that on some occasions, before leaving for a party, I made her change her entire outfit thrice over—the poor thing got all hot and bothered, she had to bring out piles of saris, while I felt this dash of amusement within myself.

But don't make the mistake of assuming I don't understand the essence of women's beauty, of their clothes. One of the reasons for my choosing Nellie was most certainly her beauty. Just the kind of beauty you never see in Bengal, but which still brings back memories of the Aryan race in northern India. At first glance, Nalini Dalal sometimes looked as though Draupadi or Kunti from the Mahabharata had come to life. 'Like a mare from Kashmir'—you remember Sudeshna describing Draupadi?—therein lay the comparison. But alas, I was no longer twenty-one, I had spent three years in England, I'd become cunning, I had remade myself differently—pruning all the weaknesses, all the stupidities that had brought me to the brink of disaster at one point. So the doe-eyed, the slim, the fair-of-skin did not have it in her to mesmerize me. I had discovered women long ago, at Bokul Villa on Lamirnie Street on an August evening. I had received that taste of womanhood, that fragrance, which was as subtle as this Chablis, as ethereal, or not even wine itself, just the breath of the wine that spirits like Yeats drank. If only I'd come to a stop there, in that breath and fragrance, my life would have been different today—not a successful one, at best I'd have been a professor in some university, owner of a house made with great effort in that huge slum-city named Calcutta. Fortunately, the women I had attached myself to at the table that evening ended up changing the course of my life.

I seem to have acquired a new vision that evening, you know. Because of the company of women, something I wasn't used to, and probably because of the grape-coloured glow outside too. The tiniest details about the appearance of women, the way they dressed, which I'd never noticed before were now—like an unexpected end rhyme in a poem, or Tagore's spectacular use of the word 'rhododendron'—obvious to me, even appearing to be meaningful. I seem to have captured for the first time the essence of the scarlet earrings peeping through Mitu's raven-black hair, shimmering as it swung now and then; the gold necklace like a crescent on the exposed part of

Kajol's breasts below her neck; of the solitary latticed bracelet on Bibhabati's lovely round wrist; Bulbul's squirrel-sharp eyes behind her black-framed glasses—the shape of their heads, the swell of their cheeks, the lines of their lips, in other words, the appearance and body language of women. The literal concept of 'women', which I had played with in my mind all this time, had been like the geography of textbooks; but today the schoolboy had become the traveller to confront the reality behind the geography—could see with his own eyes the lakes, mountains, caverns, rocks, formations; could see unending variety, an enormous possibility, none of which the atlas had even held a whiff of. My concentration was focussed on the table where I had by chance—or perhaps by Mitu's design—been given a seat. Everyone and everything else at the other tables—the argument between Anadi-babu and Jones over the spinning-wheel, the Urdu-laced Bengali that Mitu's music teacher spoke in his stentorian voice, Fotik-mama, Amulya, the other guests—faded for the moment. Everyday reality was buried under a striking new sensation—just like we forget the existence of distracting women all around us as soon as the lights go down and the curtain goes up in the theatre. As though things were unfolding only at this table, almost a play, and the most astonishing thing was, I had been given a role too, I learnt my part while watching the others perform, as it were.

Bibhabati was discussing the swadeshi fair to be held during the Durga Puja holidays. Mitu and Bulbul had both been her students, and Bulbul now appeared to be a full-fledged colleague, but Bibhabati included her new acquaintance Kajol in the discussion too; Kajol readily agreed to contribute some embroidered clothes for sale at the fair. While the discussion centred on what kind of new things could be included, which chorus songs Mitu would teach the others and which she would sing solo, Bibhabati glanced at me, 'Can we get your help too, Ranajit?' I was so taken aback by the fact that the famous Bibhabati Datta was making a request of me that I was at a loss for words. Bulbul paused in mid-sentence to look at me, I spoke with an effort, 'Tell me what I can do.'

Bibhabati asked me to prepare a chart on the subject of India's history, containing all the important dates and information, starting with the Vedic period and going up to the Non-Cooperation Movement. 'I'm sure you can do it.'

'I'll try.'

'There's something else I want from you—a piece for *Muktadhara*.'

'Me? What can *I* write?'

'I'll tell you that too,' this time Bibhabati sounded as though she were issuing an order, 'Gora's character in Tagore's novel. A discussion on why Tagore chose Gora to be an Irishman. I know you write poetry, but I need an essay.'

Now I was completely overwhelmed, because it was beyond my wildest imagination that someone as busy and well-known as Bibhabati Dutta would have noticed those poems of mine (dismally few in number) that had been published in little magazines from Calcutta. To mask my perturbation I asked, somewhat irrelevantly, 'Can I ask you something? Why is everything so expensive at your fair? A four-paisa handkerchief costs four times as much.'

'You have to take into account the people making the handkerchiefs,' said Kajol, smiling at me, while Bulbul exclaimed, 'But the fair is meant to raise money!'

But why it was necessary to raise money remained a mystery as Bibhabati changed the subject.

'I believe Dildar Navroze is coming to Dacca, did you know, Mitu?'

'So I've heard.'

'Have you heard from him recently?'

'He's sent me two new songs, including the notations.'

'Are you singing them today?' asked Bulbul.

'How can I? I cannot learn a song from the score alone.'

Mitu seemed to acknowledge her inability quite innocently. 'I'll get Dil-da to teach me the next time I'm in Calcutta.'

'Such a remarkable man!' said Bibhabati. 'I met him for the first time at Krishnanagar—we were at the same conference. His laugh is as wonderful as his singing. It was such fun, he was the life and soul of the party.'

'Oh, yes,' Mitu nodded enthusiastically, 'wherever Dil-da goes, he takes over the place. And how fond he is of tea. And singing . . . once he starts he no longer has any sense of place or time. All he needs is tea and zarda now and then—he can go on for hours together.'

'How handsome he is, too,' exclaimed Bulbul. 'Middle-parted flowing hair, such large liquid eyes, always red at the edges, yellow or saffron kurtas and shawl—brimming over with energy. He gets jailed, he fasts for a cause, he's captivated the entire country with his singing . . . extraordinary!'

'You should see Dil-da when he's sitting at his harmonium to compose a song,' Mitu continued after a fleeting glance at me. 'He has his notebook and pen before him, sings a line or two as he plays the tune, writes it down in his notebook, laughs hoarsely, loudly, then another line and before you know it, the song's done. Then he sings it for everyone—laughter spilling from his eyes, his shaggy mop swaying—an incredible sight.'

I felt as though Navroze was present there in spirit, had taken over the women with whom I was sipping tea in this reality which had failed me. A little later Bibhabati said, 'I was thinking of inviting Navroze to the inauguration of the fair, Mitu.'

'That would be wonderful!'

'I believe he's very hard to get hold of.'

'I don't know about that, but I do know he's very keen on visiting Dacca.'

'Will you write to him then, Mitu?'

'I will if you'd like me to,' said Mitu deferentially.

'Yes, of course—if he agrees, I'll make all the arrangements from the school, we can even change the date to suit his convenience. Ranajit, have you met Navroze?' Bibhabati spoke as though having had a couple of poems published entitled me to be Navroze's friend too.

'No, how would I have met him?' I said quickly.

'But I think he knows of you,' said Mitu, looking at me.

'How is that possible?'

'I'll explain all that later, but you must meet him when he's here—you'll enjoy meeting him.'

I suddenly had the sensation of being tossed onto a mountain peak, where the air was so thin I couldn't breathe properly. I'd just been told that I might soon get to know personally, not a face in a portrait like Shelley, not a legend like Kalidasa, but a contemporary poet from my own country, whom you could see with your own eyes, hear with your own ears. The very same Dildar Navroze whose poetry and music played all around Bengal, like a bunch of healthy, capable, fun-loving children, who was so accessible to Mitu that she could easily say about him, 'I will write to him if you'd like me to' or 'You'll enjoy meeting him'. But even on that peak I felt a pinprick of envy, as the poet had become 'Dil-da' to Mitu, and because he had conquered not just Mitu but also Bulbul and Bibhabati with his music; it was the art of melody that I envied: music, which is so close to poetry and yet so much sharper, simpler, more sensuous—which could penetrate the ears and reach the heart so quickly—while poetry lags far behind under the weight of its ideas and its cleverness, under the discipline of language. It flashed through my mind that even if I did ever manage to write the kind of poetry I wanted to, it would not be as much of a favourite with women—with anyone, possibly—as Navroze's music was at this moment with the women I was sharing the table with. But for that very reason I felt a longing to learn much more about Navroze—if you armed him with tea, paan, a harmonium, a notebook and a pencil amidst a roomful of people, could he really compose songs in the gaps between the laughter and the chattering and the admiration? Had he really written a poem in the fifteen- or twenty-minute interval between the end of a Mohun Bagan football match and the departure of his train to Darjeeling? Was it true that the editor of *Kallol*, unable to extract a poem from Navroze despite his best efforts, had locked him in his own office, and that Navroze had in that imprisoned state written his legendary poem 'Victory Cry'—which I memorized as soon as I read it for the first time? I was impatient to reach this extraordinary, generous, free-flowing poet—stories of whom made him sound completely unlike me in nature—using Mitu Bardhan as a medium; I felt that getting more details about him from Mitu would reveal to me the secret source of Navroze's poetic genius. But at that very moment a small incident took me away from the poet and his poetry. The electric lights in Bokul Villa went on.

In our home, kerosene lanterns were lit when darkness fell, large shadows leapt off the walls, shaking in the wind; even inside our rooms we lived in the company of night; there was no palpable distinction between the dying light of the evening and the moment the lanterns were lit. But with the sudden appearance of electric lights, the scene on the veranda transformed completely. The airy backdrop of sky, clouds and plants was replaced by the clarity of whitewashed walls of solid brick, the dark forms of the furniture, the tea-stain on the tablecloth;

the women at my table were transformed too. They appeared in new shades under the new lights; they chatted over tea; the movement of their hands, their fingers, their necks produced occasional flashes of the red and green stones on Kajol's necklace, of a dark brown glow from Bulbul's spectacles, and suddenly, because of a particular movement on her part, of the three legendary creases on Bibhabati's throat that are known as the *trivali*, which I had believed to be imaginary until now.

Till a short while ago, I had a different image of the girl who sang, an image crafted from the previous day's music session. The way she sat behind the harmonium, the movement of her lips when she sang, the hint of teeth, the way her slim fingers played on the black and white keys of the harmonium—all these I knew. But that day I saw a different Mitu. The other day when she sang, dressed in a maroon sari, her expression was pure grace, her acceptance of the admiration in every pair of eyes was easy; a short while before, in the light of sunset, she looked like a mermaid wrapped in marine plants; but then her green sari appeared peacock-blue, she spoke with short sharp gasps, her hand remained poised in mid-air after breaking off a piece of shondesh as she listened to Bulbul—the glory of her music forgotten, she became a little girl again, a flower in anticipation, still tentative, not fully bloomed yet. And meanwhile Kajol—who had the least of an aura among the four, who hadn't even passed her matriculation exams, who had lived somnolently at her parents' home for five years after getting married, whose only attraction for me lay in the fact that I would have a splendid place to stay in once Fotik-mama took her to their own home in Calcutta—

also became a mature woman in my eyes, fulfilled, a peer and a competitor to the rest simply by virtue of being a woman. This too was a source of wonder for me. And instantly Dildar Navroze changed too in my heart—or you could say he moved away from it. I no longer envied him, I was no longer curious about the uniqueness and source of his talent. For, even more than his beautiful eyes, his flowing wavy hair, his iridescent clothing, his captivating laugh, his joy, his music, even his poetic genius, even, in fact, my faint attempts at writing poetry—even more than all of this, what was far more important, what demanded greater attention and examination on my part, were these moments under the electric lights, which were evident to me but not to Navroze, and the sight of these four women under those lights, their poses, their appearance, and the movements in the curves of their bodies, which seemed to make physical contact with me with every gesture of theirs. And when Mitu sang Navroze's compositions after tea, I forgot all my jealousy and came to love Navroze too, for it was through his music that Mitu seemed to have come a little closer to me—at least, that's what I felt at the time.

Mitu? . . . No, Mitu's appearance wasn't in sharp focus yet, there were only waves of desire in my mind, desire for some indistinct nameless woman. I was young, by God's grace, we are all young sometime. So you know, I couldn't sleep for a long time that night, certain faces kept disturbing the darkness, women's faces: different women, but not fixed, they whirled slowly like a Ferris wheel. The Ferris wheel whirled, the music rose in the air—a subtle music that encompassed the sky—Mitu's voice, perhaps the voice of an angel with a voice a thousand times sweeter than Mitu's, the exhalation of some poet a thousand times more talented than Navroze; the images merging into the music, the music into the images, one face merging into another, borrowing features from one another—one person's eyes above someone else's nose, someone's lips had someone else's smile, one woman's head held another one's hair—as though several women had flowered simultaneously on the tree of my life, out of reach precisely because there were so many of them. I tried to select one, to capture her, to trap her completely with my eyes, but just as we can immerse ourselves in water but cannot hold it in our hand, in the same way that 'one' seemed to be dispersed among many, I lost her in the very process of trying to tether her to my eyes. Then, half-asleep, I concluded there was a universal womanhood somewhere, beyond material existence, beyond description, only a hint of which became discernible once in a while, sometimes on this woman's face, sometimes on that one's—that too, not always to everyone but only to a specific viewer at a specific moment—but it didn't stay, it disappeared instantly. Yet, surely, such a moment and such a condition could be realized when the essence or abstract of that womanhood could be concentrated in a single woman, maybe we could then make her a part of our life? And at once a different thought reared its head from the darkness of near-sleep; I was able to translate into a simple tongue the dissatisfaction, the sense of failure housed within me;

I felt that it might be possible to breathe normally despite this constricted, fearful, miserable environment, despite this uneducated and superstition-ridden society of ours, despite our slave mentality and the arrogance of the British, it might even be possible to be happy, if only I could find a friend—a woman—a woman as a companion, a woman whom I could speak my heart to, who would listen to me closely, who would know what I was trying to say.

Eight

Shall we sit here in this room? This is my study. At least, it was supposed to have been, for I had floated a rumour at one point to the effect that I was writing a unique autobiography for which noble task I needed a small room, in response to which Nellie had done up this room for me with the equipment estimated for use of a greater Balzac. In any case I prefer smaller rooms, I feel safer in them. I was unhappy about living much of my life in enormous bungalows, bungalows built by the British: huge rooms, high ceilings, massive windows, distant walls, gigantic compounds. There weren't even electric lights everywhere, the walls were cast with ghostly shadows, the beams in the ceilings were like the skeletons of dead beasts, ideal to hang yourself from. The wind whistled at night, it was as dark as a mountain outside. And then this house: Nellie's plan, Nellie's composition . . . her tastes had been set in her father's Malabar Hill palace . . . if she had a dining room it had to seat fifty at a go, if she had furniture in her drawing-room it had to be from London, the library had to have panels of Burma teak . . . etcetera, etcetera. This was one area where Nellie's passion knew no bounds, she had put in no mean effort behind it all. Bonheur—joy—is now an intolerable burden on me, it is of no use, emptied out; I live here with all the instruments of pleasure at my disposal. I spend the morning in that veranda looking out to the east and move to this small room in the afternoon—this one looks out to the west, I get the last rays of the sun in here. You could say I follow the sun; I want sunshine, I want light, I am afraid of the dark. But the walls of this room are intimate, the dust in this room is my comfort.

As you can imagine, nothing in this room has remained the way Nellie had done it up. As you can see, there are books on the floor, all kinds of documents scattered on the desk (unimportant, but I'm too lazy to throw them away) and look at that cushion there on the sofa, still dimpled from the pressure of someone's head—you might still find a long black lock or two of hair if you look carefully. This room is out of bounds for the servants, it's kept the way it is, every day I watch the unconquerable dust pile up a little more, primal rubbish—I can almost see the natural state of this world, this life. Sometimes the room regains a little of its original appearance under Gayatri's touch, but I have infected Gayatri with my illness too, she is beginning to enjoy this untidy life, gradually realizing the original truth that there's nothing more comforting than letting yourself go. Life is nothing but a battle every moment—with yourself, with the world, with your circumstances—is there a man who doesn't want release from all this, release from worries, release from dreams? The comfort that flows from the complete absence of effort, from being inanimate—that has been my long-cherished desire, the finest learning of life. How painful my working life was—a devastatingly claustrophobic affair, under the continuous barrage of having people as old as my father address me as 'sir', of having the orderly, resplendent in red cummerbund, run up at a crook of my finger—I greyed in my mind far before my hair became grey. I wore the mask of the judge, my eyes never closing even for an instant, the muscles in my face as motionless as that of a statue, I was the representative of the law, I was 'My Lord'. When I sat on my throne, festooned in red velvet, I was beyond the seven deadly sins, beyond hunger or thirst or fatigue, beyond anger, beyond fear. As though I had been fixed in a steel frame, nails driven through my hands and feet, over and over again I screamed silently, 'Let me go, I can't take this any more!' But no one heard that scream, no one suspected anything, no one realized I was afraid to look the accused in the eye, no one was aware that I was looking for an escape, stopping short only on seeing the police guarding every door. It was I who had not let anyone realize, kept my eyes as coldly unmoving as a stone, spoken in a voice as unwavering as death—this was all the credit, all the boldness I could claim. And wherever I was anywhere other than at court—at home, or anywhere else—Ratandas Dalal's daughter, my beloved wife, accompanied me. As though we were a god and a goddess among men, mere human beings developed cricks in the necks trying to look at us—such was our life. White, bleached, spotless, disciplined, without a molecule of grime, of moisture, of air, of slime, of rust anywhere—

confident, established, seedless. You'd know from all the things I tolerated how great an actor I am. You'd know my deception, my sleight-of-hand, my sham of a life. As though I had never been poor, as though my father didn't have to survive on a monthly pension of seventy-five rupees only, as though I had spent my life in the stratosphere from birth, just like Nellie, as though I had never shed tears, never drifted like a torn sheet of paper in the wind, never been buffeted madly by the waves . . . But tell me, wouldn't fatigue creep in some time or the other? Wouldn't one want to fall, to stoop, literally, wouldn't one feel like trampling on the roses, feel like turning off every beam of light, feel like importing defects into the shiny world created with so much effort by Nellie, feel like smuggling in germs of a disease, flowing like a sly poison? Doesn't the heart ultimately need an asylum, something to depend on . . . the unalloyed body of a woman, my cave, my fortress . . . with the beauty and simplicity of the life of animals . . . in this room, on that sofa which can be converted every night into a bed for two, far from Nellie's wealth, far from the glittering onslaught of this house which is a tourist spot of Ootacamund, far from the farce of the rose garden? I wanted to pay Nellie back for her love, to take revenge on her and on myself . . . and it was in this manner—since I couldn't convey my thoughts to Nellie in any other way—that I started my sport with women.

Allow me to tell you everything candidly. You seem like someone I have known for a long time, I feel as though you know everything about me, or perhaps you used to once upon a time but have forgotten, although I haven't. Nellie, child-woman, starved for happiness—how naïvely she believed that we are born in this world to be happy, how desperately she wanted to make me happy. As though happiness is a ripe mango or a freshly made sweet, which a person can simply hand over to another. As though love between husband and wife is some unchanging universal truth, like the trajectory of the solar system. How could I explain to her that I cannot be happy, that I don't want to be happy? That I don't want to love, that I cannot love? That I have neither the ability nor the desire. How could I explain that every living hour of my life shames me, although I haven't stolen anything, or raped a woman, or accepted a bribe even in secret—on the contrary, I have a spotless reputation for honesty and wise judgement. How could I explain the real difference between us? I married her knowing full well that happiness is unattainable, happiness in my life at least; I could have married any other woman too—she had become available by chance, conveniently for me. And the ingredients of what Nellie thought of as 'happiness' had all been available to her because of her lineage—unlimited money, social prestige, the freedom to holiday in the Black Forest whenever she pleased, all these were as natural to her as the air she breathed; almost everyone her family knew belonged to this same social category, it was beyond Nellie's understanding that things could be any other way. Only one ingredient had to be procured from outside, it could be termed a sizeable component of her 'happiness': a 'husband'—a handsome, scholarly, upright husband. As far as she and even her parents were concerned, I was adorned with those adjectives. There was no lack of competition—some of them could have bought me out three hundred times over, Ratandas could even have got a prince of one of the native states as his son-in-law—but it was I who walked away with this jewel among women. Why, how? One reason was that Ratandas, who had built his huge business empire practically single-handedly, was somewhat favourably disposed towards me—because I had gone from nowhere to somewhere, so to speak. Another, and perhaps the most important, factor was that I had adjusted beautifully to the role of the lover; without conscious effort, I seem to have touched Nalini's most sensitive chord. I rattled off romantic expressions like 'soulmate', 'heart's desire', 'together till eternity' to her, which had become clichés to the world, but which captivated Nalini Dalal, which no young man before me had chanted for her (since no wandering minstrel would even be able to get anywhere near her). But this sentimental, wide-eyed Swiss-school-educated young woman melted on hearing me—who wore narrow ties, was perfectly conversant with Western etiquette, could expound on the differences between the Indian Penal Code and Roman law for half an hour at a stretch, could spout Shelley, Hugo and Tagore. She assumed my love was of the highest order—that I was drawn 'as the moth is to the flame' etcetera. On my behalf, the Romantic poets conquered a portion of Ratandas's huge estate and a wife beautiful enough to be shown off. No one had better say after this that poetry is useless.

Even after the marriage, I played the role of lover for a year or so, the first time with the fresh juicy body of a carefully preserved virgin hitherto untouched by a man was by no means unpleasant. But in that very short period, Nellie grew dangerously into a wife. Her concepts of 'happiness' and 'husband' virtually merged. She would be 'happy', she would make me 'happy' too—oh lord! For some time after the wedding she was determined to become a Bengali, assuming that was what I preferred. Packing away her slacks, her gowns, her salwar-kameez, every aspect of the way she used to dress before marriage, she switched to the sari, and, after a visit from my parents, she even added the accessories of the married Bengali woman; she actually tried for a few days to put on her sari the old-fashioned way, like my mother; she was full of regret that she had not grown her hair. I was forced to inform her in a roundabout way that her halting Bengali pronunciation was as unbearable as the faux Bengaliness she cultivated in her appearance. 'I like you just the way you are, there's no need to change into something else,' I told her sweetly. I explained to her that sindoor contained toxic mercury, that long hair was unhealthy, that no matter how glamorous a sari looked at a party, there was no other dress as impractical when it came to moving about. The trouble was, she accepted everything I said blindly as the truth; she thought that if only she was like this and not like that, did this instead of that, Eros would appear and take a joint seat in two hearts. Gradually I had to find ways to make her realize her mistake, to break the spell so that she could appreciate the core philosophy of Romantic poetry: that because there is no happiness except in dreams, all that man's fate holds in store is unhappiness. As I told you, I couldn't but cure her of her annoying habit of painting—that's where it began, gently. What harm could it have done, tell me, if she were happy painting bad pictures? She would have grown tired of it and given it up herself one day, what did my advice achieve that would not have happened on its own? And yet she had so much faith in me that my 'dislike' made her give up her play of pastels, her tinkling on the piano, her French cooking, her Bengali look. I wanted to hurt her, but she wasn't getting hurt, she bounced back like a rubber ball each time. So I had to be a little harsher, for which her motherhood offered me an opportunity.

After the birth of our first son, Nellie sported that famous smile of proud, loving motherhood, as though hers was a huge achievement. They worship mothers this way the world over—how do I say this? It makes me nauseous, I want to throw up. Is a baby a triptych at Elephanta or Mozart's *Don Juan* that it should be labelled a great creative accomplishment? Why be so proud of something even an earthworm can do? Nellie gazed at her son in the kind of rapt wonder with which we gaze at, say, an original Rembrandt after having seen nothing but prints for ages, or at the sea, completely overwhelmed, on our first visit to Puri. 'Are you happy? Tell me, are you happy?' she kept asking me. 'See how he's looking at you!' And other hoary old clichés, which human mothers chant to teach the male beast to be a 'father', to inculcate love within him for his offspring, who is his natural enemy. Even Christian missionaries cannot accomplish what mothers can. I realized this was an escape route from Nellie's anguished 'love'—if she were to be wrapped up in her child her attention towards me would be lessened, giving me some relief—but since Nellie now wanted nothing but her child, since she experienced a heavenly bliss in cuddling that messy lump of flesh, I felt it necessary to separate the mother and the child. Excellent Occidental practices were established—the baby would stay in a separate room with a nanny, feed at the breast of a healthy wet-nurse who would be paid for it, have imported baby-food from the age of three months and be brought to his mother with great ceremony four times a day for fifteen or twenty minutes. Meanwhile, Nellie's breast ached—both physically and psychologically, but I had the civil surgeon and modern science (or what passed for it) on my side; she admitted defeat to the logic that this was the better option for the child's health, for the mother's health and beauty too, or perhaps she didn't object because I wanted it that way. That was how both of Nellie's sons were brought up—with a nanny in childhood, sent off to a missionary school in a distant healthy location as soon as they turned five, packed off to England no sooner than they turned seventeen. Nellie begged and pleaded piteously to hold back the younger one, threw many tragic glances at me, I was made to hear her sigh over and over again at night—sighs of old-fashioned, non-progressive, unenlightened Indian motherhood that broke through the flimsy covering of Western education—but I was not to be swayed from my duty. Did we want namby-pamby Bengali milksops, spineless, mollycoddled even at fourteen by mothers who offered them their laps and hand-fed meals, smothered them from birth in a demonic love that kept them babies forever? No, not in a hundred years, not in a thousand! What could be more important than ensuring that your sons are well-educated, disciplined, and will grow into real men when the time comes—successful professionals, at the very least?

But the problem which arose was that, since her sons were away, Nellie's life once again revolved around her husband; I was the centre of her world, like a wan, tiny moon orbiting the earth, she clung to me, sticking in my throat, a constant companion like an incurable toothache. I could make out from her behaviour that she missed her children constantly, but she never said anything to me, she had no complaints against me, no sense of hurt, there was no question of anger; all she wanted (and an impossible wanting it was, too!) was that I should compensate for her pain at being separated from her children, for her tortured motherhood, and fulfil all her unsophisticated, feminine, primal desires, which could not be met with the glitter of money or fashion, with my 'love'! Can you imagine how unfair this demand was! Just think of the life we led, the two of us together like a pair of lovers, living in a small town, no socializing beyond the same tedious handful of government officers of the same rank, not even any household or family problems to distract us—and *that* was the terrifying problem. There would have been some variety had there been a few showers of confrontations—hailstorms at least, if not thunderstorms—but no, that was impossible for Nellie, she would in all circumstances avoid any behaviour that she knew to be contrary to decorum (and decorum was an ingredient of happiness for her). I failed repeatedly in my attempts to provoke her. She had thrown my poisonous, cruel barbs right back at me—not by retaliating, but by sidestepping them unobtrusively, denying the possibility of conflict. And yet, if people can count themselves as happy at times, isn't it because different aspects of conflict—sometimes poverty, sometimes disease, sometimes failure—surround them?

What keeps the world ticking over, what gives life some kind of meaning, is not fulfilment but the absence of it, not unity but diversity. Only those who have been confined to their bed by illness, who have agonized over where their next meal will come from, who have seen their myriad efforts fail, who have met the need for love through pet dogs, know the real taste of everyday happinesses like good health and love and affluence and any sort of success. Leave alone man, not even the gods can survive unalloyed happiness without any opposition or conflict. Think of the lives of Greek gods and goddesses, cursed with immortality, no hope even of deliverance through death, no destruction lying in store for them in the final apocalypse—unlike our gods—nothing to do, really, till eternity, no wonder they interfere in the affairs of worm-like human beings, arguing like fishwives over Hector and Achilles, rushing around between heaven and earth, swallowing nectar and belching out the poison of envy—somehow passing their days in heaven in mutual jealousy, mutual humiliation, mutual annihilation. Now you can imagine my condition, an insignificant man stuck with the doggedly dedicated Nellie as wife! I wanted to hurt her, to make her hate me, to find release from the coils of her love, but the foolish woman understood nothing, or pretended not to even though she did. The more she played the part of the patient Griselda, the more my rage mounted, systematically I ground her peaks of wifely devotion in the dust; I decided not to maintain even the fig-leaf of courtesy or diplomacy, I would enter into direct conflict instead of issuing twisted statements like diplomats did, if need be, I wouldn't even baulk at bombing to pulverize her. That was just what happened. Eventually I had to incite my blood into action, I began my forays into the bodies of women—not because I wanted to, but to open up Nellie's third eye so that she could read the writing on the wall. With that, I went on a long journey away from Dacca, away from the women I had seen in the veranda at Bokul Villa by the light of the setting sun and then of the electric bulbs, away from my newfound desire to love.

Nine

How many students did you have in Dacca University during your time there? Pardon me, I keep forgetting you're the same age as I am, that we were contemporaries in Dacca. Do you remember what the hostel girls used to be like at the time, how they dressed? White saris, their heads half-covered, they walked to the college from the hostel in rows, marching to a beat like soldiers, divided into two or three groups—glancing neither left nor right. There were about fifteen of them, all young, students, but they appeared mature and serious, almost like nuns; covered, concealed, flocking together—like sisters of a literary order: all in white, emerging from their monastery; after a few hours of bell-ringing at the temple they would return in the evening, without a glance to the left or the right. It was hard for us to imagine that these denizens of a fortress were our classmates, that they could have anything in common with ordinary mortals such as ourselves, that they ever laughed or joked, it was even difficult to think of them as having an interest in anything other than academics. The college had an impenetrable sanctum sanctorum for them—going by the name of the Ladies' Common Room—where they spent their days behind the veil; the teachers escorted them to their classes from this room and deposited them back afterwards, guarding them across twenty or twenty-five yards of dangerous corridors. It was a sight, a spectacle, as the corridors were populated with belles for a couple of minutes when the bell rang—a flock of ewes controlled by the shepherd—pardon me, I meant to say mares following the elephant—no, that's not it either—let's say our university offered protection to the rare and graceful creature known as the 'female student' with great effort—raising fences, appointing guards, drawing lines—as though a thousand-odd carnivorous animals had circled fifty terrified does, as though a moment's carelessness would lead to the beasts of prey sinking their teeth into their succulent necks.

Their seating arrangements in class were separate too—not in the same rows as the male students but on glorified chairs on either side of the professors' desk. Of course, it wasn't as though a glance from a doe-eye never came our way, even in the classroom, or that a colourful sari never created a flash of sensation in the corridor; besides, these majestic handmaidens of the almighty were spotted at various university functions too; idiotic young men even struck up conversations with them, taking up positions outside the baize curtains covering the Ladies' Common Room—conversations meaning hemming and hawing, nodding and twisting—a few of the boldest among them tried to go even further, but, just like the thwarted tigers in their canal-enclosed space in Lucknow's open zoo, their attempts too only culminated in gestures, in greedy glances, in farcical mental licking of lips. It was simply impossible to imagine that there could ever be easy intermingling between these two completely different species.

Of course, I maintained a lofty disdain, as though I was not in the least bit interested in these pampered female monks, but that day I stopped for a moment on catching a glimpse of Bulbul in the corridor. Rebati Mukherjee from the philosophy department was walking towards the classroom, followed by the inevitable tail—a winding handful of girls, their eyes downcast . . . Bulbul was among them. But she probably didn't notice me, or perhaps she avoided me deliberately; or maybe that was how she conveyed to me that here, in this sacred educational institution, she did not want to acknowledge the person with whom she had taken the initiative to get acquainted at Anadi-babu's house. I tried to forget this humiliation, but as I was rummaging in the library stacks after the lunch-break, I heard a faint sound behind me. Turning, I saw Bulbul. Having been rebuffed once, I assumed she was there in search of a book, and I should also pretend not to know her. But the spot was secluded, there was no one else nearby, our eyes had no choice but to meet, and there was no option but to acknowledge that we knew each other. As a matter of fact, Bulbul looked at me as though she were there specifically for me, with a quick smile she said, 'Bibha-di sent this book for you.'

'Bibha-di meaning Bibhabati Dutta?'

'That's what we call her—you can, too.'

I felt as though I was being accorded special privileges; as though I had been elevated to the same status as Mitu and Bulbul—long-familiar and favourite students of Bibhabati's; as though I had taken another step forward in their world, in my newly discovered world of women, thanks to that one statement of Bulbul's. But since it wouldn't be a matter of pride for me if she realized this, I said, 'That's the problem with our country—you have to establish familial relationships with women even if they aren't part of your family.'

Bulbul wasn't pleased with the levity in my tone; gravely, she said, 'It's different with Bibha-di. She's much more than a sister. This book is a brief history of India—Bibha-di sent it in case it's of any use to you.'

I, who had to present a tutorial on Swinburne's plays in three days, who had been absorbed even a few minutes ago in the question of why no nineteenth-century English poet had been able to write a real play, took a little while to understand why I needed a history of India. Possibly guessing as much from my expression, Bulbul said, 'For that historical chart—surely you haven't forgotten.'

'The glory of India's past has to be asserted?' A small laugh escaped my throat, Bulbul put her finger on her lips admonishingly.

'Softly! This is a library—you're not allowed to talk here.' Then, in a low voice, practically whispering, she said, 'Not an assertion but a reminder. Only those who remember can do things that are remembered.'

I looked directly at her to fathom whether this last statement was drawn from her own sensibility or whether it was something she had heard, or read in a book; her small, restless eyes stilled momentarily behind her glasses. 'There's something else I have to tell you . . .' Bulbul's mouth opened, but nothing was audible, for the sound of a train was heard at that moment. The railway line ran beside the library, it was clear from the clattering and clanging that a goods train was passing, its harsh, heavy, prolonged sound did not end quickly—I had to wait nearly five minutes face to face with Bulbul, in silent expectation of the rest of what she wanted to say. To fill the gap, we were forced to look at each other once or twice, to smile. I felt a faint stirring in my heart. I was standing close to a young woman in a secluded corner, she had something to tell me—even if my mind refused to acknowledge this, my heart responded. I thought I detected a certain eagerness in Bulbul's expression too, but I couldn't reconcile it with the significance I had ascribed to it; her expression was so self-possessed for someone so young that it suggested she wasn't aware of our youth, or that this fact did not matter to her at all.

I turned my eyes away to look outside. There the grass was green, the fields wide, the branches swayed in the breeze of an overcast afternoon, a few mynahs hopped about on the ground. Couldn't Bulbul and I go sit in the shade of the tree in that field? Couldn't we take a walk under the evening sky as its first stars appeared? Surely somewhere in the background, a woman was waiting for me—the girl, the companion of my imagination—waiting for happenstance, for a connection, for a hint from fate, to part the curtains and step into view? But what Bulbul said when the sound of the train died down did not sound as green as the grass, the mynahs did not dance in the spaces between her words. 'One more thing—you don't have any objection to working for the swadeshi fair, do you?'

'But I've already told you I'll do it.'

'If you agreed only out of a sense of obligation to Bibha-di, let it be.'

Actually, the thought of poring over books to put together facts and dates didn't appeal to me at all, but then I'd even managed to get through 'The Faerie Queene' to pass my exams. 'What obligation can there be? Besides, it's not a particularly difficult task.'

'No, not difficult at all, especially not for you . . .' Bulbul stopped suddenly, as though she wasn't ready just yet to confess to any admiration for me. 'Bibha-di sent this book for you—of course, there's no dearth of books in the library, but this one's a little different, I'm sure you know the name of the author.' Holding the book up, Bulbul showed me the name of the writer on the spine, a well-known leader of the freedom movement. 'If you think it'll come in handy . . .'

'Yes, certainly!' I said, taking the book from her. 'I enjoyed his book about prison experiences, I'm sure this one's well-written too.'

'This one isn't light like the other one, but every word is steeped in patriotism.'

I paused at this last observation, it seemed to have been picked up from a critical essay published somewhere; I wanted to know whether Bulbul had read the book herself, and if she had, what she really thought of it. But Bulbul continued immediately, 'Oh, I almost forgot, I've brought a couple of issues of *Muktadhara* for you too. We need your piece in a fortnight.' Her shoulders acquired a certain angle, as though she was done with me and was now about to leave.

'What subject do you read? Where do you live?' I said quickly.

'Philosophy—second-year. I live in Kayettuli.'

'That's close to where I live.'

'I'm not home much. We'll meet again—goodbye.' She made it clear with her manner of departure that she had neither the time nor the inclination to chat purposelessly with me. But she came to our house a few days later with something for Kajol-mami to stitch. I didn't see her arrive, I only heard another woman's voice in the next room mingling with Kajol-mami's, it sounded familiar but I couldn't pin it down. I heard words like 'handkerchief', 'teapoy-cover', 'embroidery', 'hemstitch' and so on, followed suddenly a little later by, 'Is Ranajit home?'

'Ranju, can you come in here a minute?' Kajol called from the other room. I entered, Bulbul didn't pay much attention to me at first, then she got up and asked, 'Will you walk with me?'

It was nearly evening. Out on the road Bulbul said, 'Let's take a walk near the Dhakeshwari Temple building.' I was a little surprised at her proposal, because it was rather unusual in Dacca for a young woman and a young man (even for a married couple, except in Ramna) to be out strolling together.

'Aren't you going home?' I couldn't help asking.

'I'm in no hurry.'

'Do you stroll around by yourself?'

'Usually, though I get a companion too at times, like now.'

'Without telling anyone at home?'

'Yes. My parents have given up all hope.' Bulbul smiled from the corner of her mouth.

Her words, her behaviour, seemed slightly unfamiliar to me, a little strange. I suddenly remembered something from a long time ago. I was in school then, class nine, a boy named Satinath used to visit me from time to time. He was a student of law, about seven years older than me, quite a lot older considering my age at the time. The very first days, after praising my essay in the school magazine, he told me after speaking of this and that for a few minutes that he had something in his pocket which, if found in his possession, would mean at least five years of imprisonment. I didn't believe him, passing it off as a tall claim. He told me to deliver a letter to an address in Potuatuli, which I refused to do. I refused when he wanted to go walking with me near the racecourse one evening. I suspected him to be one of those who, in a literal sense, like boys—having fallen into their clutches a couple of times, I hated even thinking about them. You must remember how prevalent it was in Dacca? Not the latest imported version, though—not because that was their preference—you could call it a substitute, just something to get out of the way. Girls were out of reach, it wasn't easy even exchanging glances with them; the walls of Eden School were as high as those of jails, except within a few sophisticated neighbourhoods women didn't even set foot on the road, they drove around with the windows shut. And you had to listen to so much advice about this particular activity, couched in hints and innuendos, that some of them couldn't keep themselves from satiating their curiosity with one another's help.

But no, I never trod that path—I was a lover of the opposite sex then, still am. I may have been wrong to label Satinath as a boy-hunter, but his clandestine ways, his manner of whispering after throwing furtive glances all around, as though he walked around with a bloodcurdling mystery in his pocket, his manner in general—all of these were so loathsome that I erected protective walls around me the moment I saw him, I refused every one of his propositions. Gradually he stopped visiting me; I was relieved.

But Bulbul was a girl—not an older man worthy of suspicion—a slim young woman, a friend of Mitu's, the well-known Bibhabati's messenger, so I was quite pleased with the hint of secrecy in her behaviour, and I couldn't help but feel pleasantly surprised at her independent, unfettered ways. Didn't she know how dangerous it was for us to be seen walking around together on that secluded road? People might start saying things; how long would it be before some moral policeman tried to bash my head in? But I was a man; even if I felt apprehensive I couldn't possibly express it. As we chatted, Bulbul led me to the mango orchard behind the Dhakeshwari Temple—the spot was infamous for many reasons, there was no one to be seen anywhere. But there wasn't a shade of concern on Bulbul's face.

'The grass is quite clean here,' she said, 'shall we sit for a while? I've been walking all day, preparations for the fair are in full swing, you know.'

'Are you doing it all by yourself?'

'How could you imagine I'd manage it all by myself?' Bulbul laughed softly. 'Many of us are involved—you too. Bibha-di is amazing—she knows exactly what each of us is capable of.'

I found the opportunity to ask a question. 'You said the fair is for raising money. Is that really what it's for?'

'Partly. It's also a way to make people feel more patriotic.'

'What do you do with the money?'

'What do you mean? What about the school that Bibha-di runs, don't you suppose it needs money? What about the cost of fighting the cases for political prisoners? Where do you suppose all that comes from? This is how—through the efforts of thousands of people all over the country. The Dumdum conspiracy case is coming up in the High Court. Twelve people accused. Bibha-di says if we can get a good set of lawyers most of them will go free.'

'Will they go free because they're innocent or because of the lawyers' skills?' I blurted out.

'Do you call patriotism a crime?' Bulbul asked me, her eyes narrowing.

'I don't, but surely the judges do. It's true that their law has been broken, isn't it?'

Bulbul looked at me with stern eyes, admonishingly. 'The law is very subtle. What's important is not what someone has done—only what is proved in a court of law. That's why good lawyers are needed.'

'The kind of lawyer who can turn falsehood into truth?'

A deep colour spread across Bulbul's face, as though she was furious with me, as though I wasn't honouring the friendship she had offered me. She said calmly moments later, 'Falsehood and truth are not so simple. You have to assume that anything that helps your cause is true, and anything that prevents you is false.'

'But that's not what Gandhiji's satyagraha is based on. Truth is central to it.'

'Oh, so you're a follower of Gandhi's.'

'No, I neither follow nor oppose anyone—I have this bad habit of arguing whenever I can,' I said, smiling.

'As for me, I don't care for arguing, it comes in the way of work. Besides, it's wonderful for two people to agree, isn't it?'

I was about to say that if everyone agreed about everything all the time, the world wouldn't be worth living in, but, glancing at Bulbul's uncomplicated, eager face, I only said, 'Of course.'

Bulbul asked me whether I'd enjoyed the two issues of *Muktadhara* she'd given me.

'They weren't bad.'

'Meaning, not all that good? It isn't easy getting good pieces here in Dacca—it survives only because Bibha-di writes.'

Bulbul's words revealed that she thought of Bibhabati's articles as 'good', but it was her article that had actually disappointed me the most, it gave me a small but rude shock. She was writing the biographies of Irish revolutionaries serially, but all of them seemed to be from books, the writer's heart hadn't left a mark (although, presumably, the subject was bound to be exciting for a patriot like Bibhabati). I had not expected her to include clichés like 'sacrifice of blood at the altar of the nation', 'the dawn of independence' or 'Achilles' heel' and oft-quoted lines like 'Cowards die many times before their death'. I had assumed that someone who was so beautiful to look at, so polished in her behaviour, whose appearance at a gathering made everyone stop and stare, who had earned everyone's respect with her achievements and her character, would also write with a high degree of elegance, with the austerity of her handloom dress, with the grace of her smile. I was pained that she hadn't been able to convey even an iota of her wonderful personality to many more people, to those who would perhaps never even see her, through the medium of those Irish revolutionaries.

But of course, my disillusionment was not to be articulated to Bulbul, so I said what I had to in a roundabout way, 'Do you know whether these articles have actually been written by Bibha-di?'

'What do you mean! Do you suppose someone else wrote them for her? How could you even imagine such a thing?'

'I've been told famous people sometimes get their secretaries to write their articles for them. Nothing wrong with that—they're so busy, I was wondering when Bibha-di even finds the time to write.'

The sarcasm in my words wasn't evident to Bulbul; she said, pleased, 'You have no idea as yet how extraordinary Bibha-di is.' Stopping suddenly, she speared me with a glance. 'You're very fond of films, aren't you?'

'How did you know?'

'Oh, all the students know about you. Besides, I've seen you myself several times coming out of the cinema hall at Sadarghat.'

I didn't know anyone could have enough time or curiosity to keep track of my whereabouts, especially a young woman; I felt a little proud, but puncturing that pride, Bulbul said, 'Why do you waste your time watching films?'

'Why would I waste my time—I watch them because I enjoy them.'

'Enjoyment may be important to you,' said Bulbul after some thought, 'but not to me.'

'Haven't you ever watched a film?'

'Once or twice, Bibha-di took a few of us. That comic actor, funny moustache, large shoes . . .'

'Chaplin!' I exclaimed. 'You couldn't remember Chaplin's name? Incredible!'

'Incredible—why?'

Now I spoke loftily, like someone airing my knowledge, 'If there is anyone among film actors who's genuinely talented, a real artist, it's Chaplin. In *The Gold Rush* he's clearly proved no one can hold a candle to him—not Fairbanks, not Valentino, not Lon Chaney . . . no one. Such a wonderful smile, brimming with tears, just like Oliver Twist—no, even better, just like Lear's Fool—if only the Fool rescued Lear and Cordelia and the play had a happy ending. Isn't it possible—Chaplin's Lear, where the most important role is the Fool's?'

My flow of words dried up suddenly when I looked at Bulbul, and saw in her eyes that fine line of fatigue that cannot be camouflaged even by politeness when we are assailed by a discussion on an unfamiliar subject. Reining in my eagerness, I said, 'You haven't seen *The Gold Rush*, have you?'

'No,' replied Bulbul, tilting her head back. 'Besides, no matter how great an actor that Chaplin of yours is, what use is it for us? Will it mean enough food and clothing for everyone? Will it end the oppression of the British? Will it set India free?'

My eyes popped at this, I felt a rush of blood to my head, I met her eyes to see if she was joking. No, there was no trace of humour, her eyes were unwavering, grim—they held a combination of entreaty and reproach. Lest I say something improper in anger, I lowered my voice with an effort and said, 'Do you really mean to say that anything that will not make India independent is of no value?'

'I didn't say any such thing, I didn't want to. But . . .' Pausing, Bulbul ripped up a blade of grass with two fingers . . . 'I see Bibha-di, I worship her like a goddess, she has shown me the road ahead, I have neither the time nor the inclination to glance at the flowers strewn along the way.'

'Like a goddess', 'the road ahead'—both these expressions sounded jarring, cheap, but when I saw Bulbul gazing at me with eyes brimming with faith—faith that she had not gathered with her intelligence but discovered in her heart—I restrained the argumentative demon within me.

'It's getting dark, shall we go now?'

'I don't fear the darkness—besides, you're with me.'

I was a little surprised that the possibility of my being the cause of her perturbation was not on the horizon of her thoughts.

'I'm not particularly strong.' I smiled, 'I won't be able to save you from a miscreant's assault.'

'Perhaps I'll save you instead. But let's go—I have to go somewhere else too.'

As we emerged from the orchard, walking side by side, I suddenly discovered a tiny smile on her face. 'You know what it is,' she said, replacing the formal *aapni* she had been using all this time with the familiar *tumi*. 'I'm not a poet like you, I'm no writer, I'm very ordinary—all I know is that the house is in flames, and if I can pour even a single bucket of water on those flames, my life will have some meaning. Oh dear, I went and used *tumi*—I hope you don't mind. No, why should you, you can use it too with me. All right?' As we walked, Bulbul took my hand for a moment, and let it drop instantly.

Ten

I was astonished by Bulbul's use of the familiar form of 'you', it wasn't as though the touch of her hand didn't make me tremble, given my age it was inevitable. You do remember what a big thing it was in Bengali novels of the time for the form of address to change from the formal to the familiar, how much effort the writer had to put into getting the young man and woman to that level; a million Indian villages could have been lit up by the sheer quantum of electricity that flowed through the printed word as a result of fingers touching one another while transferring a glass of water, or of the woman's touch as the man lay on his sickbed. (You must have noticed how frequently writers made their heroes and heroines fall ill, unable to find better ways of bringing them into physical proximity!) I must admit there was a throbbing in my veins too as a result of Bulbul's sudden, unexpected behaviour, but I could see no reaction whatsoever on her part, she didn't even seem to be aware of the inherent relationship that existed between us: like the one between a flame and an inflammable object. Crossing the field, we reached the well-lit road, she kept talking as we walked, in a flat, everyday voice, continuing to use *tumi* casually, unerringly, as though we had grown up in the same house since childhood, as though we knew each other far too well, as brothers and sisters do. This counterfeit intimacy was painful for me; every time we walked under a lamppost I glanced at her out of the corner of my eye—trying to gauge how much of all this was deception or self-delusion.

She brought up Mitu Bardhan; when she heard I hadn't met Mitu since the other evening, she said, 'I'm going to visit her the day after tomorrow—Saturday—you can come too if you like. Not that you need me to mediate, she knows you far better than you think she does. For a long time now . . . Are you surprised? Now don't go telling her that I told you. She's been looking everywhere to unearth every piece of yours that's ever been published—I think she even sent your poems to Dildar Navroze.'

'What, really!' I exclaimed.

'Why are you so surprised? Mitu's not as matter-of-fact as I am—she loves poetry, even writes in secret herself. But she's very shy about her stories, never lets anyone read them, but of course she might agree if you insist—you two have a lot in common. Ah, we're at your house—all right then . . .'

Since she was about to take my leave I intervened quickly, 'Let me take you home.'

'There's absolutely no need—besides, I'm not going

home. But can't you stop using that formal "you"? I'm a little younger than you, in fact, although actually . . .'

'Actually you're the older one, since you're the girl,' I interrupted, using *tumi* this time, 'isn't that so? Just about my grandmother's age!'

'There you are, see how I provoked you into dropping the formality? I really dislike this formality among ourselves.'

'What do you mean, ourselves?'

But before I could utter the question, Bulbul continued, 'All right, you can come with me a little further—up to the level-crossing. Now listen.' Sensing her eyes on my face, I turned towards her too. 'I love Mitu very much, but I don't tell her everything—she may not be able to bear it.'

Stopping, I asked, 'What do you mean? What is it that she may not be able to bear?'

'I'll tell you another time, all right? We're going to keep meeting, after all, over the arrangements for the swadeshi fair.'

There were two assumptions in there that had me worried; first, that I had become seriously involved with the fair (was that what 'ourselves' meant?); and second, that she and I wouldn't meet any more once the fair had ended.

'Are you coming to Bokul Villa on Saturday then?'

'Saturday?' I said absent-mindedly. 'Let's see.' (As a matter of fact I was more than keen on visiting Mitu at home, but I didn't want Bulbul to know that.) 'Oh no, I have something else . . .' I stopped suddenly, for some unknown reason I felt it would be prudent not to let Bulbul know where I was supposed to go on Saturday.

I had spent a couple of minutes with Jones at Bulbul's birthday party after the singing ended; since he had read some Sanskrit he could wade through Bankimchandra, but he was finding it difficult to negotiate Saratchandra, so he asked if it would be possible for me to help him from time to time. If I could make the time, if it wasn't too inconvenient. I had agreed, whereupon Jones had asked me to tea around five on Saturday. I remembered all this at that very moment. I couldn't recollect if I had accepted the invitation (Because my glance had shifted to Kajol at that point, she was bidding goodbye to Mitu—'I had a lovely time, Mitu, you must come to our house too.' 'Please come again,' Mitu had said, turning to look—not directly at me, but in the direction where I was standing with Jones.), but I was sure I hadn't refused it either; Jones must have assumed I would go, so I had to go, or else I would become another one of those Indians who forgot that they had either extended, or accepted, an invitation, who have no sense of punctuality.

'What time will you be there?'

'I see we're standing on ceremony again!' Bulbul's eyes were full of amusement. 'Do you suppose I follow the clock? I'll be there some time in the evening.'

'I may be a little late.'

'I'm not forcing you to go if you don't want to . . . Look out!'

A jangling presence announced itself behind us, a cycle-bell like a bunch of children laughing loudly. Turning round, I saw Amulya's round, ever-cheerful face, like the moon rising through the haze of the darkness.

'I was sure I recognized you from the back,' said Amulya, moving the lower half of his body, from waist downwards, in a graceful arc as he got off his cycle.

I assumed he was addressing me, imagined he had been unable to contain himself from building the ringing of his cycle-bell to a crescendo the moment he saw me walking with a young woman, so I was more than a little surprised when Bulbul spoke in response.

'Oh, it's Amulya. Why this uncivilized bell-ringing?'

'I was practising scales on my cycle-bell. Did you know I've been invited by the young men of Jagannath Hall to pour melody into their ears this evening? There is of course the minor matter of refreshments too. Are you going, Ranajit, to this summit feast organized under the stewardship of Sudhangshu? Oh sorry, pardon me, I keep forgetting that vulgar feasting is not for you—nobody's ever seen you at any hostel feast. You only sip the nectar of flowers, the dew of the moon . . .'

'Give up this crass humour of yours, will you, Amulya,' I said acerbically. 'Asses can still be tolerated when they bray, but they're unbearable when they try to be funny.'

I felt contrite as soon as I had spoken (for I do not normally speak with the intention of hurting people), I felt a little embarrassed too, for what if Bulbul thought I was trying to teach Amulya a lesson for her benefit. But Amulya's smile widened (no barb had yet been invented that could penetrate his thick skin), and Bulbul said with a mixture of laughter and reproach, 'Oh, really! You mustn't be annoyed with Amulya, no one is. There's no malice in him. Come, Amulya, I'm going to Ramna too, walk with me part of the way.' Bulbul bid adieu to me with a single backward glance, a small smile and a friendly wave.

I walked back home slowly, questions swarming around me. That evening, the pleasant daydream that I had briefly indulged in a few days ago—there in the stacks at the library, looking out at the fields so that I wouldn't have to keep looking at Bulbul when the passing train interrupted her—seemed to have come true; at dusk, under the cool indigo sky with the first star shining, I had a woman as a companion. I had never spent as much time alone with a young woman before this. More important: I didn't seek her out, didn't chase her, she came to me on her own. The secluded spot, the eagerness in her expression that she made no attempt to conceal, the secretive air with which she said or did something, her use of *tumi*, taking my hand—there was no lack of ingredients for a romance. I should have been thrilled, in fact, I actually was at one point, but why then this fatigue, this uncomfortable feeling at the end of it all?

The thought of how minor my role was in the time I spent with Bulbul hurt my ego. Come to think of it, everything seemed to have gone according to her wish, I had merely performed her bidding all this while. 'Walk with me . . . let's go into the orchard . . . let's sit here . . . let's go now . . . up to that level-crossing . . . I won't insist if you don't want to.' As if there was any question of insisting, as if she had some sort of claim on me because of the hour we'd spent together. And then . . . she abandoned me as soon as Amulya came. So she was friendly with Amulya too, she addressed him as *tumi* too, she even praised him for not being malicious. Was she trying to make me jealous? Didn't she know it was impossible for me to be jealous of a wastrel like Amulya? Then something else occurred to me, I seemed to have a moment of insight into Bulbul's mind. No—she wasn't trying to make me jealous, wasn't employing the age-old techniques of feminine guile, she had cleverly barricaded herself against those very things. Her use of *tumi*, taking my hand, the boy-like ease of her behaviour—all of these were preventives, like vaccination for smallpox—as far as she was concerned, this was how she expected to keep the seeds of a love-affair from sprouting, how she could spend time 'innocently' with young men. I was upset at the thought, a little mortified, as—unless I had misunderstood her—my being a man held no value for her, her being a woman was of no consequence either; she wasn't even willing to acknowledge the possibility of romance, for which my desire had grown stronger ever since that evening at Bokul Villa. I felt she had deceived me with a few sweet phrases, I repented having allowed her to get as close as she had, I decided I would convey to her that I wasn't the kind of idiot who would consort with her in a brotherly way.

But who could tell, maybe this too was a declaration of womanhood for her, the other face of her feminine ploy—she sought my company precisely because I was a young man—but she wouldn't acknowledge it to herself, pretending it was all 'innocent', trying to prove that her relationship with me was one between fellow-workers, what she had consciously erected a barrier against could well be the real objective of her unconscious. But though this assumption was flattering to myself, I couldn't accept it; I could not find within me the pleasure that I should have felt at having enjoyed the company of a young woman in privacy; where Bulbul was concerned, what stuck to me was an uncomfortable feeling, a trace of annoyance, and attraction as well as doubt.

When I reached Bokul Villa on Saturday evening, armed with several books, Bulbul was on her way out. 'Lovely!' she said. 'He arrives just as I am about to leave. And with all those books too! A real storehouse of knowledge! I was talking to Mitu—Bibha-di's thinking of getting the girls to stage a musical at the fair, put thirteen or fourteen songs together into a sort of play. Hand-picked songs: from Bankimchandra to Dildar Navroze. We were discussing the selection and the sequence. 'What do you think, Ranajit?' I didn't answer, Bulbul advanced towards the door. 'I'd better go, Mitu, I really don't have any more time, my student is collapsing in my absence. Ranajit—think about what I said, about that musical. Mitu, will you find out from him, it would be best if the two of you worked on it together . . . Oh, this has Arthur Jones's name written in it.' I had put my books down on a windowsill; Bulbul was leafing through them, that must have been the source of that last exclamation.

'He gave it to me to read,' I had to explain.

'Who? Arthur Jones? Did you visit him at home?'

I said, I don't know why, somewhat defensively, 'Why, is there anything wrong with that?'

'Of course not, why should there be, we all know Jones likes mingling with young men. What did you talk about?'

I couldn't tell Bulbul in as many words that it wasn't polite to ask such a question, I only said in brief, 'This and that.'

Actually, it wasn't this and that, Jones and I had conversed about language and literature alone. I wasn't very comfortable the first few minutes after entering his bungalow in the farthest corner of Ramna. The floor was so clean and well-polished that I almost slipped on it, the furniture so immaculately arranged that I thought twice before sitting down, the cups so beautiful that they didn't appear to have been made to drink tea out of—at least, that was how I felt then, for I had no idea I would be elevated to living among luxuries much greater than those—and that too in just a few years. But within a few minutes of the beginning of our discussion, my hesitation, borne of immaturity, vanished. I found Jones quite excited about the evidence of distant kinship between some words in English and Bengali, despite the completely divergent flavours of the two tongues. *Janma*—'birth' in Bengali—reminded him of 'genesis' and 'generation'; *gyan*—'knowledge' in Bengali—of 'ignorant' and 'cunning'; *sthaan*—Bengali for 'place'—of 'stand'; he couldn't but draw a connection between *trishna* in Bengali and its English equivalent 'thirst', between *smriti* in Bengali—'memory' in English—and 'martyr'; in *bidya*—Bengali for 'education'—he found the same root as in the English words 'wise', 'witch', 'ideal' and 'idea'. Despite my first-class BA degree, I knew very little of linguistics at the time; it was beyond me how *smriti* could be related to 'martyr', but I didn't betray too much astonishment, lest Jones consider me an ignoramus. But when he happened to mention that the Bengali word for worms in the stomach—*crimee*—has evolved into the English 'crimson', I couldn't help but say, 'Really? Amazing!'

'Of course it's amazing! You can hear the proximity between the English "same" and the Bengali *shawmo*, between "name" and *naam*; it's not difficult to see how "sugar" is related to the Bengali equivalent, *shawrkawra*, or "candy" to the Bengali *khawndo*—these words have remained similar in pronunciation, and haven't changed much in meaning either—but how distant are *crimee*—such a filthy affair—and the crimson colour of the rose! Candy reminds me of something else. The underlying Latin word beneath "candid", "candle" and "candidate" is "candour", or "white"—and its Sanskrit cousins are *chandra* and *chandran*—both materially meaning "bright", "glowing". Similarly, the English "scene" is related to the Sanskrit *chhaya*. *Chhaya*, which is *skia* in Greek, does mean what you refer to as "shade" or "shadow" in Bengali, but in Sanskrit, it also refers to "glow"—like in *Meghdootam* . . .' Jones rose to fetch a book from his shelf, turning over the pages, he said, 'Here, in *Purvamegha*, "*Ratnachhayavyatikar ibah* . . . " scene, glow, stage—there are many different meanings hidden in that one word "scene", and there's no end to the number of words that flow from it.'

'But how did *crimee* lead to "crimson"?'

'I'll tell you—it's quite amusing. *Crimee* refers to worms, of course, and red dye used to be made from dead worms which the Arabs had named *kirmiz*—which is nothing but the Arabic pronunciation for *crimee*; that led, after detours through a few other languages, to "crimson" in English. Another fascinating word is "banyan"—its root is the Sanskrit *banik*—meaning "trader"—from which came the Portuguese *banyan*—what you refer to as the *bania* or the *beney*—the tree acquired the same name because trading took place beneath it. Really, there's nothing more amazing than language. The entire history of humankind is hidden in language, all races are united in it, borrowing from one another. The strongest argument against those who believe in the supremacy of a particular race or religion—like the Roman Catholics in the Middle Ages, or we British in the nineteenth century, or as Hitler has begun to now in Germany—is to be found in linguistics.'

I asked him which of the contemporary English poets he liked the most. He mentioned a name I had only heard vaguely until then: T.S. Eliot, an American; when he heard I hadn't read anything of his, Jones immediately read out a poem named 'Prufrock'. When I asked if I could borrow the book for a few days, he said eagerly, 'Of course! Have you read Yeats's latest book? There's a brand new poet born in there . . . This one of James Joyce's?'

I left with a few recently published books strapped to my cycle and several recently planted ideas clinging to my mind.

After Bulbul had left I told Mitu, 'I don't know why your friend has started using *tumi* when addressing me. And doesn't she have anything other than that swadeshi fair to talk about?'

'Yes, Bulbul does seem a bit eccentric at first, but she's very nice,' said Mitu affectionately. 'I hope you didn't mind.'

'Bulbul is full of praise for you too,' I said. 'I met her at college (not revealing the entire truth). I see the two of you have a mutual-admiration-society.'

'Why should it be a society—it's just friendship.'

I was curious to know the basis of their friendship, I asked, 'Have you known Bulbul a long time?'

'Practically since childhood. She gives private tuitions to support herself, she's involved in swadeshi efforts—she's quite extraordinary.'

'Women are even going to jail these days, what's so extraordinary about her?'

'If you knew more about her you wouldn't say that,' Mitu answered. 'Her family's not very well-off, her father wants to get her married, somehow. Bulbul insisted on studying at the university, she even does all the cooking at home whenever her mother gets asthma attacks, and on top of all that she stays up nights reading the proofs for *Muktadhara*—she amazes me. And besides . . .' a faint smile appeared on Mitu's lips '. . . I can't do any of all this myself, I do nothing at all, I stay home all day—for that reason too I can't help but admire Bulbul. I still hesitate to go out by myself, I get a headache when the sun is too strong—I'm probably a little old-fashioned.'

I was extremely relieved to learn that Mitu's nature and proclivities had nothing in common with Bulbul's. I said with extra enthusiasm, 'Not everyone has to be an all-rounder, surely—and it's not true that you do nothing—singing is a big accomplishment, and . . . you sing so beautifully that you don't need to do anything else.'

I was a little surprised when Mitu went red—she heard her singing being praised all the time, why did she still feel embarrassed? After a pause, she said, 'Please come and meet my mother, she's not very well today—would you like to sit upstairs? My father will soon be home too.'

I left Bokul Villa only at nine that evening; on the way

back, like a mild breeze over the water, or dry leaves flying through the summer air, or the murmur of distant pines, a thought wafted across my mind intermittently, gently, but repeatedly: Am I falling in love? Am I falling in love?

Eleven

Were they the same—the person I was then, and the person whose photograph was published in all the Bombay newspapers a few years later, arm-in-arm with Nalini Dalal: the newly married couple, envy of their peers and a symbol of wish-fulfilment for the masses? You know, when I arrived with Nalini at the location of my first posting, in a small town in unfamiliar Madhya Pradesh, far away from Bengal, among people who spoke a different tongue, and then, when a life began in which the others almost never let me forget that I was an upper-class member of the governing classes, a judge with a sceptre, I felt a sense of self-satisfaction at the thought that I had been able to bring about a complete transformation in myself. I mastered the behaviour expected of me in public life as a government servant so perfectly that my reputation as a brilliant officer spread within just a few years from the regional governor all the way to the Department in New Delhi. I laughed in my head at this achievement, I became curious about testing myself in other ways, I felt inclined to examine how far I could get away from my past. Examine, that is to say, conduct an experiment. The laboratory of this experiment was my heart; the apparatus, my intellect; and the guinea pig, my wife.

Couldn't it have been possible to love Nellie? Of course it could have been. Where there's a will there's a way—and this wasn't a particularly difficult task, just a matter of giving the young and beautiful Nellie the opportunity for a fragrant flavour to rise from the churning of the flesh, which is called fondness in everyday speech. Was there anything preventing affection, tenderness—more than which the majority of couples never get to experience? Our hearts don't die after all, they only fall asleep at times, waking up when something violent happens—but no one can force them to wake unless we ourselves are willing, unless we cooperate, unless we join in too. I wasn't willing to love Nellie, I was opposed to the idea—that is the long and short of it. There is a technique with which you can generate the chilliest of winds even in moments of overwhelming lust—it involves splitting yourself into two persons, like those two mythical birds in the Upanishads. That was just what I did; at the precise moment that I melted in Nellie's embrace, another I stood alongside watching the two of them, a twinkling smile on his lips, maybe with a cigar in his mouth, an inch of ash dangling from it—watched an amusing bout of wrestling, a circus act, panting, groaning, shallow breathing like a dying man—but far too jaded, routine, tiring. It was the same when I started my sport with women afterwards. The little pleasure that I could wring out of the grotesque gymnastics of my invention—hammering, ripping, clawing, contorting, spending the night with a flesh-and-bones-covered skeleton on either side—came from observing myself, the pure scientific satisfaction of tracking every step of my own progress. It certainly was progress—I was on my way to overcoming hatred and embarrassment and fear, I was absorbed in those very things that were abhorrent to my taste, I had in me the potential for sainthood—at the very least I would succeed in achieving a great deal more.

But no—you're bragging a little too much, Ranajit—you still have to go to a lot of trouble to arrange the resources for these games, you have not yet lost all common sense, you never set eyes on a commissioner's wife or a colonel's girlfriend, you greet even the diamond-studded mistress of a local ruler with courteously bowed head, as though she's a well-connected lady—simply put, your flawless, polished behaviour with those who are part of your defined social circle—those who practise cordiality during fixed hours at specified places like the club, the racecourse, the ball, the governor's party—has kept your reputation as spotless as the house that Nellie keeps . . . That was how I berated myself at times, disciplined myself, provoked myself, when I sent Nellie off to her mother's on some pretext, and my loyal, economically dependent servants produced a village belle for me at night, a tribal girl, a virgin daughter of a famished man, or perhaps a smouldering middle-aged widow. Don't imagine I harmed anyone, as I told you it was pure commerce: if a virgin burst into tears I let her go (and not empty-handed either)—if I sinned it was against myself. But still, my curiosity, my desire to know myself didn't let me stop; gradually I learnt the methods for myself, I realized that the ingredients for my research were not particularly rare; wherever I went for a holiday—whether in the country, or in Europe—I discovered playmates ready and willing—some happy with ten rupees, some with an asking price of fifty pounds, that was the only difference. I scrupulously avoided those who were willing without charging a price, simply for pleasure, lest they entrap me afterwards with demands for paying back their debt in other ways. I grew as cunning as Nellie remained naïve and credulous; that was how it became possible to keep her in the dark, even though she always accompanied me on my holidays.

Did she know nothing at all? Did she suspect nothing? Is that possible? But how would she live if she ever lost her faith in me? The biggest accomplishment of her life was her marriage, she had expected it to spread itself over every tree and branch, bear seeds and fruits, offer her shelter for the rest of her life, that was what she had seen in her mother's life, and in the lives of many women her age—it seemed beyond her imagination that there could suddenly be an exception in her case. So she kept suspicion at bay with all her strength, convinced herself continuously that all was well, clung to her adolescent definition of 'happiness', watered the same rootless plant every day. Meanwhile, I remained guilty in my own eyes for being unable to rid myself of the weakness of secrecy—if I kept it all secret from Nellie I wouldn't get to know the eventual outcome of my experiment, the self-knowledge that I had acquired over this period had to be shared with my spouse, only she could provide the real proof of my achievement. So, when she had this house, this garden, built in Ootacamund as an embodiment of her dreams of happiness, her beloved Bonheur, source of joy, I decided that this was my opportunity, I mustn't let go of it.

My first task was to escape my blasted job. Of course there was another reason too; after the glorious British sun had set on the Indian empire, I couldn't stomach the idea of servility to our handloom-clad ministers. I could have become a minor star of independent India if I'd managed to survive—but no sir, I can't stand politics, that snake almost bit me once. Nellie never gave herself those meaningless airs either, it never even occurred to her to exploit the unlimited influence that her father enjoyed in Congress party circles, that she could, if she wanted, become a member of Parliament or a cipher-like Minister of State; God had created her in the mould of a wife, a mother, a housewife. She was pleased with my early retirement; she expected a second honeymoon in this second life. We possessed everything necessary: health, wealth, leisure and this newfound romantic environment. Our sons flew in to spend a month with us, praised the new house sky-high; after their return to England I had to hear every comment of theirs (although I had already heard them with my own ears) many times over from Nellie. Her grown-up sons charmed her; her days were painted by new dreams—of their return to India, of their marriage, of our grandchildren. So incredible was her propensity for love that she bubbled at the mere thought of daughters-in-law who were still unknown, grandchildren who were nothing but future foetuses. Still, nothing wrong there, I had no objection, but she wanted to share this dream with me, as though it was some unique delicacy that she wouldn't enjoy completely if I were deprived of it. All told, her behaviour suggested that a sudden fragrant breeze was blowing everywhere, even to my jaded eyes Nellie appeared beautiful at times; the roses in the garden seemed to advise happiness, I even spent a few nights in Nellie's bed after a long long time. But immediately afterwards I felt worried, what if I lost at the last moment, what if Nellie took advantage of this endless leisure to wreck my efforts of so many years. This time I went for the jugular, getting women to come to the house. In Nellie's presence, under her nose.

I did, however, sequence it so that there wasn't a sudden breakdown, so that I could savour the whole thing for quite some time. First the burning embers, then the soothing balm. Abject apologies, 'you're a goddess, I'm a worm from hell', even a few tears. Nellie knew—had finally come to know—my real character, but she still didn't have the willpower to dismiss my apologies, my tears. Sometimes I gave it a break so that Nellie did not give up on me completely, so that a woman's wanton laughter heard in half-sleep could once again stab her in the back. And then again the apologies, the splashing of water to revive the one who had fainted. I pressed on with my superb technique in this fashion, alternating fornication with false contrition. Are you astonished? Are you wondering why Nalini tolerated all this, why she didn't revolt, didn't leave me, didn't take recourse to the law to inflict some harsh punishment on me? She was Ratandas's daughter, what did she lack for, whom was she in awe of; it wasn't as though she couldn't have left me a pauper begging on the roadside. But it was easy to see why she didn't do anything, why she didn't walk out. No—she wouldn't be able to, she would never be able to inform the world, not even those closest to her—her parents—that her palace of happiness had been destroyed, that it had never even actually been built, that her entire life was nothing but a handful of dust, and that she hadn't realized all this earlier simply out of foolishness. She wasn't able to admit this defeat—which I eventually forced her to accept—to anyone; she chose death, instead, to avoid this humiliation. No, not suicide—self-defence, rather, that amazing ability of the living being to develop an illness in order to protect oneself from mental pain. She fell silent, insensate, burning out slowly like a candle—terminal anaemia, in medical parlance. I made an enormous fuss over her treatment, flew in specialists from Bombay and Calcutta, but her body did not cooperate with the treatment. Nellie declared her revolt, not through words or deeds but through the continuous rise in her white-blood cell count, through her failed heart, through the breakdown of her liver. One night, you know—when, to pass those unbearable hours, I was researching the black rose—very late that night I was reading a book I had had sent to me from Holland, here in this room she came to me. Raising my eyes from the book, I saw her suddenly. Her complexion had changed completely—it had turned grey, like ash, there wasn't a single touch of red anywhere on her lips or cheeks. 'Why did you throw me out?' she asked in fluent Bengali, very gently. I saw her three or four times, she came, stood near me, made eye contact, asked the same question, and disappeared. So I had to advertise for a housekeeper, and found Gayatri.

Excuse me? A murderer? Don't pass judgement prematurely, my friend, you haven't heard the entire case yet. Come, let's go back to Dacca for some time. To our youth, yours and mine. Are you a young man still? . . . No, that's where you're mistaken, you cannot measure age by chronology alone. My old age began at twenty-five—I've been the same kind of old man for a long time, though I don't look it, but I know there's no difference between my being twenty-five and ninety-five. And yet—I was young once too—for a few years, a few months, a few days at least. Those afternoons in Bokul Villa. It was October, the sky changing by the minute. Dark clouds, silver clouds, drizzles and sunshine, sometimes so astoundingly blue that there had to be heaven on the other side, but sometimes stormy in the late afternoon. And, like a more intimate version of that distant, enormous sky, Mitu. Her slow drawl; tender, reserved, as though keeping a part of herself coiled up, locked away. Slightly distant, her eyes black, grey, brown, but never stormy, always calm, brimming. What did we talk about? I don't remember, don't remember either how the hours went by. The evening was for practising music, for people to come and go—which was why I had chosen the afternoon; around one-thirty I went directly to Wari from college, by the time I left under the declining sun in the west, Bokul Villa had cast a long shadow over the compound in front. The answer to the question that had shaken me a few days ago now resonated to the sounds of my heart, like a woman pregnant for the first time I felt within me the birth of a new life—not merely wish-fulfilment or imagination, but real, certain, growing love.

But there is nothing pure in our lives—everything is

an alloy, even what we refer to as greater pursuits have something or the other in them that's adulterated. An uncontrollable passion propelled me towards Mitu as soon as classes ended at college; but when I emerged a few hours later I was no longer the ardent lover, I could sense in myself a trace of irritation—fatigue, discontent. Nature, without waiting for my permission, was doing its work within me; the company of a young woman who had not thrown away her womanhood by exposing herself as much as Bulbul had, who had, on the contrary, made it flower by actually concealing some of it, was fanning my desire—even making me impatient at times. I was embarrassed to acknowledge this to myself, I tried to push it away from my mind—this wasn't difficult either, because during that same period, something else also took place, for the same reason, something that could be called the expansion of my personality. I seemed to be unravelling, spreading myself in different directions, evolving well beyond myself, becoming much better, stronger, as though everyone in the world were my friend. I no longer disliked Bulbul, for she no longer existed as a woman for me, every symbol, every scent of womanhood was now packaged in someone else. I had done everything that Bulbul had asked me to do—the history chart for their fair, the essay on *Gora* for *Muktadhara*, I had even chosen patriotic songs for their musical—and it had been no trouble doing all this, no annoyance—everything seemed easy. I didn't consider Amulya intolerable any more either—the doors of Bokul Villa were always open to him, like a 'member of the family'; he addressed Mitu's parents like members of his family, ran errands for them, rushed off on his cycle if a message had to be sent to

Mitu's music teacher, bought Mitu copies of *Probashi*, *Bichitra* and *Nabashakti* from Sadarghat. I, with my newly acquired suitor's personality, could forgive Amulya's stupidity and crass humour now, I even pitied him a little—since he had to work so hard in order to gain proximity to Mitu, had to serve the family in so many different ways. I had even spoken to Arthur Jones about him—whether it would be possible for Jones to give a recommendation to a friend of mine—I had by then become friendly enough with him to make such a request. I spent an afternoon or two with Jones every week; we exchanged mild banter about my inability to pronounce the 'th' sound correctly, and about his similar inability, despite knowing Sanskrit, to pronounce some of the unique Bengali sounds; but from my conversations with him, I got much more in return for whatever little assistance I gave him in reading Bengali, for nothing he said was lifted from a Bradley or a Mathew Arnold; and reading the books I borrowed from him was rapidly changing my own notions of literature too. I was trying to write my poetry in a completely different style, wondering whether Amit Ray had spoken the truth after all, even in jest, maybe compositions with 'strong lines, erect lines' were indeed what were needed—correcting Amit Ray, I even thought (for the woman's face was now an indispensable ingredient of my world) that only if the rose or the woman's face touched the reader like the pain of neuralgia could the feeling in the heart be captured correctly in language; this ache I felt in my breast whenever I thought of Mitu—expressing it probably needed a language that was compact, dense, sharp, not very smooth, a little splintered, as though the force of emotion had made the words develop cracks. A hope grew within me slowly, like a sibling to my love, that I would eventually be a writer—that I would succeed; even this sudden acquaintance with an Englishman with a passion for literature was an omen.

I became more intimate with someone else too at this time—Kajol. But there is a history of heartache behind this . . . Pain? Or was it the same trite story, the traditional property of Bengal, the futile sighs of women like roses in the desert? There was an entire philosophy of life behind what I did to Nellie—no self-interest, I wasn't besotted with anyone, just pure curiosity—an attempt to kill those well-known ghosts: love, marriage, family. But it isn't always like that—people suffer simply because of circumstances, because society is unmoving, because the sentries are indomitable. Tell me, can you possibly feel sorry for those who just submit to assault, who don't protest, who haven't even learnt to protest—are they even worthy of sympathy? Pardon me? Oh, my wife. I can say this for her at least: she loved me, and people don't have control over their own hearts. You'd be completely off the mark if you compared her to Kajol. You must have understood much earlier how Kajol's life had been destroyed. You must have realized that Fotik-mama was not in the least bit interested in the daughter of the truck-line owner who had fulfilled his wish to go to England; that he probably did not remain celibate in England for five years, that maybe some 'foreign slut' may even have consumed him fully. This wasn't difficult to surmise, the older people in the family had grasped it in an instant, when Fotik-mama visited us for a couple of days even my mother knew—I was the only one who wasn't aware of any of this for a long time. Immature, a fresh and callow young man, paying no attention to family matters—that was me back then. Everyone in the family loved me—it wasn't anything special, it was natural, I didn't have to give anything in return, didn't have to consider anyone else's feelings—that was what I thought at the time. How selfish that spring of life is—made famous, glorified by poetry!

But still—one day I suddenly looked at Kajol for herself, when Fotik-mama announced that he would have to return to Calcutta soon. My mother was unhappy—'How can you do that? Durga Puja is coming up, is this any time to go?' But her requests, pleas, tears didn't work; Fotik-mama simply had to go, his business partner had written from Calcutta—there was urgent work. Besides, what use would it be to stay on in Dacca, even after all his efforts he had succeeded in persuading only three people to invest in his company's shares—one of them was Anadi-babu, the other two were his acquaintances too—no one could be convinced that electric bulbs were so useful that there was no question of the venture failing, Indian bulbs would be cheaper than imported ones, and the swadeshi tag would make people buy the Jyoti—named for brightness—brand bulbs; the next product would be fans, named Moloy, or spring breeze—dividends would be given in only two years.

But no, people in Dacca were not 'industry-minded', they were generations of job-seekers, they didn't see value in anything but the same old 'government paper', unwilling to risk their money, having lived cocooned lives by virtue of their land-owning legacies, and those who *were* traders in millions of rupees stocked their currency notes in safes at home marked with symbols of devotion to the gods, and all they were familiar with by way of business anyway were shops for garments and for stationery, which they ran from their cushioned seats on the floor. What *would* this country come to—where a medieval darkness still pervaded, where some people were actually under the impression that electric light harmed the eye, where huge sums of money rotted in the belly of the god of business, or was locked into gold on women's bodies or in drawers. 'Indian women's gold ornaments should be seized and invested in business, we won't lack for anything any more.' Saying this, Fotik-mama looked to me for support. A few weeks earlier I would have agreed whole-heartedly, but at that moment Kajol-mami's crescent necklace swam before my eyes. That evening, on Mitu's birthday, when I was having tea with the ladies, my eyes had shifted a few times from Kajol's face to her necklace, it made her neck and breast look even more beautiful, I thought, and wasn't some of the warmth from her body being radiated by those cold stones and gold? Besides, I had realized by then that my mother, despite her boundless affection, mentally blamed Kajol for her husband's disinterest—this came out obliquely sometimes in the things she said; Kajol was apparently not 'adept' enough, she didn't know how to assert her claim over her husband. I felt this was unfair, and because of that too, I was somewhat biased towards Kajol, I didn't want to say anything that could even indirectly be held against her. So I said a little warily in response to Fotik-mama, 'Yes, you're right, of course, but I'm sure you'll agree that it's nice when women look beautiful.'

'Ah, young man!' said Fotik-mama in English, clapping me on my back and laughing, but the very next moment his face seemed to darken slightly, he said softly, 'Some of them look beautiful even without ornaments.'

I had always been a nightbird; I was up that night too, writing a letter. There were sounds in the next room—my mother had relinquished the room to Fotik and Kajol—he was leaving the next day, his things were being packed. Quite some time passed after the packing was complete, it was late at night, my lips moved silently, the pen moved, when a conversation began suddenly in the next room, I heard my uncle's annoyed, sleepy voice, 'Shut up, let me sleep.' The object of his reprimand, however, didn't shut up, kept murmuring—it seemed to be an argument. It wasn't right to eavesdrop on confidential exchanges between husband and wife, and besides, the letter was far more important, but because their voices rose at times, the quiet, silent atmosphere which I needed for my letter was disturbed every now and then. Two phrases—'lump of jewellery' and 'your father'—in Fotik-mama's angry voice came to my ears—did he really want to take away Kajol's jewellery to invest in his business, or did he want Kajol to get capital from her father on behalf of her husband? 'Aren't you ashamed of yourself,' began Kajol. I had no idea her soft voice could be so sharp (just as you couldn't make out on hearing Mitu talk that her singing voice could effortlessly swirl upwards from high notes to even higher notes) but I couldn't hear what she said after that. They talked softly for some time—soft, muted, but with sharp undertones (I could make that out even from the next room)—then Kajol's voice suddenly tore through it all—'Whose photo is it! You *have* to tell me!'

'Shut up!' Fotik-mama roared like a lion. Then silence descended.

I was annoyed at being disturbed when I was writing my letter, but I couldn't concentrate on it immediately, I remembered a small incident from a few days ago. I had sent my cycle in for repair, and was walking back home, around ten at night. When I neared home I saw Fotik-mama about twenty yards ahead of me. He walked slowly, a trifle tired, his head bowed. I lengthened my stride to catch up with him, but Fotik-mama stopped under a lamp post, pulled out something from his pocket to look at with great concentration—a small piece of paper, a letter or a photograph, perhaps—he was looking at it with so much attention that he didn't hear my footsteps, and was so startled when I called his name that the piece of paper fell from his hand. Retrieving it at lightning speed, he turned to me. 'Met your friends, Ranju? Let's go home quickly, I'm starving, didi's made mutton rezala today I think.' This was his natural way of speaking, but it didn't quite suit him at that moment, he seemed to be smiling with an effort and I saw worried creases on his brow. It was obvious that until we met he had definitely not been wondering how soon he could get back home for dinner. I had forgotten the incident the very next day, but that night in bed I recalled it—I suddenly thought I had, after all, caught a glimpse of the piece of paper that had fallen from his hand—a photograph, a face, a woman's face?

Sometimes I saw my mother whispering to Fotik-mama—advising him, possibly—and it was impossible to fathom what my jovial, large-hearted uncle, lover of good food, pondered with his head in his hands. Sometimes he got letters with foreign stamps on them—it was quite natural, he must have friends in many countries, but when Minu took the stamps for her stamp-collection, I saw they were all German; although he didn't know much about Goethe he was full of praise for the Germans; and though he didn't normally discuss politics, the papers had him agitated sometimes. 'Have you seen Hitler's barbaric actions, Ranju? How he's persecuting Jews! If this demon is allowed to grow, there will be a disaster. Looks like another war is inevitable.' At that time, like many other people in our country, I wasn't worried about Hitler either, that's why I couldn't make out why there was a real strain of anxiety in what my uncle was saying, even if say Hitler did cause some harm to Germany, what difference could it make to him? I had thought that the other side of our hatred for the British was love for the Germans, I had even heard that Germany was the ideal country for engineers, but it had never occurred to me that Fotik-mama could have some other relationship with Germany, or that he might have a personal reason for fearing Hitler. I didn't notice either that whenever he received his letter from abroad, he looked melancholy.

This time too my mother raised the issue of his taking Kajol with him, although very mildly. 'Don't worry any more, didi, I've managed to get things organized, I'll find a new house as soon as work begins on the factory, after that . . .'

My mother interrupted him, 'I keep telling you, you

don't need to move into a new house, what you have is fine for the two of you. Kajol is the perfect housewife now, she'll keep your home as pretty as a picture, you'll see.'

My uncle came up with some cheap humour in response, 'I'm fed up of hearing you praise Kajol, didi, I'm going to be jealous now, I tell you.' After a pause, he continued in the same light vein, 'Listen, I'm thinking of taking Kajol's jewellery with me this time—all this clumsy heavy jewellery is outdated, why don't I get her some new jewellery in the latest fashion instead?'

My mother thought for a moment and then said, 'That's a good idea, but as a man you don't know much about these things, what if the jeweller cheats you? It's better to ask our local jeweller here, he's trustworthy, his work is neat; besides, Kajol must approve of the design too.'

'All right, whatever you think is right,' said my uncle grimly. Matching these trivial incidents with what I had accidentally overheard cast a shadow of suspicion in my mind, but I didn't think about it too long, nor was I inclined to, since I was upset at not being able to finish the letter to Mitu.

The next day I went with my uncle to the station to see him off; when the tiny metre-gauge train slowly clanked its way around the Tikatuli corner and disappeared, I sighed deeply. This train left Dacca station at 11.50 every day, the steamer was ready at the Narayanganj jetty—why didn't I buy a ticket and get onto the train, why didn't I get off the next morning at the half-lit, half-dark Sealdah station with its echoes and its big clock, in that city where the clock was set thirty-two minutes ahead, where the asphalt roads glinted in the early morning sunshine, where you could buy every book, every magazine, where people spoke without an accent, and where—most importantly—Mitu was now? What could be easier, why didn't I go, why did I deprive myself? Fate seemed to be playing with me; just when the afternoons at Bokul Villa had become the focus of my existence, when I could hear their resonance beneath every other hour of the day or the night, Mitu was called away to Calcutta, to record Dildar Navroze's new songs. Who would have known that Navroze—whose poetry I was devoted to—and Edison's invention—that fragile disc which had embedded in my memory the line '*Amaar jaabar byalaay pichhu daakey*' ('Calling me back as I was leaving') in Kanak Das's voice—would stab me in the back this way? What if I went off to Calcutta on some pretext, and then came back on the same day as Mitu? The steamer on the Goyalanda in the morning, the autumn mist on the river, the taste of tea after the sleepless night on the train, the view of the Padma's waters while leaning on the railing, turning silvery under the sun, the hot steam rising from the engine-room downstairs, the bo'sun's bells, the up-and-down movement of the pistons like lions' heads, the smell of the water, the foamy whirl under the wheels of the steamer, the aroma of the deckhands' cooking, the chicken curry with steaming rice, the musical cries of the sailors as they laid the planks at a jetty—if I could only share these sights, sounds, smells, tastes, with her, what greater happiness could there be in my life? On that two-storeyed steamer on the Padma—named the *Emu* or the *Ostrich*—where we had a break of seven hours from all responsibilities, where there was nothing to do but pass the time, and with the things all around not yet become stale out of habit, surely I would be able to get a little closer to Mitu, perhaps I would finally grasp the mystery that made me love Mitu, but which I had not been to unravel correctly as yet. But no—Mitu had written that her recording would take place next week, and that her father too was getting anxious about his patients, so they would be back soon.

'Mitu had written': how easy it was to say that, but when Mitu's letter arrived only three days after they left, it took me the entire evening and half the night to feel at one with the recipient of the letter. I hadn't expected her to write, maybe it's not right to say I hadn't expected at all—maybe we had said something with our eyes, but I did not have the courage to translate that silent exchange into a clearly written, correctly addressed letter. Not only the content or the summary, but also every single aspect of the letter became the subject of research; in the same way that a critic of poetry examines in minute detail every rhythm, metaphor, use of words, punctuation and, if possible, the abandoned drafts, in the process extracting the implicit meaning, half-concealed by the words in order to rouse the reader's passion even more, I too examined the letters written in violet ink on bluish notepaper, the large letters, the handwriting slanting to the right, the long strokes on some letters, touching the lines above and below and creating a new script, as it were, the excessive use of dashes instead of commas (possibly the influence of some recently famous young writer), a couple of amusing spelling mistakes (such as the addition of redundant vowels)—all of these contributed to my happiness, provoked my senses, I also tried to make out from what she had written and then scratched with two diagonal lines how much of her feelings she had concealed, and what those concealed feelings were. I touched the letter very gently, leaned forward to sniff it, touched it lightly with my lips, as though that one sheet of paper were a very tender, valuable object, as though too much pressure from my hand could make the letters disappear.

My notion that travelling with Mitu on the same steamer could provide some wondrous result was probably incorrect; there would be other people on the steamer, other tasks, hunger, even drowsiness arising from tiredness later in the day; movement among the rows of people sitting and lying on the deck with their luggage and children wouldn't be easy either, nor was it impossible that there might be other passengers whom Mitu or her parents knew. Besides, if it turned out that Anadi-babu and his family were travelling second class, I wouldn't even be able to reach them. But a letter, a letter was completely personal, intimate, the world had no power to put up a wall between the letter and me—beyond everyone's prying eyes, two individuals had come together, face-to-face, though apart, they could almost touch each other. A real touching of hearts with someone—how infrequently that happens in our lives; how rare those moments are, when there's nobody but she and I, our hearts tuned to the same note, travellers on the same road. Such peril everywhere—so many pits and ditches and craters and abysses all around; just when one of the friends, having almost finished *War and Peace*, cannot think of anything beyond Tolstoy, the other one is thrilled by an actress's fourth marriage; while the man seeks an opportunity for a private conversation at the restaurant, the woman's attention is captured by the music from the stage; while the young wife awaits her husband's return, her hair done up, the husband gives her a meticulously detailed account of the tennis match he's just watched, none of which makes any sense to her—this way, for the most trivial of reasons, hearts don't meet. But there's no such danger where a letter is concerned—the essence of those we love are captured in it, only for ourselves; it is unburdened by the weight of unexpected factors like headaches, hunger, the company of other people or any other complication; you could even say it isn't remotely under the control of fate, unless of course the postal department makes an error in delivery.

Another realization came to mind on reading Mitu's first letter, of which I found ample evidence later in life. The physical presence of a person is seldom similar to their letter; spending time in a person's company doesn't always tell you what their letters will be like; sometimes we lose interest in a person whom we had quite liked on meeting as soon as they write a letter, for the words they've composed reveal some silliness or pretence or lack of education or coarseness whose existence we had not thought possible. It also happens that those whom we had labelled very ordinary prove themselves intelligent and sensitive in their letters. And those whose presence and letters are equally enjoyable also reveal a new personality through their letters—of which Mitu was an example. I saw that her writing was as uninhibited as her behaviour was reserved, although she was deferential in conversation her written language held no weakness—she would never have directly told me something like 'I'll wait for your letter'. Letters are like literature—at least, potential literature (Madame de Sevigne was considered a writer only on the strength of her letters to her daughter); because lesser methods of self-expression, such as a look, an inflexion of the voice or a gesture with a hand or the eyebrows are not available for help, words have to do all the talking in letters; besides, it is easier to say things because you cannot see each other, because there isn't anyone in front of you who would turn pale or blush. After receiving Mitu's letter, I wrote back to her the same night, when everyone at home had fallen asleep, staying up till two in the morning. I posted it with my own hands at the post office in Ramna on my way to college the next day. My life acquired a new flavour, as though a fresh wind was blowing over me, I was stirred by a new thrill and excitement. An undercurrent of happiness flowed beneath the fact that I was missing Mitu. I paced up and down in front of my house every afternoon, waiting for the postman (it even happened that letters arrived from Mitu on two successive days); even before tearing open the envelope I thought of the first line of my reply (although it inevitably changed when I actually sat down to write); and the day she wrote in black ink instead of violet, and on white notepaper instead of blue, I had the same sensation of wonder that I had felt when I saw her in a new light in her green śari and yellow blouse at sunset.

One day, when I was late getting back from college, Kajol-mami handed me a thick envelope, saying, 'It's from Mitu, isn't it?'

'So it seems,' I said casually, disinterestedly.

'The peon delivered it this minute,' Kajol spoke as though she was justifying herself. 'Does Mitu write to you every day?'

'Oh no, not every day. Just . . . once in a while.' I felt a little abashed, suddenly remembering that Fotik-mama never wrote to Kajol from Calcutta—he only wrote a couple of lines to my mother sometimes, and everyone in the family had accepted this to the extent of not even commenting on it, and even I had not considered before this how unnatural this was, how unfair too from the perspective of daily life.

'And do you reply as soon as you get her letter?' asked Kajol with a smile at the corner of her lips.

Turning a little red, I said, 'You know me, my fingers are always itching to write, if nothing else even a letter will do.'

Kajol's expression turned serious, her eyes met mine for a moment, and then suddenly—but deliberately, not unexpectedly—a question dropped from her lips, 'Are you marrying Mitu?'

I felt a thousand pinpricks on my face for an instant, pulling myself together I said, 'What on earth are you talking about, I'm not even remotely thinking of marriage.

Do you suppose writing to someone amounts to marrying them?'

'Don't bother to protest, you've turned so red it's all quite obvious. Come and have your tea.'

After this, Kajol told me every now and then how wonderful it would be if Mitu and I were to get married. 'You're made for each other—not immediately, but you're going to be done with your MA soon, then a job, why not finalize things right away? I know Mitu's parents won't object, in their hearts this is what they want as well, and we won't find a more suitable bride either for you. What do you think, should I raise the subject with them when they're back? I can't tell you how happy I feel at the thought of Mitu being your wife!'

With someone else I'd have become very angry, maybe I wouldn't have spoken to them any more, but since I had heard in Mitu's letters what her heart was saying, I felt guilty before Kajol; as though the love that was Kajol's due had come my way instead—this was the kind of discomfort I felt when she painted these colourful pictures of our married life—Mitu's and mine; or you could say falling in love had made me a better person to the extent that I had now learnt to pity Kajol, I had no objection to indulging her; to tell the truth, I quite enjoyed listening to her speculate about Mitu and me—perhaps this was what everyone referred to as 'sympathy'. I liked the idea that there was someone who supported my love, I was happy that I could bring that other person some joy too by spending a few moments talking to her. In this manner Kajol and I developed a different kind of relationship; it was she who brought me my cup of tea when I came back from college, gave me something

to eat; (to please her) I asked her to put a few drops of her eau-de-cologne on my handkerchief, after the first day I got a whiff of the fragrance from my handkerchief every day without asking. When Mitu wrote they would be back the following Friday, in my joy I couldn't stop myself from letting her know. But the very next day—Durga Puja was almost at hand—Hindu-Muslim riots broke out in Dacca.

awake or just-awake two-in-the-morning, a golden, fragrant cup of tea. It wasn't just the tea, I was also beginning to enjoy Kajol's company more and more, because I had no one else for company, nothing else to do. I was stuck within the walls of the house all day—at best I walked around the neighbourhood, but there was no one close enough to talk to, I couldn't concentrate on writing, even reading was becoming unpalatable; in this situation only Kajol appeared like an oasis in the desert, at least a little shade, a little water, a little variety. Kajol was no longer as silent and listless as before, she talked, moved about freely, called me upstairs to the terrace some evenings. I tried to get her to identify the constellations, explained to her the difference between planets and stars; sometimes, instead of surrendering herself to her bed after lunch, she sat on the deckchair in my room to chat with me. She didn't have many subjects to discuss, but I got so fatigued by the ever-new strategies to kill Muslims proclaimed by the hardworking, brave and altruistic young men of the neighbourhood—who patrolled the streets at night with sticks and supplied groceries and vegetables to everyone during the day, even fish and duck eggs sometimes—that I preferred Kajol's memories of childhood from Jalpaiguri, her dreams of a future for Mitu and me, which she wanted to be a part of as the messenger, the go-between.

I was careful not to let slip any reference to Fotik-mama (even the news of the riots hadn't made him anxious enough to write separately to Kajol, I didn't care to think about him either) to ensure I didn't hurt Kajol. I couldn't avoid the presumptuous conviction that it was my duty to be kind to this beautiful and neglected member of the family; then again, I also felt extremely grateful to her, since she was a fine bridge between the absent Mitu and me, like some small recompense for Mitu's absence. When I got sick of the lack of activity, of the weight of the emptiness, I even played a few games with her, hinting that I liked a couple of other young women too—for instance Bijoya Sen from our university. Kajol was really perturbed by this—I had to satisfy her curiosity on whether the aforementioned—and imaginary—Bijoya Sen was pretty, which year of university she was in, how old she was, whether she had glasses or not; she recoiled on hearing that Bijoya was reading for her MA—'Oh my god, an old woman!'

'Not at all—she's my age—maybe younger.'

'Stupid boy, don't you know that young men of twenty-one are still tender, but young women of twenty-one are over-ripe.'

I was amused by this metaphor. 'But you're over twenty-one too, you don't seem like an old woman.'

'So impertinent! You saucy boy!' Kajol reddened a little, then found another point of objection. 'Bijoya Sen. Then the caste doesn't match yours—you can't marry her.'

'Why not? As if anyone takes all that into account these days.'

'What do you mean? If the castes don't match, a Hindu wedding isn't possible.'

'So what? We'll marry in court.'

Kajol became serious, then said after a pause, 'I know

you're making all this up, there's no one named Bijoya Sen.'

'Of course there is—we meet at college every day, how can you say she doesn't exist! She's a very good student—came first among the girls in the Dacca board exams.'

'All right,' she met my eye, 'touch me when you say that, and I'll believe you!' Kajol extended an arm towards me, I laughed, so did she, her lovely compact teeth gleaming—she felt better knowing that my devotion to Mitu hadn't developed cracks. But the very next moment there was a shadow of apprehension on her face. Grabbing my hand, she said, 'Tell me, promise me you'll never think of another girl besides Mitu!' She said this so intensely I was surprised; as I slowly released my hand from her soft fleshy grasp, I felt that it was because of Kajol that Mitu had taken a bigger place in my life, become more real. I regretted having teased her about my invented fellow-student, looking into her eyes I believed that surrendering all that your heart desires entirely to one person is fulfilment. Seeing that I was distracted, Kajol asked, 'What are you thinking about? Is a letter due today? It isn't time for the postman yet.'

Mitu's letters! A new wound in my heart. When the riots started the city was in such a state that letters weren't delivered for two days, then three letters from Mitu arrived at the same time. Her father had postponed their return after a telegram from a relative in Dacca—'The newspapers make it sound quite terrible, are all of you well? Please take care, what more can I say. Baba and ma are both very anxious because the house is unoccupied, what if it's robbed, why do we have to have trouble like this. We'll be there as soon as the situation improves even slightly.' Three short letters, virtually the same things said in each. In the last one she wrote, 'Write every day if you can, I can't sleep for anxiety.' She had put several stamps in the envelope, so that I didn't have to risk going out for them.

I kept writing every day, but increasingly I felt I was running out of things to say, I was no longer infatuated with Mitu's letters. Those letters, which I had gushed over mentally, which I had considered even more valuable than her physical presence, now turned out to be foggy, a gloomy insubstantial substitute—momentary, partial, fragmented, or a trundling bullock cart which my stallion-like desire overtook in leaps and bounds. I realized that a letter was representative of only a moment in a person's entire life; the ten minutes or the one hour that it took them to write was the only part of them I could assume as mine—I didn't know how they spent the rest of their day, it was entirely their wish what information they provided or withheld. Jealousy attacked me, I was jealous of those whom Mitu knew in Calcutta, of those who were fond of her music, of those whom she had met for the first time during this visit; they were sharing laughter and happiness and friendship in a secure, civilized Calcutta, replete with a thousand attractions, with which I had not the least of connections, in exchange for which I got . . . a piece of paper, a few words, a few skeleton-like letters. The spontaneity disappeared from my letters, they gradually began to get smaller, then one day (because, even when in love, we're sometimes tempted to posture) I wrote a twisted, artificial letter, in a tone of implicit accusation, as though, even after the riots had ended, she was deliberately—for some reason she hadn't told me, or out of indifference towards me—delaying her return. The reply came: 'We arrive next Thursday, we'll talk then. You don't understand anything!'

By then, after nearly three weeks of pandemonium, with the Durga Puja dates having passed by, a miserable, bitter, dreadful peace had descended on Dacca. In this situation, the first person who came all the way home to find out how things were with me was Bulbul. I was pleased to see her, but she didn't say anything that appeared encouraging; just as I was trying to get the riots out of my mind, going into denial over them, thinking of them as unreal, like a nightmare, trying to convince myself that being civilized was our natural state, Bulbul made it more real with accounts of macabre incidents, some of which she had herself witnessed in her neighbourhood.

When I said, 'Thank goodness I didn't have to see anything like that,' Bulbul's expression hardened.

'Is it enough that you didn't? Does that make everything all right?'

'Since I don't have the power to make right what's wrong, what alternative do I have but to avoid it?'

'Who says you don't have the power?'

'Maybe *you* do, but I don't,' I replied with a smile.

'That's why we're in the state we're in, because everyone thinks that way.'

'Let's go for a walk,' I responded.

Crossing the railway lines and entering Ramna, I sat with her on a culvert. It was a November afternoon, the roads deserted as the university was closed, a trace of winter in the air, signalling a change of season. At last it was possible to move around without fear, there was no need to protect our backs, where somebody could plunge a dagger in without even giving us the chance to turn around. But this newfound sense of security, the enormous bowl of the sky upended over the field, the yellow of the sunshine on the grass—which reminded me of the Pre-Raphaelites' poetry, of a sunken-cheeked, sunken-eyed girl, her blonde hair loose on her back, from a Rossetti painting—none of this claimed her attention even for a moment, she started talking immediately. What she said was like a newspaper editorial, an inspiring speech at a public meeting—bubbling with emotion like a kettle on the boil—but the same subject, which had been the only topic of discussion these last few days all over the city. Had I thought about the massacre, the carnage that had taken place in the city? There had been riots before, but violence like this had never been witnessed—people seemed to have stooped to the level of beasts. Even Durga Puja could not be celebrated, the occasion that people looked forward to all year, those few days of joy weren't allowed either; Eid was just a couple of months away, people were already scared, what if there was trouble again, what if there was an attempt at a counter strike? But who was at fault for this happening over and over again? Who was responsible? The Hindus? The Muslims? Neither. It was the third party that was responsible—the British—those cunning devils, playing one off against the other, making us forget who the real enemy was. They would cling to our land in this way, suck out our last drop of blood. What did I know of what the police had done this time? They had supplied the petrol used to set houses on fire, kept the riots alive by providing arms, even entered people's homes to confiscate kitchen knives and sticks used for household work, anything that could be used for self-defence. In Armanitola, Digen Majumdar's two sons tried to stop them, the British sergeants whipped them unconscious. In Farashganj, the animals kicked Shibeshwar Pal's pregnant daughter. Do we have to tolerate this too without protest? Shall we not avenge this? Shall we not make them realize we're human beings too?

Bulbul's face reddened, her breath quickened, I noticed her breast rising and falling sharply. 'Don't you have anything to say, Ranajit? Doesn't it make your blood boil?' I was embarrassed about myself—embarrassed because I couldn't be part of her agitation, couldn't burn in the flames of vengeance. On the one hand were the gruesome things she'd described, and on the other—how shall I put it?—my disobedient, distracted mind was caught in between, making me helpless. Should I too forget about everything else and slave day and night to eject the British? Was no other expression of duty, of conscience, possible? But what if my heart said something else? I recalled arguing with Jones about Kipling just the other day. I still harboured rage against the British within me, I could still see everywhere around me the signs of what Gandhi had termed the slave mentality. I still felt a prisoner, imprisoned within the walls of a boxed-in tarnished antiquated society. But since then, in a space of merely a few months, although the condition of the country was unchanged, or could even be said to be worse, I had undergone some changes. The company of

Jones had lessened my hatred for Englishmen, I had learnt to look at history a little differently. I had a notion that if the British were today the emperors of the entire world that lay between the oceans, it wasn't as though they were not worthy, and our flaws were responsible too for our wretched state. Besides, I had a new inspiration in life now—love: the horizon had opened up before my eyes, it was no longer impossible for me to leave the pond and set sail on the turbulent river. I didn't want to hate or be angry, I only wanted to see the good in this world; I didn't know how the problems of our country would be solved, but I had found out what I wanted to do with my own life, that was what I wanted to toil for constantly. I asked Bulbul about the fate of her swadeshi fair.

'What swadeshi fair!' Bulbul sighed. 'All the effort, all the hard work—all gone to waste. But that's irrelevant too. Bibha-di says she'll skip the fair this year, it's time to take up harder tasks. It's no use putting ointment on a poisoned wound—it needs surgery. Do they imagine they can stop us by putting us in jail, by hanging us from the gallows? Even after three magistrates have been killed in Midnapore? There's going to be some action in Dacca too.' Bulbul breathed heavily, her eyes met mine for a moment.

'I understand what you're saying, Bulbul, but . . .' The words escaped my mouth, 'but you're not going to be part of it, right?' Bulbul smiled gently. 'Don't worry, we won't involve you. You can see how they're rounding people up everywhere, can't you? They took away fifty of our boys under deténu during the riots, nobody knows whose house the wolves will attack next. I'd better not visit you any more.'

Her last statement hurt my male ego, and I said quickly, 'Why not? Why should we be so scared?'

'I'm not scared for myself,' answered Bulbul, 'but it's different in your case. Maybe you will write an extraordinary book one day—it's Mitu you need, not me.'

I—daft young man—couldn't help feeling pleased that Bulbul considered me worthy of something, she respected my literary ambitions too, although I didn't actually like her all that much.

'I'll be off now.' Bulbul got to her feet hurriedly. The sun was setting, half the world was covered in darkness, that field in Ramna was empty in every direction; I suddenly felt a kind of gloom, a world-encompassing sensation of emptiness, and in the gaps, like the stars twinkling in the cold evening sky, a few incoherent memories popped up.

'Stay a while, Bulbul, let's talk of other things.'

'Tell me.'

'Not the British, not Hindus and Muslims, I'm thinking of other things. You'll probably laugh, but I'll tell you anyway. Have you ever walked though Shankhari Bazaar on a summer afternoon, Bulbul? How strange that narrow, tiny, ancient lane is, the three- and four-storeyed houses jostling with one another on either side, sunlight never gets entry into that lane—you get a musty, clammy, damp smell as soon as you set foot in it, you can hear the sharp buzz of the saws all the time, they've probably been doing that same thing for two or three hundred years, their complexions have gradually blanched from the lack of sunlight—their entire life, their earnings, their existence lie in that one lane. Doesn't it astonish you to think of it? And that smell as soon as you enter! One more thing, Bulbul. When you rode in a coach as a child, didn't it startle you to look out of the red, blue and green glass windows? You know, I used to gaze through them, charmed—the roads, houses, people all turned different colours—a different kind of sunlight, so soft; the sky became deeper, it seemed to come closer, and with it the clip-clop of the horses' hooves, the coachman's whistle, whip, bell, the cool leather smell of the seat, all of it making you drunk, almost—don't you ever remember all this? Do you only think of your country all the time, only do as your Bibha-di tells you—aren't you a person of your own, don't you ever live as yourself? Shall I tell you what I think? These seem to be the only real moments of happiness in our lives, the only memorable things—when I entered the clammy cold of Shankhari Bazaar from the sunshine, when I saw the sky like a fairy tale through those coloured pieces of glass.'

Bulbul listened to me in silence, her expression turned sad for a moment, then she shook herself and got to her feet again. With a small smile, she said, 'Please don't mind, Ranju, but it's impossible for me to wander around the world of emotions like you do. I have nothing but my duties in my life.'

This was just the answer I had expected from Bulbul, but I felt lighter at having been able to say what I had; I remembered Mitu was arriving the day after tomorrow, this sense of loss of something precious was meaningless now, I was on the verge of a reunion.

I met Bulbul again at Bokul Villa, three hours after

Mitu and her family arrived. She had arrived before me. When I got there, Anadi-babu was sipping tea in the ground-floor veranda with his family. Bulbul was talking of the same things—riots, police, the 'third party'—I thought she and Anadi-babu were having an argument over the best method for securing independence; he wanted to follow the Gandhian path, while Bulbul was probably advocating a quicker and somewhat more violent method. The freedom that I needed at that moment—the freedom of being alone with Mitu—seemed to have turned into a distant dream thanks to Bulbul. I realized my expression was hardening gradually, I felt angry, not just with Bulbul but also with Mitu, for she was listening attentively to the argument—at least, she was pretending to—and looking away, avoiding my eyes. Yet she didn't join the argument—her expression was tired, distracted. I heard Bulbul say, 'Gandhiji actually favours the British, why else did he take their side during the war? The enemy has to be uprooted by any means, there's no room for goodness in politics.'

Now I couldn't help speaking up. 'But is it because of the British that we have fallen, or is it because we had fallen already that the British could swallow our country so easily? Our poverty, superstitions, lack of education—aren't we responsible for all this?'

'Of course we are. You've raised a very good point, Ranajit—perhaps we're drowning in our own sins, our untouchability, passivity, fatalism—there's no end to it. From Rammohun Roy to Gandhi, there's been no lack of effort to change all this, but how much have we changed, really?'

Encouraged by Anadi-babu, I started speaking

emphatically. 'What have we done in the last five hundred years, in the last thousand years, to demand happy and comfortable lives today? Did we cross the Atlantic to touch the soil of America, discover even the smallest of islands, plant some new crop? Did we ever imagine that steam and electricity could be of such important use for us? Did we learn to dig into the earth and extract oil? Why even go that far—tea grew wild on our mountain slopes and forests like weeds, probably from the time of the Rig Veda—we couldn't identify that either, so ignorant and blind were we. All this was done by white-skinned people, they're the heroes of this age, so what's so surprising about their being the monarchs of this world?'

'So you're suggesting we have to be heroes too, dominant too?' asked Bulbul, clapping her hands.

Glancing at her, I stopped short. In a different tone I said, 'I'm not suggesting anything. I'm an ordinary creature, I don't have a prescription for saving the country.'

'But we need to think about the kind of heroism, the kind of power that's involved,' said Anadi-babu.

'The more we think, the less we'll be able to do,' explained Bulbul, shaking her head.

Anadi-babu smiled. 'That's another question you've raised, Bulbul. Is what we call civilization the creation of the thinker or of the doer? Of both, surely, but . . .' Anadi-babu scraped back his chair, 'I don't have time today, I'll explain to you another day that all action arises from thought. I need to go out.' Looking at his wife and daughter, he added, 'Two of my patients have sent word urgently—let me find out whether the carriage is ready. Why so quiet, Mitu, not ill, are you?'

Mitu was lost in other thoughts. Throwing a glance at me, Bulbul got to her feet. 'I'm off too, will you drop me at Rajar Deuri?' she said to Anadi-babu.

Mitu took me upstairs, to the veranda where we had spent many fulfilling afternoons a few weeks ago. But reality failed to scale the high peak on which I had, in my imagination, placed this long-awaited moment of reunion. My mind was out of tune, my emotions seem to have dried up, I felt as stale as after a long nap on a summer afternoon, the things that Bulbul had said just now—and also at Ramna a few days ago—which I should have wiped out of my memory the very next moment, which were offensive to my taste, which went against my nature, which destroyed my happiness—those very things seemed to be lodged at the back of my mind, like the prolonged bitter taste of medicine, they seemed to be circling me like black spectres, or like some subtle poison that I had taken by mistake and could not throw up, could not prevent from flowing into my bloodstream. I had tried to touch Bulbul with memories, with dreams—I couldn't. My mind was like an unfamiliar land to her, or a forbidden room, where she would never set foot. It made no difference to me, I didn't love Bulbul, but it wasn't as though I had no feelings for her, I was assailed by the apprehension that she was heading towards danger. And, most agonizingly for me, a part of my mind had even accepted that what Bulbul had said was the bitter truth, and against that backdrop I had the uncomfortable sensation at times that I was guilty of wanting to love, of wanting love, of wanting happiness; that I lost myself even today thinking of the sky that I had seen as a child through the coloured glass panes of the carriage was also my crime. Meanwhile, Mitu, too, perhaps because I was distracted, sounded inhibited, or perhaps a new shyness had wrapped itself around her like the mist on this autumn evening.

We indulged in small talk for some time: what they had done in Calcutta, when her new record would be released, whether Dildar Navroze had written a new book, had they really done away with the open-roofed double-decker buses. But we ran out of things about Calcutta very soon, because she had already given me all the news in her letters, besides, with Mitu back in Dacca the attraction of Calcutta was no longer as strong, I wasn't even curious any more to know how she had spent her time there. And Dacca only meant riots, a topic that Bulbul had wrung dry already. Mitu asked when our university would reopen.

'Next Monday.'

'When are your MA exams?'

'They're still some time away, next year, in July.' After a pause Mitu said, 'In Calcutta this time . . .'

'What? Why did you stop?'

'Yes, I'll tell you.' Suddenly the possessive lover within me seemed to awake, shoving aside my state of silent somnolence with both my hands, I looked at her sharply. 'In Calcutta this time someone said he wants to marry me.'

My heart quaked, in a dry voice I asked, 'And then?'

'My parents weren't unwilling—the man was extremely suitable in every way.'

Without noticing that she had used the past tense, I exclaimed, 'So it's final?'

'Why should it be? I don't have to marry someone just because they're suitable, do I.'

'You didn't agree?'

'Is there any question of agreeing?' Mitu glanced at me for a moment.

I read her mind in her eyes.

'What if your parents insist?'

'You know they aren't like that. It's going to be my decision.' Then her words fell like a breath, 'Do you want to talk to my father?' I sat in silence, unable to exhale, the hammering in my heart drowning out all other sounds. Slowly, Mitu put her hand in mine. Then, getting to her feet, she said, 'I'll wait, as long as you want me to.'

I returned home with my head in a whirl. This wasn't just a case of falling in love, exchanging letters, spending long afternoons together—this was marriage. Another person's happiness, her future were all in my hands. Putting my happiness, my future, in someone else's hands. Could I take such a big responsibility—I, who had achieved nothing yet to speak of, a poor, uncertain, unknown young man of twenty-one. To think that Mitu—the famous Amita Bardhan, object of so many talented people's affections, to whom Dildar Navroze had dedicated his book of songs—wouldn't even glance at other eminent men, those who were 'extremely suitable in every way'! I felt smothered under the weight of joy as well as anxiety, as though a huge demand was being made of me, which I could neither refuse, nor accept; at night, rubbing my face on my pillow, I screamed silently, 'Mitu, make me worthy of you, make me worthy of you!'

Thirteen

Can you see how the colour of the sunshine has been changing gradually, from yellow to pinkish red? The sun-god is about to go to bed. The sun sets between those two hills over there, I sit and watch until the last drop of light dies. But the sunrise is not all that spectacular in Ootacamund, you know. There are no clouds, so the play of colours isn't particularly brilliant; even in summer a thin mist sometimes clings to the air; some days it even happens that the ball of fire up there, losing its lustre, forgetting its dialogue, like a silly round-faced actor, disappears backstage quietly, its last speech incomplete. But still, I enjoy gazing at the day as it fades away; the world beyond the window pane seems like a well-arranged stage, the hills become hollow, light, like theatre sets, and those scattered houses in the distance don't seem real either, they have no inhabitants, they have no purpose but to fill these scenes. You must have noticed that the light in the late afternoon is much brighter than that in the morning. Maybe it isn't actually so, but the late afternoon descends so softly, injects a sigh so secretly into its light, selects such tranquil colours that to our eyes their luminescence becomes much more dazzling, much more gorgeous. Farewell, end, grief; evening is as alluring as it is simply because there's nothing as beautiful. But after that? Then it's grey-black, the night, me alone, nobody nearby, I'm afraid, I'm afraid at night. I cannot sleep, even alcohol brings no sleep, I have nothing—I don't meet the eyes of the flowers that bloom in my heart in the darkness, my eyes lack the strength to climb those long flights of the night's stairs—I want closed-in walls, this small room, where Gayatri turns this very sofa into a bed for two at night or doesn't even bother, drinking ourselves into oblivion, we slump against each other without any effort.

No—this isn't a hint for you to leave. I've told you already, I abhor women; I need them only because I am afraid to be alone at night. Why? I fear Nellie, I fear Kajol, I fear the bullets of East Bengal's terrorists. 'Watch out, Ranajit, don't imagine you'll escape our retribution even in your dreams,' Bulbul told me once—did she really tell me that, or did I make it up in my head? 'Don't forget me, Ranju,' Kajol told me once—did she really tell me that, or did I make it up in my head? Can you tell me, do those who die really die once and for all—for ever? Never—shall we never meet them again? Can you tell me what death is? A person who was once closest to me, and whom I have not seen for thirty-five years, whom I will not recognize even if I do, who today will seem so very distant, like a Martian, aren't they dead for me too, and I for them? And this 'I' we refer to, that too is changing by the year, changing by the day; just as the cells in our body die continuously and are reborn continuously, our 'I-ness' is not fixed either—it's temporary, accidental, fluid—take that twenty-one-year-old 'I'—he is as dead now as some emperor of ancient Babylon, it's a descendant of his who survives, with the same name, the same body. So what it amounts to is that we're all dying a little continuously, and we've named a collection of many small deaths life, and when all relationships with other people end, we call that condition death. But we do not comprehend our own death, as long as a person exists in the world, we forget that they will die; but whenever someone's existence ends, we declare them dead, since there is no possibility of our having a relationship with them any more. But in that sense am I not dead too, this I, who's sitting here, talking with you? Pardon? All right, you may say I too have relationships with others, since I have their memories. In that case, those who have died haven't really died, even those I haven't set eyes on for thirty-five years are still with me, then memory is nothing but immortality. I see you understand everything, that you know—you're a hypocrite too, just like me. I would be grateful—truly grateful—if you agreed to spend the night here. I'd talk to you all night, just like this, face to face. Face to face, as though before a mirror. You're my age, you were in Dacca at the same time as I, in the same neighbourhood, you look sensitive. Tell me, didn't you know me in Dacca? Maybe I'm only telling you what you know already—the only difference is that you've forgotten, but I haven't. I haven't forgotten how, for nearly a month after Mitu returned from Calcutta, I spent my days in a claustrophobic, breathless, nerve-wracking state. It came in many forms, that agony, filled with illusions . . . You're surprised? 'I'll wait for you—as long as you want me to', these words should have taken me to seventh heaven, shouldn't they have? Of course! It wasn't as though I wasn't immersed in the whole thing, I too felt I couldn't contain myself any more, as though I was permanently drunk, I floated on clouds in the sky, I had found the pot of gold of my dreams, my rose garden in the Sahara, the formula of that magic alchemy that could change the entire world. But all said and done, we're only mortal humans, how can we cope with heaven?

Something very strange happened; when the possibility of Mitu and I getting married went beyond Kajol's fanciful imagination and became real, even inevitable, I found it difficult to reconcile myself to this outcome. Someone within me seemed to be resisting, seemed to be protesting. It was strange—whether a year later or five, I would be tied down by Mitu, and truth be told, the process of being tied down had begun that very day. How odd that my love—which I had all this time thought of as a melody, a fragrant breeze, a quivering nerve—now had to be measured with the tape of domesticity, as though it were a piece of fabric at the tailor's, to be used eventually to stitch a usable covering under which Mitu and I, who had even a day earlier been lovers, free, unique (for, just like a child to a young mother, his love is unprecedented and unparalleled to a young man—he doesn't even consider that it is a repetition of the age-old), would overnight be converted into husband and wife, merging with billions of other people on earth. As soon as the child in your arms grows up enough to go to school, as soon as love receives the seal of social sanction, comparison with others can no longer be kept at bay, worries over failure—for the child at school and for the married couple in their duties—seem to dilute the pure milk of romance. Are you wondering? Have you concluded that I didn't really love Mitu, that it was all childishness, emotional exuberance, a balloon full of gas? I won't argue with you; all I'll tell you is that I still get tremors in my heart sometimes when I think of Mitu, even now I know that it was the only time in my life I had ever loved a woman—just the once, just for a few days. And hence—since I sensed within me an inappropriate hesitation, the dilemma of an improper uncertainty, a weakness whose existence I had never suspected—hence my unhappiness. Not imagination, not fiction—this was life, real life, that was approaching me, but why couldn't I put my arms around it to hold it close? Why did the same I, who was jealous of everyone in Calcutta—till the day Mitu returned to Dacca—now believe that without a little distance, a little doubt, love isn't complete?

I had another reason for unhappiness, which was even more embarrassing. As soon as I absorbed the fact that Mitu would live with me—in the same house, round the clock—the physical, flesh-and-blood part of me seemed to become doubly aggressive. Unknown to herself, possibly without meaning to, Mitu indoctrinated me in lust—scorching, unfulfilled lust. For the first time I noticed how her nipples became erect sometimes—no matter how much her blouse and her frequently adjusted sari covered them, they didn't seem able to prevent themselves from announcing to the world, with a mixture of amusement and curiosity, that they existed, they were prepared. I seemed to realize for the first time that the face was not the only ingredient of a woman's beauty, so was her body. Looking at the movement of Mitu's moist lips, I forgot to respond to her; when she shifted her position, or rose to her feet, or walked from one room to another, her body appeared to me to be a fusion of a multitude of curved, restless lines, sometimes radiating outwards in different directions, racing towards me, as though demanding a response. The line where her breasts split into two entranced me; I looked for its metaphor in the newly risen crescent moon, in the moonlight broken up by a torrent of water, but I could not convert it entirely into poetry, could not escape the desire for physical contact. I felt as though I had gazed upon her long enough, as though there was nothing left to say—now our bodies had to get to know each other.

That desire burned within me was not a new discovery, but all this while I had managed to keep it submerged under the appreciation of beauty; the lustre of the necklace around Kajol's throat, the vision of Mitu like seaweed in her green sari—all of these were self-contained experiences, which charmed me, distracted me, but didn't turn me wild. Alas for those thoughts of beauty, the luxury of those dreams, why had they turned to sensual longing today? At times I just couldn't bear it, when the desire became intense—to touch Mitu, to embrace her, to kiss her; in fact, an evil thought also reared its head, that Mitu should prove her love by giving herself to me physically straightaway. But I knew how chaste Mitu was, how sensitive, how tender, how heartbroken she would be if she were ever to see me behaving harshly. 'Will you talk to my father?' Which meant a religiously sanctioned union, or at least the pledge for it. 'Let's get married, not before that, until then both of us will fast . . .' It was on the ancient bough of this tradition that the lovely flower of her love had bloomed, I didn't have the courage to shake that bough, I still retained enough of a conscience not to do it. But this attitude—which was entirely natural at her age, given the times and the circumstances—bothered me secretly, it felt as though she couldn't trust me completely, her patience appeared to be worldly wisdom, even a lack of love. Then again, I couldn't forgive myself for this lust-stricken condition either, I felt unworthy of Mitu, I was lowering myself in my own eyes every day and dragging Mitu down with me from the open sky of pure feelings to a tiny claustrophobic cubicle. This way, under the onslaught of one tumultuous wave after another, the days passed; there was no ground beneath my feet, I couldn't find that moment of resolve whose favourable wind could take my life to the opposite shore. I visited them every day, but I couldn't tell Anadibabu what I wanted to, what I would have to—or what they could certainly surmise—because one day, in keeping with our customs, and embarrassing me, they brought up the subject themselves. 'Let's wait a little longer, what's the hurry, you and I are sure in our hearts . . .' I told Mitu, she didn't reply, only looked into my eyes, unable to meet her eyes I bowed my head.

Bulbul kept supplying me with an antidote to my pain. An antidote, but the treatment was itself another illness. Just as the wise doctor sometimes induces a new disease to combat an existing one—getting a madman's fever up to a hundred and three degrees, or bringing on eczema for an asthma patient—or the way the body sometimes finds equilibrium in its reaction to two opposing poisons—two cups of black coffee after eight whiskeys ensure you can drive yourself home safely—in the same way, I too suffered from two different illnesses—sometimes the one, sometimes the other, both equally harmful, but the harm caused by one was compensated for by the other. Bulbul visited me from time to time; she had chosen the orchard behind the Dhakeshwari Temple for our conversations; I quite enjoyed meeting her since she was not the object of my affections, I had no demands of her—legitimate or illicit; I did not need her like I needed Mitu, it wasn't as though even a month's absence would make me feel an urge to seek her out.

That Bulbul, a woman, a young woman (even if she had consciously rid herself of her femininity) was attentive towards me (despite the divergences in our nature) was flattering to my self-esteem; I could stroll alone on the streets with her (a freedom that was not possible with Mitu), I could chat with her lightly, easily, these were things I quite enjoyed. But still, what I derived from consorting with Bulbul was not pleasure but mere respite from my unhappiness, from emotional pressure, that too for a short while only; just as when, on your sickbed, you turn on your side and feel quite comfortable suddenly, only for the bed to turn hot the next moment, the pain in your joints becoming palpable, in the same way it didn't take much time after my conversation began with Bulbul for my mood to turn sour, it became clear at every stage that the same god had not created both of us. One day, when Mitu and her family had only just returned from Calcutta, Bulbul suddenly brought up Arthur Jones. Had I met Jones recently?

'But Jones is in Darjeeling,' I said.

'Don't you know he's back?'

'Is he? I should visit him then, I have several of his books with me.'

After a pause Bulbul said in a low voice, 'Let me tell you something, Ranajit. Stop consorting with Jones. You can return his books, but don't visit him again.'

I laughed. 'Do you really imagine that I will follow your instructions, Bulbul?'

'It's for your own good.' I recalled the litany that Amulya had reeled off about Jones in Bokul Villa, saying in an oily tone the very next moment, 'Can you get me a recommendation?'

'Never mind Jones,' I said. 'I have an appeal to you.'

'An appeal? From you? To me?' Bulbul's voice sounded different, as though in a moment of absent-mindedness she had revealed she was a woman.

'There's a good Buster Keaton film on—I want to take you and Mitu—will you come?'

'You want to take Mitu, isn't that so? They won't let her go alone with you, so you need a chaperone too. Why don't you take Kajol-mami?'

'Do I need your permission to take Kajol-mami?' I said harshly.

Bulbul paled slightly, then said, gathering herself, 'It's also news to me that you need my help to take Mitu out.' She smiled, twisting her lips, and an unnatural yellow glow flared in her eyes.

Suddenly a different thought flashed through my mind, which had not occurred to me before, but which I realized was correct as her eyes met mine: she was jealous of Mitu, jealous because I loved Mitu. I threw bait at Bulbul, 'Can't you believe that I'd like it if you came?' I was trying to deceive her, Bulbul had grasped my motive accurately, I did want her as a chaperone, but having been caught out I was forced to pretend that my joy wouldn't be complete if Bulbul didn't go. Bulbul's intentions were exposed even more clearly when she said, 'Even if nobody but I came?'

My deception rose another degree in my reply. 'Mitu is your friend, I had thought you'd be pleased if she came too.'

Bulbul shook her head slowly and her eyes and voice regained their arid 'unwomanliness' in that instant. 'No, Ranajit, I won't go for the film, I don't have the time. Even if I did, I'm in no mood to enjoy myself. You have no idea, I'm absolutely furious.'

'That's why I was saying that laughing with Buster Keaton would make things easier for you.'

'My mood isn't going to improve so easily.'

'Is that why you make others feel unhappy too?' Bulbul responded to this harshly, 'No one in this country has the right to be happy . . .' then continued in a softer tone, 'except you.'

Several days went by. The university reopened, the days became shorter, winter wasn't far away. My time passed the same way, at least externally: college, Bokul Villa, the occasional afternoon in Jones's company, Bulbul now and then, chats with Kajol at home sometimes. But one day I was taken aback by a trivial incident. As soon as I went out that afternoon, I saw Bulbul. Walking up to me quickly, she said, 'I won't keep you long, I know you're going to Mitu. I just came to tell you something.'

'What is it?'

'You visited Jones again yesterday?'

'How did you know?'

Without answering, she said, 'There's still time, listen to me, Ranajit, don't visit Jones any more.'

'How can I honour an unfair request?'

'But do you know why I'm saying this?'

'I can guess, but I'm not going to argue with you today, Bulbul, I really am busy today.'

'Can you give me five minutes—two minutes?'

She looked wretched: her hair dishevelled, her garments coarse and dirty, her appearance unkempt; I felt she was deeply agitated, that she wanted to share her anguish with me and unburden herself.

'What's the matter?'

'Nothing new, Ranajit. I feel very sad to think you can have tea and biscuits with an enemy of the country.'

'Don't give me the same hoary clichés,' I sneered.

'What makes you so conceited that you dismiss anything not to your taste as clichés? Have you ever considered why Jones moves around so much in Bengali circles? Considered why he's learning Bengali, reading Bengali books, why he goes to the university to debate, to music sessions at Bokul Villa? No . . . I know what you're going to say, let me speak. Maybe he *is* well-read, intelligent, maybe he does love music, maybe he *can* pick up foreign languages rapidly, but aren't you going to think about what use he's putting these abilities to? He's using them to gain admission into people's homes and then extract inside information, betraying us! Have you forgotten that it was this very Jones who instigated the riots in Dacca and then disappeared for a change of air to Darjeeling, that our young men are trapped in his net, that they're being snapped up as frogs are by snakes and despatched to camps in Hijli and Buxar? A spy, a vicious spy, a cunning, manipulative devil—that's your Arthur Jones!'

'I don't believe it,' I shouted.

'We know—we have proof.' Bulbul spoke coolly, but I could see the flames of anger in her expression.

'I don't know what you mean by "we",' I replied. 'Nobody is "we" to me, everyone is an individual "I".'

'"We" meaning "we"—the people of this country.'

'Then I'm among them too. That I or "we" is telling you that all "your" proof is spurious, and that your impression is absolutely off the mark. Jones is a genuine person—I know—he's embarrassed that the British rule India, he has taken this job only to learn about our country, to understand it, he will never do anything knowingly to harm India. British rule is a machine, and Jones is a human being, a person—can't you tell the difference between the two?'

Bulbul smiled. 'You're such a good person yourself that you think everyone's the same. How well do you know Jones? He spouts a few lines from books and you melt. You float in your world of emotions and ideas, you cannot even imagine that a honeyed tongue can hide a poisonous soul. But I beg of you, don't mingle with Jones any more, you never know what happens on those desolate roads in Ramna, I'm warning you.'

'Are you trying to scare me?' I spat out.

'I cannot claim there's nothing to be scared of! What if the others don't believe that Jones isn't using you?'

'You mean to say I'm supplying information to him—so I'm a spy too.' I laughed loudly, Bulbul looked at me in silence. I continued, 'Are you going mad, Bulbul? What *is* the matter with you?'

Sighing, she said, 'So you won't honour my request?'

I didn't answer, Bulbul didn't say anything either, there was silence for some time. The argument was pointless; the very things that gave me proof of Jones's goodness made him a criminal in Bulbul's eyes. Jones's love for literature and his research in linguistics were masks according to Bulbul. That he moved around freely, spontaneously, seeking friends among Bengalis—that too in this famous and notorious Dacca, where a year ago Loman had become no man, where the pugnacious Hodson hadn't been let off either—was, in Bulbul's words, his most deceitful ploy—that was how he was hoodwinking decent people like Anadi-babu and me. Apparently he was trying to show us that he wasn't like other Englishmen—he didn't go out with bodyguards, he would accomplish his tasks under the disguise of a 'friend of India', that was his real plan . . . But did Bulbul really suspect me too? No—that was impossible, whatever she was saying was all tutored, made up—she clung to those notions as though they were all she had in life.

'Bulbul,' I discovered a new line of argument suddenly, 'you're saying all the Dacca boys have been arrested because of Jones's manoeuvres. But doesn't the fact that you're still out of jail prove his innocence?'

After a short silence Bulbul said in a low voice, 'I won't be out of jail much longer either. That's why I came here to tell you all this, before disappearing from sight. Ranajit, you love Mitu so much, but what about your countrymen, who are being ground to dust under the boots of the British—can't you love them a little too?'

'Whatever else you do,' I flared up, 'don't bring Mitu into it.'

'What! You can't even bear to hear me speak of Mitu?'

'You and I have nothing in common, Bulbul,' I said, stricken. 'Let me go.'

'Let you go? You're telling me not to come to you any more?'

'If all we do when we meet is quarrel,' I said firmly, 'it's best to stay away.'

'I see. So this is what you really think?' Bulbul sighed. 'All right, so be it.'

Silence descended on the mango-orchard (we had arrived at our usual spot almost unconsciously)—side by side, without looking at each other, we emerged on the road. Neither of us said another word, I didn't pause to say goodbye to Bulbul when we reached the head of our lane.

Then—in half an hour—I was at Bokul Villa. The stars were in my favour; I found Mitu on the first-floor veranda with her parents, without anybody else nearby. I didn't delay any more, all my hesitation dropped away, I let those much-speculated words slip easily from my lips: 'I want to marry Mitu.' I gave myself up to the bond that was my salvation, which could never again be taken back. I was calm; I slept soundly that night.

Fourteen

Could you press that button near you please? . . . That one, on the extreme left. Thanks. Evening is getting on—my whiskey-evening. Drinks, bearer. For you? Nothing? No, we cannot have that, have something, at least a drop of sweet sherry . . . Cheers! Ah, what a relief now that I've taken a sip. Come, let's welcome the evening, holding our glasses up like flags, fearlessly. Doesn't the evening feel like the end of a lifetime for you every day? From day to night, and again from night to day—how enormous these changes are, and yet how easily people accept them, even crossing the sea with a single leap like Hanuman doesn't tire them out. But I find it far too fatiguing, only with a lot of effort over many hours am I able to get past each of these junctures, climb from day to night, sink again from night to day. In the early hours of the morning I feel sleepy, but even in my sleep I can make out I'm sleeping, I know when dawn breaks, when Gayatri leaves in her dressing-gown, I turn over, and suddenly I fall deeply asleep, but it takes much longer to wake up than the time I spend asleep. I feel like I'm swimming, sinking, surfacing sometimes to breathe. When I open my eyes I cannot tell where I am, the meaningless dreams I had seem to cling to my eyes like fish-scales; sometimes I think I'm in my bed at our Bakshibazaar home (I even remember that Kajol is in the next room), sometimes the scent of Mitu's hair while half asleep at the George V hotel at Athens, the Parthenon outside the window, I remember, but when I open my eyes I realize that I had mistaken Nellie for Mitu. Sometimes I imagine I'm in Cannes, only for a couple of days, I should set my eyes upon the azure Mediterranean Sea right away, no, it's not morning yet—it's night, late at night, no one awake anywhere, the upheaval of the sea in my head, Mitu's eyes like stars in the darkness, Kajol's body like a mermaid soaked in foam. But what is that tinkling sound? Jabbalpore, Nellie's piano, is it time for me to go to court, will the clock-hands stay at eight o'clock till eternity? That's the kind of hide-and-seek the room plays every morning, I feel as though my life is fragmented into a thousand pieces and scattered everywhere, at this moment of waking up I try to gather them and piece them back together—so much effort, I'm exhausted—in trying to get myself back I'm being torn apart all over again. How will it matter if I do not wake up again, if I wrap myself snugly in the remnants of my sleep and go from one darkness into another? But no, so long as the body exists there is no respite from time; I need to have my coffee, use the bathroom, I can't do without shaving either, then there in that veranda to the east, I feel that light is good, I want light, the clarity of daylight restores my courage to live; I am no longer in doubt over who I am, where I am, what the date is, what time it is. And for that very reason I have to go through another battle in the evening; after several hours in daylight the darkness appears unfamiliar; the fragments of life that I had managed to arrange fall apart again, seem to melt in night's high tide—not forever (in which case there would have been nothing to worry about) but for twelve hours only. That's why I'm so wary about going to sleep, I'm aware that I cannot afford to be completely submerged, I must clutch at a straw even in my sleep, so that when I wake up, I can feel my way around to rebuild this house, the town of Ootacamund, this world and my identity, all from that same straw. Tell me, is life so wonderful that you have to toil so hard for it?

But no, it isn't as though there's no reward for labour. Those two periods in our life, the moments before falling asleep and before waking up, when we're endowed with almost supernatural powers, during which we can practically grasp the past in our hands—as fragile as a drop of water, which we refer to as a dream, but which is actually our own creation—an invitation, a response, a dialogue, a re-enactment. Our hearts look on without bias then—understanding everything, forgiving everything. A luminous day nestling somewhere in there comes back, when I knew for sure that I would marry Mitu, that her parents would come over soon to talk to mine—I was happy, but not filled with impatience, I could calmly wait long years, very long years, for Mitu, I had found my life's objective, I would no longer be confused. The wind was my friend, the sunlight and the stars my support, I was fearless, I was safe. I had a friend at home, she was the only one I had confided in—I couldn't stay without doing it—about what I was immersed in, just like these autumn mornings are immersed in light. 'Kajol-mami, don't tell anyone else, but Mitu and I . . .' Kajol's face was suffused with a wonderful joy as soon as she heard, her eyes looked brighter, her cheeks redder; even after she had run her fingers over my cheeks, through my hair, she wasn't satisfied, she took both my hands in hers and looked at me in silence for a while. At that moment even that selfish young man realized how much Kajol loved him; realized how good a person has to be, how pure, to be so happy at someone else's happiness despite their own deprivation; maybe he loved her too. Those few days, those were the only luminous days of my life. Kajol was stupid, Kajol had no sophistication, no personality—that was what I had always heard from my family; even I—even after the revelation that evening at Bokul Villa, even after becoming much more intimate with her out of compulsion during the riots—had not been able to overcome my attitude entirely, combining indifference with pity for her; even the dream that I had nurtured involving her and Fotik-mama was only for selfish reasons. But during those days Kajol had become important to me because of her own self, she and I had developed a new relationship, she had multiplied my happiness, had grown to be my confidante.

Every night, after my return from Bokul Villa, when my parents went to bed after dinner, I spent some time chatting with Kajol—light, juvenile conversation, the exuberance of my happiness, which Kajol had made her own too, which allowed our hearts to touch each other through a trivial exchange or a shared laugh. I forgot that for Kajol this was merely the kind of fulfilment her sad life had not provided, like savouring the pleasures of love by proxy, maybe Kajol forgot too as she merged herself into these beautiful moments of my life, into our joint future—Mitu's and mine. I no longer remembered her languid, half-asleep appearance, she seemed to have discovered a new personality, as though the woman within her had only just awakened, the woman whom I had seen only once before for an instant, that evening at Bokul Villa, first by twilight, then by electric light. In a group of three women her individuality had not been clear to me—today, however, there was no one next to her; as a result, we had formed such a personal relationship that I could not but make her a shareholder in my future. My imagination still played with that pink house on Heysham Road, but Mitu and I were its occupants now—and my former role had been given to Kajol, she visited us from time to time, our companion in pleasure, our friend in happiness.

That Fotik-mama lived in the same city, in that same Bhawanipore, that Kajol was his wife, that she lived under my parents' guardianship—none of this occurred to me; I had separated her from her social environment—as though I had first claim to her affection, her attention—I, and Mitu. Just as it's not only the horizon but also much of the eastern sky that turns red at sunrise, in fact, by some atmospheric trickery, the glow spreads to the west too, in the same way my love for Mitu had extended beyond her to reach Kajol. And Kajol, on her part, had also climbed the stairs taken by Mitu to reach my heart. That's why I can still see Kajol sometimes, beneath the swirling waters of my half-sleep, like some tender, wet mermaid, a line of silver light piercing the darkness and instantly—like a fish escaping a net to dart away at the speed of lightning—sinking again into the darkness, into the farthest, deepest waters. Sometimes a black dot appears in that light, the dot grows, spreads; I see Bulbul, on the street outside our house. 'I've come again—I had to.' I look at her without speaking, after a moment's pause she says, 'You're getting married? To Mitu?' I bow my head, I feel embarrassed suddenly. 'Are you wondering how I knew? I knew the moment I looked at you—you look so happy. And besides, that's what we have been hoping for all this time, wasn't I the first one to say the two of you are made for each other?'

'How are you?' I ask. 'How?'

She smiles from the corner of her lips. 'Come for a walk? For a few minutes?'

'All right,' I say, trying to be polite.

It was a withered autumn evening, the grass beneath our feet wet under a light dew, the mango-orchard still and silent, slices of sky visible through gaps in the trees—yellow, blue, discoloured. Bulbul began casually, 'Arthur Jones is giving a lecture at Curzon Hall tomorrow, aren't you going?'

'I don't like listening to lectures.'

'I'm going—I want to hear what Jones has to say about Indian civilization. Why don't you come too—we're expecting some fun tomorrow.'

'Fun! Why?'

'Isn't it going to be fun if Jones starts singing praises to India?'

'Listen to me, Bulbul, if you start spouting that rubbish again I'm leaving right now,' I said.

Bulbul was silent for a while, her head bowed; I could hear the call of birds. Suddenly she raised her face swiftly and said in a scratchy voice, 'No, no more rubbish—only action now. Want to see something?' Suddenly inserting her hand into her blouse, she pulled out a . . . a . . . I trembled all over, my vision blurred, when I saw her clutching a pistol in her thin hand.

'Are you trying to scare me with a toy?' I whispered.

'A hero's toy, made in Germany, see? It's for Jones.'

'What are you saying, Bulbul?' I screamed.

'Shh, don't shout.' She covered my mouth with her hand. I twisted her wrist and snatched the pistol from her hand. 'Careful, it's loaded,' she exclaimed.

But I had lost the power of speech, unknown to myself, just the one word emerged continuously, 'No! No! No! No! No! No! No! . . . Bulbul! Not Jones! Not you!'

Bulbul's face was suffused with a smile, the victor's smile—arrogant, brilliant. 'Now you know why I came—although you had asked me not to. I came to say goodbye. Jones may be a good man, he may be a saint, but he's English, he represents those who are turning India into a graveyard, for that reason—for that reason alone—we need this. To make them understand yet again that we don't want them—using the language they understand. The idol isn't the goddess but we worship at her feet nevertheless, this too is something like that. A photo isn't a human being, but even when we see a photo of Michael O'Dyer which of us doesn't want to spit on it, to kick it? This too is like that. And if Jones really is innocent, that's even better, we'll be able to tell them that we won't forget even if they're good men, we don't want kindness, we don't want favours, we want to get rid of them, get rid of them!'

Bulbul's voice sounded like a knife being sharpened on a stone, she breathed like an injured beast. Swarms of words fastened themselves to my brain like insects, I had no words—silent—experiencing with all my mind and body a sensation that I had never even imagined, my blood boiled, the pores of my skin were on fire, my eyes were riveted to the pistol which I held in my hand—cold steel, but still warm from contact with Bulbul's skin, also loaded with fire, the combined warmth spreading to my veins, I forgot the world and everything in it under some sorcerer's spell. Leave alone touching one, I had never even seen a pistol in my life—except in a film—probably none of my ancestors had—but it was in my hand now, an incredible machine, flawlessly made, with a beautiful narrow barrel through which the hero's semen emerged at lethal speed, with unrestrained force, assault, plunder, victory. I was dizzy at the thought of so much power being condensed into such a small object, so small that a slim petite woman could carry it around concealed in her blouse, and which could be used in an instant, without anyone being aware of it, to comprehensively kill someone. How strange it is that in this world where love is so hard to find, so painful, surrounded by the barbed wire of complexities, violence is so extraordinarily simple, and the gratification of that violence so easy. I glanced at Bulbul with the same eyes that were dazzled by the pistol; her eyes glowed in the half-darkness. I saw her differently at that moment: taller, irresistibly attractive, her posture radiating authority, as though she held the judge's sceptre, as though the judgement was hers to deliver.

'You're trembling, Ranajit, give it back to me.'

I walked up to her, standing very close, and breathed, 'Really? . . . You'll really be able to?'

'That's why I'm asking you to be there tomorrow. You'll see for yourself.'

Joining her conspiracy without knowing it myself, I asked, 'Isn't there anyone else?'

'They've been arrested, Ranajit, some are on the run. Besides, I want to do this, it's my job—I must do it myself. This is what will bring fulfilment to my life. I'll never be anyone's wife, anyone's mother, there's nothing else I'm good for—I just have this one desire, dream, hope, whatever you want to call it: to stand before a Englishman and say, "Here's what we owe you, fair and square." Not with words, but by putting a hole in his chest.'

'What if you can't? What if you miss?'

'Even so—let me try. That's no mean achievement either. At least I'll be able to convey what I wanted.'

'And if—if . . .'

'Andaman? Hanging? That's what usually happens. What value does my life have anyway, that I must nurture it?' Bulbul tried to smile, I looked at her, entranced. What she was saying was like some sweet morphine, I became numb, I had nothing to say in response—the clear advice of good sense, principles, conscience, all seemed irrelevant, meaningless; like a lantern in daylight, all my logic had now paled. Bulbul gently retrieved the pistol from my hand, put it back inside her blouse and wrapped the end of her sari tightly round herself. 'I've told you what I had to. You're free now. I don't know why I told you—but I wanted to, I wanted to very much. I'm going now, Ranajit.' When we emerged from the mango-orchard she said, 'Don't come any further with me, Ranajit. I'm off now.' She looked at me for a while; I felt her eyes were sucking out my blood, my marrow. Then she walked ahead swiftly, I saw her disappear in the mist at the head of the road.

But as soon as she disappeared from view I seemed to awake from a trance. What had I done, how could I have let her go? Could I not have stopped her, could I still not do it? A silent scream rose in my breast, a cold sweat ran down my spine. No—I wouldn't let it happen, it was impossible! I went back home, took my cycle and pedalled full-tilt to Bulbul's house in Kayettuli—no, she wasn't back. Then to Bibhabati's house in Rajar Deuri. Bibhabati was in Calcutta, Bulbul hadn't been there all day. Was she going to spend the night at some secret hideout—and stay there tomorrow too, till the evening? Would I not be able to find her then? What should I do now? Should I inform them at the police-station? . . . No, how could I? Go to Jones? . . . That was impossible too. I had to save them—not just Jones, but also Bulbul. Who would tell me how to do it? Bulbul had turned my world upside-down. Where was I? There—the thick pillars of the collegiate school, the yellow church with the clock-tower—when I was in school, how often had I craned my neck during afternoon classes at that clock-face lit up by the setting sun, in the hope that it was four o'clock—why wasn't I still a child, why did I have to grow up, why this agony, why had Bulbul imposed this enormous responsibility on me? I cycled around blindly for some time, randomly going past places like Digbazaar, Banglabazaar, Sadarghat, before circling back to the Collegiate School, Victoria Park—I got off my cycle, lifted it over the park fence and lay down flat on the grass. Wet grass, dewdrops falling now and then, and in the sky—I was suddenly startled—the moon, lightly golden like an egg, calm. My heart jumped, I remembered Mitu, whom I had forgotten all this while.

The night was well advanced, Lamirnie Street was deserted. A misty moonlight had spread everywhere, the cool moon, the melancholy sky, the trees, having lost their reflections in the moonlight, were silhouetted, hazy—all was quiet and beautiful, filled with sadness and silence. Such moonlight usually made me want to sink deep within myself, but today I had been drawn out of myself, as it were, I didn't seem to exist. The momentary consolation that the sight of the moon had given me as I lay on my back on the grass in the park was destroyed as the world crowded in on me—things I knew nothing of, understood nothing of; the moonlight was irrelevant to me now, on the contrary, I was surprised that on such a night, while a dreadful incident was in the making, the moonlight and the mist could be so unmoved, as beautiful as on any other night. I didn't race off in distress to Bokul Villa, I actually slowed my cycle down, as though the relationship between Mitu and me was no longer undamaged, I was doubtful myself about how worthy I was of going to her. The road was flanked by houses, people at peace in each of them, none of them knew anything—but I—why did I have to be the one to know, why did this enormous burden have to be mine to carry, why had Bulbul left me in the grips of this unbearable agony? Did I really have the right to be happy when such an intense, venomous agony could build up around the edges of my existence, threatening to burst in a gigantic explosion? Lives—the lives of two people—and two people who were very real to me, radiant, those lives were now threatened—how could I ignore that? Assassination—a dreadful word, profane, unutterable! And involved in it was—incredible, but true—not some criminal, not some dacoit, not someone driven mad by greed or rage, but a young woman, a girl, a friend of Mitu's, the selfless, hard-working nationalist Bulbul. Yet it wasn't as though I could evade my responsibility by ruling her guilty—she was throwing away her own life too; by combining an extreme transgression with an extreme sacrifice, she had elevated herself beyond criticism. There was no question of right and wrong here—I was suffering, for Bulbul, for Jones—if I couldn't save them, with what honour would I face Mitu, love her, marry her?

As soon as I entered the drawing-room at Bokul Villa, I met both mother and daughter. They were sitting in stunned silence, their faces like thunder. The moment she saw me Mitu's mother said, 'Something terrible has happened, Ranajit. Mitu's father's pistol has been stolen.'

I felt bile rise in my throat. 'What did you say?' I muttered indistinctly.

'He sold all his hunting guns long ago, he had only kept this one German pistol—it used to be a favourite of his father's, he had kept it as a remembrance. I told him so many times this is not a good time to have such things at home, get rid of it, at least deposit it at the Treasury, but . . .' Mitu's mother's voice choked, she couldn't finish.

'Has it really been stolen?' I asked. 'Nowhere to be found?'

'Nowhere. It used to be kept in the safe at the head of his bed, he always kept the key with himself, but he's a little absent-minded, must have put it down carelessly somewhere, who can tell how it happened.'

'When did he last see the pistol?'

'Last . . . I'm not sure . . . it stays in the safe usually, once in a while he'd take it out to clean it . . . that's as far as it went.'

'Did he bring it out recently . . . to clean it?'

'Yes, he brought it out about ten days ago,' answered Mitu.

'And you found out today it's gone?'

'Today, yes. Just a short while ago—when getting something else out of the safe. Mitu's father has gone to the station to report the theft—I hope the police don't start harassing him.

'A glass of water, please, Mitu,' I said, following her. Draining the glass, I said, 'Let's sit on the steps here.'

That same veranda where I had my first awareness of womanhood, that same garden where the sunlight had filtered through the trees to light up Mitu's face. The trees looked unfamiliar now in the moonlight: distant, cut off from the world of people; the tender, mist-shrouded night seemed only the scenery on a stage without a play, without actors. And Mitu, my future wife, whom I loved most of all, who was sitting by my side, appeared to be someone distant, as I could not tell her what I knew, could not tell her that I'd seen her father's pistol, touched it—barely three hours ago. Happiness, will you ever come back to me? Where was that golden land, the land of dreams, where love was simple?

'I'm scared, Ranju,' said Mitu. 'They won't do anything to baba, will they?'

'Of course not! Why should they do anything to the person whose gun has been stolen? Tell me—did Bulbul come today? To your house?'

'No. I haven't seen her in days.'

'How many days?'

'At least nine or ten days. She visited once in between, but we were out.'

'I see.' The words escaped my mouth.

'What? What're you getting at?'

'Nothing. Mitu . . .'

'What?'

A plan was taking shape in my mind slowly, initially as unclear as the misty moonlight, then—just as a line of poetry in perfect rhythm suddenly leaps into the poet's mind out of a nameless uneasiness, when he knows that he has found his poem— I suddenly realized with great clarity what I had to do now. I looked at Mitu, a scream rose in my breast, 'Let's go away somewhere, somewhere far away, Bulbul won't let us live here.'

But no, there was no way to say anything—all roads but one were closed—I would probably choke to death.

'You were about to say something,' said Mitu.

'No, I just said your name, I wanted to.' I moved closer to Mitu, sensed the delicate fragrance of her hair for a moment. 'Mitu! What a beautiful name, how beautiful you are!' I continued. Hoof beats were heard outside, we went into the drawing-room.

'Well?' said mother and daughter in unison as soon as Anadi-babu entered.

'Well, what? I made a complaint at the police station.'

'And now? There won't be any trouble?'

'Trouble? Why should there be trouble? Is there anyone in Dacca who doesn't know me? They won't give me a gun-licence again, of course, but that's just as well, I don't want to keep evil in my house any more. It was an heirloom—it's gone now.'

Mitu's mother asked in detail about his conversation with the police, but Anadi-babu waved her away. 'Never mind all that. Hello, Ranju. Why are all of you looking so grim? We should invite people over one of these days, of course we needn't tell them anything just yet . . .' He looked in turn at his wife and at me '. . . but the celebrations can start immediately. Have you heard, Mitu, Kanai Basak's fourteen-year-old son is apparently a real wizard with the tabla, I'm going to ask him to play with you one of these days.'

Anadi-babu tried to lighten their mood, but a cloud flitted across his own face every now and then. I sensed the anxiety he was concealing; a Gandhian who believed in non-violence, the altruistic homoeopath, he couldn't rid himself of the fear that his pistol could be used to perpetrate an assassination. There was no other significance to a gun being stolen in present-day Dacca. I was sorely tempted to draw him aside and tell him what I knew—but no, let him, his wife, their lovely one-in-a-million daughter . . . let all of them sleep peacefully tonight at least, let the suffering, let the agony be all mine. For a moment I felt as powerful as the gods—the fate of others was in my hands, I was the overlord of the happiness, the peace, the life, the death, of someone else—at least for a few hours, till tomorrow evening. At that moment I felt the passion of the sacrifice and the arrogance of those who stepped up, pistol in hand, to assassinate the British; I felt that if for some time it were possible to transform oneself into a god, to rise above principles, ethics, conscience, even the fear of death, who wouldn't agree to throw away this life as though it were worthless? But my eyes met Mitu's at once; her face was wan, her lips dry—my body, my soul, my heart, all that I was made of, seemed to rush towards her uncontrollably, I turned my eyes away, every heartbeat said, making sure I could hear, 'Mitu, be safe, be happy, be happy.' Anadi-babu asked me to stay for dinner, I agreed—just so as to stay with Mitu a while longer. I had to pretend to eat, pretend to converse too. Then—the compound of Bokul Villa, the misty moonshine, Mitu and I walking side by side, Mitu walking with me up to the gate. I paused. Before leaving. 'Come tomorrow,' said Mitu. I looked at her once more—my dream, my refuge, my life, my innocent, well-meaning existence . . . I left them all behind and leapt on my cycle with a single movement.

I came home, night deepened, everyone fell asleep one by one. But sleep had deserted me, fatigue had abandoned me. I thought only of the following night—when I would go to Curzon Hall, keep my eye on Bulbul, stop her at the crucial moment. It was easy—what could be easier? The outcome? Let it be what it will. Fate had no common sense, why else did I have to be the one to have to do this, I, who was the least capable? I kept playing the scene out in my mind—I lay down, I sat up, I paced around; anything I tried to distract myself with collapsed like a house of cards. I recalled Arthur Jones—his comely appearance, his reserved manner, his gentle way of speaking. I recalled the petite Bulbul, disappearing dimly in the mist. I had been once more to Bulbul's house on the way back, I was told she was visiting her aunt in Coormitola, she would be back the next day. In other words, she was going to stay out of everyone's reach till tomorrow evening. I would confront her tomorrow. But . . . would I really be able to pull it off? Of course—I had to. And after that? What if people didn't understand, what if I was accused, what if the twists of the law proved that I was guilty? What if the gun went off in a skirmish, killing Jones? But how would I prove then I was not a murderer? Jail? Andaman? Hanging? No . . . no . . . I can't, I can't. Let me go, Bulbul, let me go—I want Mitu, I love Mitu. I love poetry, love the sky, the clouds, the smell of books. I want to live—let me go, Bulbul. Tell me, what can I do for you, in return for which you will return Anadi-babu's pistol to me? Bulbul, don't you want to be happy, to make others happy—have you never loved anyone? I didn't do you any harm, why did you punish me so? . . .

I'd kept the lantern burning on the desk, turning it up I opened a book, but in spite of all my effort I couldn't make sense of a single word. Did the world where people read poetry, listened to music, wrote poetry, made music, exist any more? What if the bullet from the pistol pierced me, right here, where my heart was about to burst? Would I die? Was this the last night of my life? I pushed the book away, leaned back in my chair and shut my eyes, I suddenly felt there was still a lot of time, I would still be alive for many, many more hours. Should I leave a couple of letters behind—one for Mitu, one for my parents? What if there was no time afterwards? But listen—maybe I had exaggerated everything; if I wanted, if only I wanted, I could come out of this circle of fire. Should I simply stay home all day tomorrow? Take the first launch to my aunt's house in Munshiganj? Wrenching my nerves repeatedly, someone seemed to say, 'Why are you worrying so much about Bulbul, about Arthur Jones? Are they more important to you than your parents? More important than Mitu? Mitu, your Mitu, whom you've promised, who will wait for you as long as you want her to, whose happiness, life, future all depend on you—are you going to sacrifice her for an obstinate young woman's whim, someone who means nothing to you, whose mission, ideas, action are all the direct opposite of yours? What can you do if a lunatic murders an innocent man? Bulbul's hand will probably tremble and the bullet will miss its mark, there won't be a scratch on Jones, or maybe Bulbul will not be able to muster up courage eventually, or maybe her humane feelings will assert themselves, her love for her own life—maybe she'll fall ill tomorrow, or her father will pass away—so many things can happen between now and tomorrow evening. Calm down, go to sleep, think of Mitu—if Mitu and you can be happy, if you can ever manage to write some good poetry, will that not make this world, this India of Bulbul's, truly richer?' Bubbles . . . like bubbles the thoughts rose, only to disappear instantly; I was like the prisoner who goes back in his dreams to his home in the village; I was compelled now, I didn't know who had compelled me; I was free no more, my own desires had been buried. No matter which way and how many times I thought about it, I ended up at the same place—Curzon Hall, Bulbul, Arthur Jones. No—I cannot, I won't think of it any more, I can't think of it any more—forgive me, O Lord.

There was a rustling noise behind me, I turned round with a start to find Kajol near the door. I remembered she had come into my room before going to bed—for our usual night-time chat—I had told her I had something important to read. I had forgotten her completely all this while, I was surprised—a living being appeared to have entered the world of spirits. Taking a step forward, she said, 'What is it, Ranju, why haven't you gone to bed yet?

'I was about to, why did you get up?'

'I woke up suddenly, were you pacing up and down a little while ago? I thought I heard someone groaning.'

I rose without answering.

'What have you done to yourself?' said Kajol. 'You aren't ill, are you? Let me see . . .' She put her hand on my forehead and my cheek to check for fever. I looked at her—eyes swollen with sleep, her sari billowing in an attempt to cover her voluptuous body; I saw in her all that I was about to lose—well-being, a normal existence, life itself, the taste of life; she stood before me full of anxiety, affection, tenderness for me, her garment the national flag held aloft by the last surviving soldier on the battlefield, or she was like a lighthouse spotted from a sinking boat, or she was like the lifeline held out from a boat as I drowned. A mad desire rose within me, a torrent burst out through the rock: I would tell her, tell her everything, I would leave at least one witness to my suffering, I would share this tragic night with at least one other human being. I turned into a foolish helpless child at that instant, into an overcome drunkard; holding Kajol close to me, I put my head on her shoulders, I trembled uncontrollably, then the sobs burst through my breast, the tears through my eyes. Relief—I was saved—swimming endlessly after the boat had capsized, I finally found the ground beneath my feet. Kajol's fingers running through my hair, her voice like a hornet's in my ear—'What is it? What is it, Ranju? What is it?' My tears slowed down, I raised my face, she wiped my tears away. 'Tell me, won't you?' But by then the fire from a different pistol was spreading in my body, I no longer saw Kajol, I only sensed the touch of a woman, her breath on my throat, her body filling up my emptiness. If that was indeed so, if my familiar world was indeed going to disappear the next day, if I had to die tomorrow, would I never know a woman, never know love? Would I have to die with my deepest desire unfulfilled? My longing, kept under control all these days, became unstoppable, I drew Kajol into my bed. 'Ranju, Ranju, Ranju, Ranju . . .' she tried to stop me, weakly, then suddenly she burst out sobbing, her breath working up a storm, her heart thumping, her tongue in my mouth like the flames of a frothing supernatural fire, her moist mouth on my lips forcing . . . making me swoon, me breaking down into electrified atoms on her breast. Nothing remained—no world, no responsibility, no suffering—just she and I—no, we didn't exist either: this was release, nirvana, death.

Fifteen

Have you noticed, night has fallen, it's completely dark. The world outside has turned unfamiliar. But I, I am secure. See how small my room is. Enclosed by walls, the light is switched on, a heavy curtain is drawn across the window. I have plenty of alcohol, I have Gayatri. I am not afraid. The Gorkha guard and the two German Shepherds patrol the grounds all night. Pardon me? Oh, I'm not surprised you're astonished by my capacity for drinking. You could call me a minor champion where that is concerned. But don't worry. It doesn't do a thing to me. Go ahead, test me, ask me to pronounce any difficult word of your choice, ask me spellings, geography questions, history dates—whatever you like. Oh, I see, you want to find out things from the past, secrets, on this pretext. You're very clever, my friend, you want to make me say what you know already, what you've known for years altogether. Why, were you not there that evening at Curzon Hall, were you not watching Bulbul, watching me, from a distance, doesn't all of it come back to you? Bulbul sitting in the front row, me hiding behind a pillar in the corridor, Bulbul couldn't see me, her gaze was riveted on Arthur Jones, just as mine was on . . . her. I had eyes only for her, watching her with close, very close, attention. Indistinct sounds: Jones's lecture, the rustle of leaves, of the wind—meaningless. All other faces were blurred, they didn't exist. Arjun saw nothing but the eyes of the bird, that was Bulbul's sport with Jones, mine with Bulbul. My eyes were bursting, every moment seemed like an eternity. There . . . there. Bulbul got to her feet, her hand snaked into her blouse, I ran up to her and put my arms around her. A deafening sound, smoke, the smell of gunpowder, screams.

Tell me, I was in custody for a few days, wasn't I? You're sure you remember? And then? Oh yes . . . when I was released I heard Jones had pleaded for me, but not even his efforts could save Mitu. Mitu was arrested under deténu, in Dacca Jail for now, she would soon be transferred somewhere else. I asked for permission to meet her, I didn't receive it. The pistol was her father's, Bulbul was her friend, the empire of George V couldn't possibly remain intact unless she were detained. Bibhabati was arrested in Calcutta, Jones was transferred to Rajshahi. Two months later I boarded the *City of Calcutta* at Chandpal Ghat. I had no choice but to go to England. If I stayed back the police wouldn't leave me alone. Apparently the district magistrate had assured my father that all charges against me would be withdrawn if I were sent abroad immediately. Besides, I got anonymous letters from time to time: 'You may have saved Arthur Jones, but don't expect to save yourself from our vengeance. Bulbul was arrested because of you, we will not spare you.' The police on one side, the 'we' whom Bulbul had mentioned on the other. There's no justice in this world, I tell you. For me, Kajol pawned the very jewellery that she had not given up for her husband; it was on the strength of that money that I set foot on the shores of England on a bitingly cold night.

Was I unhappy to leave India? Not at all. The ship sailed, Bengal's shores disappeared from my view, I noticed with surprise that I felt no sadness; Bulbul, Kajol, Mitu—even Mitu—had all become silhouettes already. Kajol came to the pier too with my parents, but her eyes, red with crying, left no shadow on the afternoon sky; and that night, when she and I had became one with each other like two rivers flowing into one, that too seemed to have disappeared from my life, leaving not a sign, no resonating echo. I felt no regret for leaving these shores, nor did I feel any curiosity about the land that I was sailing towards; what difference would it make even if I were to leap into the Bay of Bengal. But I didn't have the initiative left for something like that; I was finished, shattered. It was a matter of great fortune that no one had been hurt, that there had been no physical deaths, that all that had happened was that chunks of plaster had fallen from the magnificent ceiling of Curzon Hall. But I died at twenty-one—that evening, that day. I was rent asunder from the pivot around which my life had revolved, which had become the heart and soul of my existence; just as the expulsion of the earth from our solar system would mean that not even a blade of grass would grow any more on it, so too was this for my spirit.

Not even the day I set foot in the England of my dreams, the glimpse of Blake's manuscript at the British Museum, of Shelley's poetry notebook at the Bodleian, Sybil Thorndike's performance in Bernard Shaw's *Saint Joan* . . . none of these could thrill me; I felt that wherever there were people, hell yawned, death loomed in a hundred different forms and names—there was, therefore, no difference between one country and another. I felt my old life had ended, but a new life had not begun—all that remained, like a ghostly voice, like a message from a half-unknown dark continent, were letters from my mother. One day, two letters arrived together, one from my mother, the other postmarked the detention camp at Hijli. Mitu—it was a letter from Mitu. Mitu from Bokul Villa. The golden-voiced singer. The homoeopath Anadi-babu's daughter. My lover. My future wife. Her last line was, 'Don't be sad, we'll meet again.' Just as the sound of the rain, or a breeze at dawn, or the temporary effect of a new medicine, makes even the terminal patient think he's recovering, so too did Mitu's letter make me regain for a moment my will to live, I felt life could begin all over again. But after reading my mother's letter, I couldn't fathom its meaning for the longest time. 'The accursed woman has left us, taking with her the wages of her sin.' Who? What sin? Where had she gone? Bitterly cold, the wind like a knife, a blizzard, a snow-covered, blurred London by night, taken over by whores, scoundrels, drunks and the lonely—I was on the street, tramping for miles, tramping and saying to myself, 'Kajol is dead, she was carrying a child in her womb—her husband not with her but still pregnant—that's why Kajol hanged herself.' An enormous city, I knew no one, an enormous world, I knew no one; the night was as cold as a corpse, my limbs were turning numb. To keep warm I entered a pub—my first encounter with alcohol—I have no memory of how I returned home that night, whether I slept at all.

Are you feeling upset for Kajol? Forget it—it's futile. You blame me? How strange, did I ask Kajol to kill herself? . . . You know, I was briefly tempted to tell my mother everything, to write her a long letter—fortunately I had the sense at the last moment not to give in. She loved Kajol, she was grieving, why add to her burden of sorrow. She never wrote or spoke of Kajol again; I remained silent too. No one knew who had gifted that foetus to Kajol—no one ever will—except me—and you. You know in what bizarre circumstances it happened—the outcome of a sudden surge of passion—I hadn't imagined such a thing even five minutes earlier; Kajol felt pity for my traumatized state, she tried to protect me with the heart-churning tenderness of her starving womanhood, which was why she lost her head, responded so easily to my desire. And why shouldn't she have—what had she got in her own life, after all, what had she got from her husband besides callous neglect—was she not a human being, did she have no heart, no physical needs, no right to claim compensation from life at least once? And I, I brought rainfall to her desert; we were swept away in a torrent of mutual consolation that night. You know everything, you understand it all by now, would you still call it wrong?

If anyone indeed was responsible, you know who it was? Bulbul. Because she was a woman and so young, the High Court judges showed her some clemency, her sentence was reduced from fourteen years to eight. But her real trial never did take place, except in my head. 'You love Mitu so much, can't you love your countrymen just a little?' Does it take even a minute for men of the world like you and me to understand her real meaning? Bulbul fell in love with me, but she refused to acknowledge it to herself, so she channelized her emotion towards a terrible alternative. She wanted to kill not Jones, but my love; to take revenge not on the British but on Mitu and me, for we had fallen in love with each other. She had hit her real target unerringly with her jealous bullet—a perfect bullseye. If that were not so, why did she reveal to me her shocking plan? Does a person embarking on such a mission let slip anything even to their best friend in the world? Does such a person even have a friend, for that matter, *can* they have a friend? How could she—she had sacrificed herself to teach me a dreadful lesson. 'See for yourself how I've punctured the balloon of your dreams, will you be able to lose yourself again in your world of feelings, your world of love?' Tell me, wasn't this extortion, blackmail, cruelty, torture for the heart, torture for the conscience? What can cause more torment than misery, tell me, is there anything else with the same overpowering ability to turn the innocent into the guilty—where will you find a person so hedonistic, so intent on pleasure, so selfish that he won't shrink back in the presence of the dying man, before the sobs of the starving, at the scene of superhuman bravery that breaks through the shackles of harmony, of conviviality, of self-control?

Pardon me? Why do you think I'm mistaken? Oh, Bulbul's patriotism. Her willingness to die. Tell me, why are you telling me once again what I had thought true too? I accept that I was overcome when I saw the pistol in her hand, I was overwhelmed by this frail girl's audacity and the extent of her self-sacrifice, for a moment I felt insignificant in comparison, for a moment I agreed with her that Arthur Jones was not fit to breathe the air on this planet. No, why blame Bulbul, the fault was mine; idiocy, idiocy—what you might call crass stupidity. I didn't realize how easy it could have been to prevent her, if only I'd just told her one thing—'Bulbul, your life is valuable to me too, I love you.' In the seclusion of the mango-orchard, when the last drops of sunset were oozing through the gaps in the leaves, and I held in my hand the lethal weapon made warm by contact with Bulbul's breast, if only I'd taken her hand in mine and said, 'No, Bulbul, I won't let this happen, come with me, I'll explain it all to you.' Or I could have echoed her words, 'You love the three hundred million people of this country, don't you love me even a little?' But no, how could I say that, I was a saint, incapable of lying—it was Mitu whom I loved, not Bulbul. I couldn't pretend, I had not learnt to be a hypocrite, I was entirely under the control of my idiotic heart. With that one little lie I could have kept the pistol with myself, could have returned it to Anadibabu—how everlastingly happy the ending of this story could have been. And if I could not do that, why could I not shake off the ghost of that Himalayan blunder—why did I have to be altruistic, to try and save lives? Shoving my oar in, butting into other people's affairs, treading where I had no right to be. What obligation did I have—

what did Bulbul and Arthur Jones mean to me? Nothing at all, nothing compared to Mitu. Why had I not been able to reason: let people make their own choices, what difference did it make to me? In trying to save them, I killed Kajol. Destroyed my own life, Mitu's life.

But you know, around the same time, there in freezing London, I discovered that my intellect had turned leaner and sharper—I read for the Bar, prepared for the ICS examination, and made passionate love to economics, political science (oh Lord, even those tall, useless ideas were referred to as 'science'!) and law, visited Parliament to listen to political debates; and admired the cleverness of human beings more and more each passing day—that satanic cleverness which enabled the advocate to get a murderer exonerated; which empowered strong races to massacre weaker ones and then act as their saviours; which Bibhabati had relied on to teach Bulbul that there was no such thing as the truth, that whatever was convenient had to be assumed to be the truth; which I later employed like a hacksaw on my wife Nalini; which is still the excuse and the pretext for my existence; whose victorious colours I hoisted over pots of money and lumps of women's flesh—that same cleverness. I gradually removed every stain from my character, you know, you could say I turned spotless—a brilliant student in England, an outstanding officer, unmatched in my ways, behaviour and etiquette—but actually nothing, only a machine, just an amalgam of gestures, zero within. But then there's no such thing as zero, the smallest whole number is one, just as it will never turn to zero even if you keep splitting it into smaller and smaller fractions, in the same way there's an immortal, invincible, infinite decimal lurking within us, it's in our blood, the germ of a dead heart—perhaps this is what is known as memory, this is what is known as eternity—the equation that never allows the past to disappear, brings back whatever has happened, doesn't let us forget.

No, I didn't reply to that letter of Mitu's, Kajol had plundered the last spark of my feelings. I didn't enquire after Mitu even after I came back to India. Sometimes my mother told me about her—I listened in silence, without commenting. Mitu was released after four years, her mother was no longer alive when she went back home. The woman had given in to depression, she wouldn't eat, had developed a stomach tumour. Surgery may have saved her, but because of Anadi-babu's stubbornness she died under the orthodox homoeopathic school, barely a month before Mitu returned home. Anadi-babu gave up his practice, the foundations of his life imploded. Mitu—nurtured so lovingly, the only child of her parents, reclusive, shy and tender in disposition, who used to get a headache if the sun was too strong, who used to share a bed with her mother—that very same Mitu, having lost her beauty, her youth, her mesmerizing voice, returned to a father now become inactive, inanimate, aged.

Do you know who married her in honour of her former glory? Amulya—the well-built, dim-witted Amulya, given to profane humour. He was arrested at the same time as Mitu; he tried very hard to be arrested by writing a preposterous letter to Bibhabati—he wrote it secure in the knowledge that it would end up with the police—that was how he escaped his father's disciplinary yoke, the tyranny of education, the infamy of being unemployed, how he managed to think of himself as a peer of those better than him. He wrote no novel when in jail, didn't read Hegel, Marx, Jung or modern poetry, didn't spend his days on a deckchair, hand on his brow and sighing at the sky; he kept the entire camp at Buxar in high spirits with his singing, his jokes, his stories; after large meals, long hours of sleep, many games of cards, plenty of volleyball, and vastly improving his health, he left the camp with his suitcase full of handwoven dhotis and silk panjabis . . . You look surprised that Mitu chose him . . . But why? Why should you be surprised? Her mother was dead, her father was incapable of supporting himself, what choice did Mitu have but to get married? Me? Do you suppose everyone didn't know that by then I was already Ratandas's son-in-law? But then don't imagine Amulya is a nobody. Haven't you heard the poet Amulyacharan's songs in Calcutta? The star of modern music, who 'composes songs' in the guise of the lice on Tagore's body? The coyness emanating from whose throat has swept away the eternally young men and women of Bengal? Amulyacharan, with his fleet of cars, the toast of all 'funkshuns', the heart-throb of young women, the news of whose marriage to the film-playback singer Madhukshara Majumdar had overjoyed most people in Calcutta. Apparently his first wife was not worthy of him, she was far too ordinary. The demands of time are astounding—in a mere eleven or twelve years everyone forgot the once-famous singer Amita Bardhan whose records took Dildar Navroze's songs across the country, who used to correspond with eminent musicians from Calcutta, from Lucknow, from Pondicherry, and who had now lost all interest in music, so much so that she didn't even accompany her plump, glamorous husband to musical programmes. Pardon me? No, Amulya wasn't fortunate enough to become a widower—I don't know for sure what happened exactly, whether they were divorced in court, or simply separated, whether Amulya had conspired to drive her out so as to replace her with a worthier wife, or whether she had walked out on her own one day with her ten-year-old son. No, I know nothing, no wind bore her name to my ears—but still the heart, my heart, my bankrupted treasury.

Quite amusing, isn't it? The very cycle of events in which so many lives were destroyed yielded fame and fortune to Amulya. And my Fotik-mama—you remember him, don't you? Who thrust his wife into the arms of another man, into suicide—he was rewarded too. My mother gave me the good news even before I had completed a year in England. Fotik's business was booming in Calcutta, he had brought his German wife and child over, they were well, his wife had black hair, black eyes, she was beautiful. For a moment I felt a hot flush, but the very next moment I reflected: at least one Jew had been saved from the Nazis, she had had been able to escape vicious Germany thanks to her Indian husband, years of anxiety for herself and her daughter had finally ended, let's assume for the rest of her life—I too had a role to play in all this, for sure I did. Had Kajol not died, Fotik-mama may have waited even longer out of embarrassment, and what assurance was there that by then his German wife would not have been burnt in a gas chamber with other Jews? Or maybe Fotik-mama would have thrown up his hands, consigning both his wives into the hands of fate he would have got married a third time. At least there was this one silver lining—there's no such thing in the world as only a dark cloud.

Leaving already? Do stay a while longer. These Ootacamund nights are far too silent—it gets cold, no one steps out, everyone retreats into their holes. Can you hear the sound of silence, in your ears, like the buzz of crickets? I find it intolerable—let's talk these crickets of silence into oblivion. You may think I'm done talking—but no, I can keep talking all night, all my life. But it's your turn to say something, why don't you say something? Don't you want me to justify myself? Aren't you going to ask me why I didn't go back to Mitu? Why I didn't stand by her when she was in distress? Why I compelled her to marry Amulya? Why I didn't wait for her release when I went back to India, why I didn't contact her, had I forgotten her last line—'don't be sad, we'll meet again'? You don't need to ask, I know, I know. I know I could have kept her alive, brought her back to life, if I had written to her regularly from England, if I could have been with her as soon as I came back—if—if—if all this had been done everything would have been different, I would have had a different life. But do I have to spell out why it did not happen that way? Don't you understand? There was an obstacle—a terrible obstacle, insurmountable—Kajol. With what honour could I go to Mitu—golden-hearted Mitu—who was brimming with trust? Nalini Dalal meant nothing to me, I could cheat her any way I wanted to—but Mitu? It was impossible to confess to her about Kajol, equally impossible to look into her eyes while keeping it a secret. So, here I am.

Besides, I wasn't the same person any more by then; day by day, with conscious effort, I had given myself a different character, reshaped myself. I loathed emotion, I loathed love; I loathed all those famous words—greatness, heroism, ideals. I had concluded they were only colourful gift-wrapping for poison, daggers, fire, damnation. I had concluded that those who live for themselves are the most worthy. Those who don't love, don't sympathize, those who are level-headed all the time, in any circumstances, are the only wise ones. That was how I had wanted to spend my life—in that desperate effort. That was why I killed my wife a little bit at a time, why I became a connoisseur of the flesh of women. I took my lovelessness, my vengeance, to an extreme level. And yet I didn't succeed. I couldn't forget, you know. I didn't go back, but why can I not forget that I did not? Why does Kajol keep coming back? Is this my punishment then? But punishment for what? I committed no crime, I only wanted to do good, to love. Was that my crime? Or did I not love enough, and so I have to suffer? Tell me, tell me something before you go. Am I guilty? Am I unfortunate? Which? Am I detestable? Am I the lover? Which? Am I a murderer? Or a martyr? Which? You heard the testimony of the accused, aren't you going to deliver your verdict now? . . . All right, I won't force you, you don't have to give your verdict right away, let the trial continue for some time more; day after day, night after night, you against me—cross-questioning, arguments, twists of logic, dissect it, tear it apart, take the innards out—and still there's no end to it, there's no one to have the last word. Very well then, I won't keep you any longer, my chauffeur will take you home. Good night. Please come again tomorrow.

1. **Remembering Buddhadeva Bose, 'The Compleat Writer' by Ketaki Kushari Dyson**

2. **Arunava Sinha in conversation with Damayanti Basu Singh, Buddhadeva Bose's daughter**

P.S.

Insights
Interviews
& More . . .

Remembering Buddhadeva Bose, 'The Compleat Writer'

Ketaki Kushari Dyson

This article is essentially based on a lecture I gave at the invitation of the Sahitya Akademi, Delhi, on 11 December 2008. I have retained the informality of the speaking format, developed a few of the ideas a little more fully, which I couldn't do at the lecture because of the constraint of time, and made a few additions in the light of discussions that took place after the talk.

It is a great pleasure, and likewise an honour, to be asked by the Sahitya Akademi to talk about Buddhadeva Bose in Delhi in this year of his birth centenary. We are here to remember one of South Asia's most brilliant writers in the twentieth century, who belongs to both India and Bangladesh, and to the wider world. I have, of course, written a general introduction to him in my book of translations from his poetry,[1] which many readers seem to find helpful, so I shall happily draw your attention to it. If you are interested in the subject, please do read it. Needless to say, I shall be drawing on some of that material here. And I have also written on him in Bengali several times, in various articles and in my new book, *Tisidore*,[2] which is just out, but when I sat down to write this talk, I began to wonder how I could present the gist of such discourses to a Delhi audience within a limited time, and where I should begin. Then, in what seemed like an auspicious nanosecond, the name of a seventeenth-century English classic, deeply buried within me for over half a century, flashed upon my inward eye in my solitude. That book is *The Compleat Angler*, published in 1653, written by Izaac Walton, who lived from 1593 to 1683. It occurred to me how well a phrase like 'The Compleat Writer', modelled on *The Compleat Angler*, would describe Buddhadeva Bose: 'complete' in the sense that all the parts or elements that are needed to make a whole are there, nothing is missing, with the additional suggestions of 'consummate' and 'quintessential'.

It occurred to me how well a phrase like 'The Compleat Writer', modelled on *The Compleat Angler*, would describe Buddhadeva Bose: 'complete' in the sense that all the parts or elements that are needed to make a whole are there, nothing is missing, with the additional suggestions of 'consummate' and 'quintessential'.

Buddhadeva Bose (1908–1974) is the most versatile literary figure in Bengali after Rabindranath Tagore, someone about whom it could be said that Tagore's mantle had come to rest on his shoulders. As a writer, he was a Renaissance man, excelling in every genre, and has left a substantial output; everything hasn't been gathered together in book-form yet. An outstanding poet, he also wrote short stories; novels, ranging from the major family saga *Tithidore* to novels specializing in intense psychological analysis, such as *Raat Bhor Brishti* (Rain Through the Night) and *Golap Keno Kalo* (Why the

Rose is Black); brilliantly word-crafted plays in both prose and verse; and eloquent non-fictional prose such as travelogues, memoirs, and belles-lettres. He was a distinguished editor-publisher, a central figure in the post-Tagore modernist movement in Bengal who helped to change directions, a passionate literary polemicist, a great letter writer, someone who helped to launch the careers of several of his contemporaries and of many younger writers, a creative literary translator who inspired others, and although an intellectually inclined writer and a critic of great acumen, a writer for children also. His entire life, from childhood to his last day, was packed with literary activity bursting at the seams. He was exemplary in his total dedication to his literary vocation, his detailed understanding of what that vocation meant, and his enormous stamina in pursuing it on a daily basis. He lived and breathed literature through good and bad times.

His entire life, from childhood to his last day, was packed with literary activity bursting at the seams. He was exemplary in his total dedication to his literary vocation, his detailed understanding of what that vocation meant, and his enormous stamina in pursuing it on a daily basis.

And what times they were, those times through which, for some of us, our parents' generation lived—the very heart of the twentieth century with all its turmoils, two World Wars and the inter-war years, the Great Depression, the rise of fascism, the decay of the British Empire, the different freedom struggles in India, violent and non-violent, for Bengalis the famine of 1943, the Great Calcutta Killing of 1946, the Partition, of course, with its aftermath, and the subsequent effort to rebuild shattered lives. Now that some of Bose's letters to his younger daughter have been published as a book,[3] we can see him reacting to and commenting on some major political events in the subcontinent in the post-Independence period: from cross-border conflicts and the rise of the Naxalites to the liberation of Bangladesh. He read and travelled extensively, and demonstrated through his life and works that one could be a cosmopolitan and a writer committed to his mother tongue at the same time. Although a fluently bilingual writer, he reserved his most sustained energies for enriching his mother tongue, something which he regarded almost as a sacred task.

It was because of all these thoughts crowding like shadows at the back of my mind that the book-title *The Compleat Angler*, suddenly recalled, gave shape to the phrase 'The Compleat Writer'. I began to derive comfort and inspiration from those two phrases, as from two blocks of dark chocolate. The mind is in some respects like a continuously expanding chest of drawers, which gets crammed with all manner of items we love to hoard, some clearly of value, others seemingly junky, but we cannot always tell which item will suddenly prove its sterling merit one day. Some items disappear into a black hole from which we can never

He read and travelled extensively, and demonstrated through his life and works that one could be a cosmopolitan and a writer committed to his mother tongue at the same time. Although a fluently bilingual writer, he reserved his most sustained energies for enriching his mother tongue…

retrieve them. Others linger in a ragged state, and the expanding chest clings obstinately to them, refusing to let go, until one day, in one of the obscure recesses, we spy a glint, lynx-eyes in a dark bush, and we recognize something precious, something that could be put to use. Thus did the name of a book, stored in my mind from my student days, come to my rescue when I was fishing for a cue on how to begin my task of writing this talk. Fishing is an apt metaphor in the context of the name of the book: *The Compleat Angler*.

Thus did the name of a book, stored in my mind from my student days, come to my rescue when I was fishing for a cue on how to begin my task of writing this talk. Fishing is an apt metaphor in the context of the name of the book: *The Compleat Angler*.

As a gesture of thanksgiving to this process, I want to read you two of Bose's sonnets on this very process of retrieval, which I translated in my *Selected Poems of Buddhadeva Bose*.[4] There is a third sonnet too, which I didn't translate; all three are very famous poems in the canon of modern Bengali poetry.

To Memory: 1

It's you I accept as Goddess. There's nothing that's not yours.
What I call the well-spring, the root cause, is really your sleep:
intact even on the horizon, stealthily it creeps,
but if, half glancing, you turn in bed, a lush wonder flowers,

and glossy grapes kiss the earth, turning it to wine.
So the canvas lies blank, stone's inert, the vina just a jarring
    whine
till you teach us how to cross the surf, navigate the main,
till you lead us beyond the track, the rugged terrain

of warring night and day, to eternity's peaceful plain,
from far to farther, to another birth, the prehistoric cerulean
where, in a matrix, like a cluster of stars, burn

man's destiny and your unending treasures.
Darkness is what you own, but greater than light is that dark,
and utterly valueless is what you idly discard.

(6–7 May 1955)

To Memory: 2

'Tree', 'flower', 'pond', 'cloudy day': are dry mathematical symbols,
merely abstract, till you raise the curtain and show that my
eyes too are yours.
The vine trails over my body, a field bursts into sudden yellow
flowers,
dyeing the sky-line. And thus I come to claim the earth, stars,
and all else.

War flares; the citizen runs abroad, roaming from shore to shore,
losing in an instant letters, pictures, manuscripts, all that cold
store;
but still he won't lose you, for the pole star is your sign,
which never sets elsewhere and is of all hoards the inner gold mine.

On a straight road we walk. Ants in procession, along the
diligent miles,
carry the corpse of a huge insect through childhood, the youthful
years,
even dragging from age to age documents, signatures, files,

till gradually men's countless children grow old and disappear.
But through your heart must he walk—whoever wishes to go
back,
for only you know that pathway—that fine, curved, effortless
track.

(8 May 1955, afternoon)

Buddhadeva was born on 30 November 1908 in Comilla, now in Bangladesh, the first-born child of his parents. His mother, just sixteen years old at that time, died of postnatal tetanus within twenty-four hours of giving birth. He was brought up by his maternal grandparents, who doted on their only grandchild. For all practical purposes, they were his parents. He addressed his maternal grandmother as 'Ma'. For some time, while the family lived in the country town of Noakhali, he was educated at home by his maternal grandfather Chintaharan Sinha, a mild-mannered man who served in the police force, but who should have really been a schoolteacher. Noakhali, on the destructive river Meghna, later to hit the headlines because of communal riots and then become famous because of Gandhi's presence there (about which Buddhadeva has written eloquently), was in those days a sleepy outpost of the British Indian Empire, but again not so sleepy in other respects. It had a town hall with Doric columns, housing a public library, an indoor sports centre, and an auditorium with a well-equipped stage for cultural activities. The young Buddhadeva became the child prodigy of this mofussil town. Chintaharan taught him English, introduced him to Sanskrit, and showered him with books and magazines in Bengali. The boy became a voracious reader in two languages, started writing torrents of

> **The boy became a voracious reader in two languages, started writing torrents of poetry and prose in his mother tongue and sending them off to magazines, and soon saw himself in print. He launched his own handwritten magazine and organized amateur theatricals.**

poetry and prose in his mother tongue and sending them off to magazines, and soon saw himself in print. He launched his own handwritten magazine and organized amateur theatricals.

In 1922 the family moved to Dhaka, where Buddhadeva had his formal education, first at school, then at the Intermediate level, and finally at the university, where he read English Literature, and from which he duly took his bachelor's and master's degrees with great distinction. 'Dacca' University, as the name was spelt then in English, was in those days a well-appointed new campus founded by the British along Oxbridge lines. Its library was well-equipped, its teaching staff highly qualified, and it was vibrant with cultural activities in which both students and teachers participated. Buddhadeva spent a crucial, formative period of his life in the city of Dhaka, some nine and a half years in all. It was during his years there that he published his first novel, his first collection of stories, and his first two collections of poetry, one consisting of his juvenilia and the other gathering together his first batch of 'adult' poetry, poems which drew the admiration of Tagore. Dhaka was where he first heard Tagore speak and where he met Nazrul Islam. It was in his Dhaka years that he wrote in the avant-garde magazine *Kallol*, staged his own play in the campus, started his

Buddhadeva spent a crucial, formative period of his life in the city of Dhaka, some nine and a half years in all. It was during his years there that he published his first novel, his first collection of stories, and his first two collections of poetry…

own magazine *Pragati*, with friend, fellow student, and fellow poet Ajit Datta as a co-editor, first in a handwritten and then in a printed format. Noakhali was where he had become aware of the non-cooperation movement, where he had taken to spinning cotton thread as thick as ropes and as matted as a sannyasi's locks, but it was in Dhaka that he learnt to reject violence as a political means. Dhaka was also where he first met his future wife, Protiva, who eventually became an author in her own right.

In the context of Bengali writing, Buddhadeva belongs to the cluster of writers whom we group together in the convenient category of post-Tagore moderns. Such labels are rough-and-ready, and need to be understood as such.

In 1931, after obtaining his MA degree, Buddhadeva migrated to Calcutta in pursuit of a literary career. Calcutta was, of course, the hub of the Bengali publishing industry. And he did succeed in establishing himself as a professional writer there, though financially it was a hard struggle for him in the thirties and forties, and it continued to be intermittently so through the fifties and sixties, right up to his death in 1974. But economic struggles could never break his resolve to pursue a literary career.

His writing career had several phases of development, and obviously I cannot deal with them in any detail in a talk like this. All I can do here is pull out some important threads from a rich story. In the context of Bengali writing, Buddhadeva belongs to the cluster of writers whom we group together in the convenient category of post-Tagore moderns. Such labels are rough-and-ready, and need to be understood as such. Chronologically, Tagore's long life meant that his last phase coincided with the emergence of the new writers. Tagore was continuously renewing himself, and every writer of grit is of course a modern in his or her own time. Yet some demarcation is useful to separate someone who grew up in the second half of the nineteenth century from those who clearly belong to the twentieth. Tagore had shaped the modern literary Bengali which the younger writers could not help using: it was their natural heritage. It was Tagore's gift to them, and for this they were forever obliged to him. Yet they wanted to express new themes in it, reflect in its mirror the new concerns of a less stable, more complicated, more fractured and angst-ridden period of history. They never disowned him or lost their respect for him. But he was a mountain-range, and they fretted at being in the rain-shadow area of such a mountain. They wanted to put their own marks on the landscape. To those born almost half a century after him he was a grandfather-figure, and at some stage grandchildren need to go their own way. Bose, as a representative of the youngest generation of these aspiring writers, played a crucial role in this process of differentiation. As he recalled in his later years, his generation had to arrive at some kind of negotiation with Tagore:

Tagore had shaped the modern literary Bengali which the younger writers could not help using: it was their natural heritage. It was Tagore's gift to them, and for this they were forever obliged to him.

'a negotiation—that is to say, an arrangement, or it might be called, from our point of view, an act of getting ready, so that we did not remain forever trapped in his vast net, so that he could become bearable and usable for us.'[5] Bose retained his affectionate relationship with Tagore till the very end, visiting him in Santiniketan, and Tagore recognized him as a new voice, but a degree of rebellion against the older figure was inevitable, because the zeitgeist was shifting. Professor Sibnarayan Ray, whose words I have quoted in my introduction to Bose's poems, has summed up the confrontation between the generations very aptly, so let me quote him again:

Bose retained his affectionate relationship with Tagore till the very end, visiting him in Santiniketan, and Tagore recognized him as a new voice, but a degree of rebellion against the older figure was inevitable.

> Against his [that is to say, Tagore's] intuitive apprehension of cosmic and personal harmony the accent now was increasingly on the inevitability, even the desirability, of conflict and disorder; to his joy of existence were opposed passionate feelings of frustration, anguish and anger; his aesthetic gracefulness was challenged by underlining the social reality of violence, exploitation and squalor; and the mystic-religious dimension which related his love lyrics, especially of the middle period of his career, to the tradition of the Vaishnavas, Bauls and Sufis, was rejected in favour of a more overtly sex-oriented, secular and tormented eroticism.[6]

This is the core of the modernist project in Bengal. Strangely, I have noticed that some people seem to locate the arrival of modernism in Indian writing in the fifties or sixties,[7] but that is because they are not looking beyond English-language writing for its signs. In the pan-Indian perspective, the native Indian languages must surely be included in the map. The adjective 'Indian' makes no sense otherwise. From the point of view of Bengali writing, the twenties and thirties of the last century were a period of intense creative turmoil. The prose poems of Tagore's *Lipika* (1922) were a significant formal innovation; his novel *Shesher Kavita* (1929) incorporated a discourse on modernism itself, and Tagore almost reinvented himself in his collections of poetry in the last decade of his life. The magazine *Pragati*, run by Bose as an undergraduate in Dhaka between 1927 and 1929, with the help of his friend Ajit Datta, made a remarkable contribution to the modernist movement which was brewing in Bengal in the twenties. It was here that Jibanananda Das, senior to Bose by nine years, emerged as a new voice in Bengali poetry, where Bose 'discovered' and established him as a poet, and where Bose defended him against jibes emanating from certain critics of the Old Guard. New writers were vigorously defended on the platform of *Pragati*, but for doing so, Bose earned the relentless

The magazine *Pragati*, run by Bose as an undergraduate in Dhaka between 1927 and 1929, with the help of his friend Ajit Datta, made a remarkable contribution to the modernist movement which was brewing in Bengal in the twenties.

hostility of the conservative magazine *Shanibarer Chithi*. In 1926 Bose wrote his rebellious poem 'Bandir Bandana' (A Prisoner's Song of Praise), in which the teenaged poet recast the relationship between the Creator and his own creative self. Typically, in a mature Tagorean image, the human poet would be a flute on which God played his tunes. But the youthful Bose rejected such images. 'A perpetual prisoner in the instincts' inescapable cage—that's how you've made me, my ruthless creator!' According to his testimony, he was born a prisoner, but improved his lot through his own creativity.

In 1935 Bose founded the poetry magazine *Kavita*, which he edited with loving care for a quarter-century. *Kavita* became the leading Bengali poetry magazine of its time, where all important poets aspired to be published.

You gave me desire, as dark as a moonless
night:
from that I've moulded love, mixing it
with the honey of my dreams.

......

I am a poet, and this is my pride—
I have created this music in exalted
delight.
This is my pride—that your mistakes I
have rectified
with my own dedicated enterprise.[8]

In 1930 Bose published his first adult collection of poetry, which took its name from this very poem 'Bandir Bandana', thrown to God as a mocking challenge in the guise of a song of praise. The collection marks a new, defiant beginning in Bengali poetry. In 1935 Bose founded the poetry magazine *Kavita*, which he edited with loving care for a quarter-century. *Kavita* became the leading Bengali poetry magazine of its time, where all important poets aspired to be published. It was also an extremely important magazine for the discussion and review of poetry. Bose was a superb stylist in critical prose, and some of us learnt how to write book reviews and other forms of literary criticism, using him as our model. He also set up a publishing unit for his magazine, calling it Kavitabhavan, 'The House of Poetry'. He took on the role of an editor-publisher while fellow poets paid for the printing of their collections. All activities were run from the poet's home. Between 1937 and 1966, he lived with his family in a first-floor apartment at 202 Rashbehari Avenue in southern Calcutta. Affectionately known as '202', this apartment home of the poet became an institution in the city's arts world, where writers, intellectuals, publishers, and their friends dropped in for endless cups of tea and animated addas late into the night. It was a platform and a network of which poets anywhere in the world would be proud. Bose's influence was seminal on younger poets and critics, and he was invariably generous and helpful to anyone in whom he detected literary promise.

In Calcutta, a city he loved and was very loyal to, Bose nevertheless faced the struggles of a migrant from East Bengal

In Calcutta, a city he loved and was very loyal to, Bose nevertheless faced the struggles of a migrant from East Bengal and never really got the academic job he deserved, except for a brief period at Jadavpur University.

and never really got the academic job he deserved, except for a brief period at Jadavpur University. Humayun Kabir got him involved in the setting up of an Arts Faculty at Jadavpur, and Bose set up a Department of Comparative Literature there, joining it as Head in 1956. In 1963 he had to resign from this job under circumstances which have never been satisfactorily explained, but it is clear that there was some academic politics behind it. There must have been an anti-Bose lobby which eased him out. Bose has referred to this incident as 'a deep wound' in his life. He deserves to be remembered as the person who introduced the discipline of Comparative Literature to India. He was devoted to his department, was a successful and popular teacher there, and several of his students and colleagues in that department have become noted writers in Bengali.

This interest in Comparative Literature, which he gained from his teaching experience and travels in America, ties in with his long-standing interest in literary translation. Bose believed passionately in the importance and validity of the creative translation of poetry, and practised this art from the beginning of his literary career. His most famous translations in this field are his verse translation of Kalidasa's *Meghaduta*, for which he forged a suitable Bengali equivalent of the mandakranta metre,

He deserves to be remembered as the person who introduced the discipline of Comparative Literature to India. He was devoted to his department, was a successful and popular teacher there, and several of his students and colleagues in that department have become noted writers in Bengali.

with long, meandering lines of astonishing fluency and beauty, and his translations of the poetry of Charles Baudelaire, Rainer Maria Rilke, and Friedrich Hölderlin into Bengali, which made these foreign poets our kinsmen, without destroying their slight alterity. These spectacular achievements made a deep impact on our generation and influenced the style and diction of original poetry written in Bengali in the fifties and sixties. Indeed, the activity of poetry translation had an influence on the evolution of Bose's own poetic style in the mid-fifties. One can see it clearly in his collection 'Je-Andhar Alor Adhik' (The Darkness that is Greater Than Light, 1958), which is regarded as a second thrust towards modernism in his poetic career, after the initial thrust with 'Bandir Bandana', published in 1930. The two sonnets I read out earlier are from this collection of 1958.

Bose's experience of teaching in various American campuses also bore fruit in his own work. The need to teach courses in epic poetry drew his attention afresh to the great Indian epics and led him to study them in depth. This study led him to write some remarkable plays using and reinterpreting old stories from that hoard, and his mature poetry also shows a penchant for weaving both foreign and native Indian myths and legends into the fabric of his work. He is equally at home with the Indian story of *Rishyasringa* and

He is equally at home with the Indian story of *Rishyasringa* and the Greek story of *Icarus*, with the story of Arjun and the story of Elektra. The renewed study of the Mahabharata led also to the essays in interpretation published as *Mahabharater Katha*.

the Greek story of *Icarus*, with the story of Arjun and the story of Elektra. The renewed study of the Mahabharata led also to the essays in interpretation published as *Mahabharater Katha*. He was working on a planned second volume of this book when he died. The first volume was translated by Sujit Mukherjee as *The Book of Yudhisthir*. I must say that I find it difficult to forgive the people who denied Bose a research fellowship at Simla, when he was soldiering on with this work with very little money, his wife ill and immobilized, and his own health deteriorating.

A fascinating aspect of his personality is Bose the traveller. His travels within India and abroad have left powerful ripples in his writings, and are recorded in memorable travelogues which are charged with poetry, humour, and intellectuality.

A fascinating aspect of his personality is Bose the traveller. His travels within India and abroad have left powerful ripples in his writings, and are recorded in memorable travelogues which are charged with poetry, humour, and intellectuality. They still have the power to hold our attention and provoke us to ponder and mull social and political issues. I would like to read to you my translation of his famous poem 'Chilkay Sakaal', written when he was approaching his twenty-sixth birthday.[9]

Morning in Chilka

Ah, how very happy I have felt this morning—
how can I say it!

How spotlessly blue is this sky, how unbearably beautiful,
like a master singer's raga variations spreading unrestrained
from horizon to horizon!

Ah, how good I've felt gazing at this sky—
green hills curving all around, hazy in the mist,
Chilka glinting in the middle.

You came over, sat by me awhile, then strolled to the other side
to see the train that had come and stopped at the station.
The train left.—How much I love you –
how can I say it!

The sun floods the sky, dazzles the eyes.
The cows graze with total attention—how tranquil!
—Had you ever thought—coming here, beside this lake we
would find
what we hadn't found so long?

The silvery water lies dreaming, while all the sky
streams on its bosom in a flow of blue
with the sun's kisses.—That here a gorgeous rainbow would blaze
circling the ocean of your blood and mine—
had you ever imagined it?

Yesterday sailing on the Chilka we had seen
two butterflies coming along—flying over the water
for such a long distance.—How bold! You'd laughed,
and how I had loved

that wonderful, radiant happiness of yours! See, see
how blue this sky is.—And in your eyes tremble
so many skies, deaths, new births—
how can I say it!

(11 November 1934, Chilka, Orissa)

Likewise, he observed and incorporated foreign landscapes in his poetry and prose, adding a fresh dimension to the Bengali language. Travelling abroad matured him as a humanist intellectual of his times, and he met and interacted with eminent contemporary writers such as Henry Miller, Allen Ginsberg, George Oppen, and Stephen Spender.

His journey towards an international outlook had indeed begun long ago, when he was growing up in Dhaka, not only through his voracious reading, but also through sustained correspondence with Prabhucharan Guhathakurta...

His journey towards an international outlook had indeed begun long ago, when he was growing up in Dhaka, not only through his voracious reading, but also through sustained correspondence with Prabhucharan Guhathakurta, a friend and relative, a mentor-like figure slightly senior to him, who went abroad for higher studies and wrote to him regularly. Let me go to a passage from Bose's memoirs about this, which I translated in my book:

> During Prabhucharan's stay abroad my communication with him was without a break. Ceaselessly I wrote to him, and ceaselessly got his letters. When letters take three months or so to go back and forth, it is not really possible to conduct a proper dialogue; it is only possible for each to describe his present moments, a speaking out through letters in the literal sense. Happily, both parties were extraordinary in their zeal and speed in the matter of composing letters. We were both what is called effusive types of personality, and we did not lack subjects in which we were both equally

interested. From Boston, from Los Angeles, from Santa Fé—sometimes from the compartment of a Pullman train—then from London, Rome, Paris, Berlin, Stockholm came letter after letter from him, and with them books from different countries, and monthly and weekly magazines—piles of them—such diversity! From the moment I got one of his letters in my hand, my enjoyment of it began: rows of foreign stamps, paper as crisp as ironed cloth; names of streets and hotels in so many unknown languages—and inside, so many stories, so many items of new information, such affectionate greetings! Books came: Ibsen, Maeterlinck, Gorky, Andreiev, Oscar Wilde, Sean O'Casey, volumes of contemporary American poetry. Illustrated programmes of Moscow Art Theatre's New York season found their way to me. Enclosed with letters, newspaper cuttings came too—on the dancing of Pavlova, the acting of Duse, performances of Chopin's music. Even those items that I didn't entirely follow had something to give me—an intoxicating scent on the bodies of the books, the polish of printing, pictures, and the touch of breezes from far lands. The whole of the Western world, spread from California to Russia, its art, literature, way of life, its living geography, so many rivers, cities, and men and women not seen with my eyes but waxing real in my mind—this it was that Prabhucharan gave

From the moment I got one of his letters in my hand, my enjoyment of it began: rows of foreign stamps, paper as crisp as ironed cloth; names of streets and hotels in so many unknown languages—and inside, so many stories, so many items of new information, such affectionate greetings!

> me as a gift, from my fourteenth to my sixteenth year, when I was emerging from the ground like a sapling, wanting to lift my thin branches up to the sky that arched over the whole world.[10]

His political thinking, as evident in his writings and published correspondence, was strikingly mature. In his faith in non-violence, democracy, secularism, and pluralism, he was a true child of his times, and his deep distrust of violence, dictatorship, and Stalinist-style autocracy was far-seeing…

What began so auspiciously matured in his later years into a deep wisdom which rejected narrow, tribal-style nationalism in favour of international humanism—ideas in a direct line of descent from Tagore, but backed up by his own experience. This philosophy finds memorable expression in the letters he wrote to his younger daughter Damayanti when she was studying in the USA and later when she was living in Kanpur.[11] His political thinking, as evident in his writings and published correspondence, was strikingly mature. In his faith in non-violence, democracy, secularism, and pluralism, he was a true child of his times, and his deep distrust of violence, dictatorship, and Stalinist-style autocracy was far-seeing, though his refusal to align himself with the political left did have some consequences for his image and publicity when the left came to dominate political life in West Bengal. There has been some cultural politics around his name, and his cosmopolitanism has been misinterpreted. After his death, his figure was to some extent neglected and marginalized. He was given credit as a critic, as a translator, as an editor, as an impresario in respect of other poets, but not given enough credit as a poet in his own right. While his plays have received some attention, not enough attention has been paid to his novels and short stories, which have made a unique and brilliant contribution to Bengali fiction. However, through the dedicated efforts of his daughter Damayanti over the past decade there is now a genuine revival of interest in his works and he is beginning to receive from posterity the attention he deserves.

This discussion will not be complete unless I acknowledge my personal debt to Buddhadeva Bose. Dhaka is the crucial initial link in the chain. My father was also a student at Dhaka University, two years junior to Buddhadeva, and they also had common friends.

This discussion will not be complete unless I acknowledge my personal debt to Buddhadeva Bose. Dhaka is the crucial initial link in the chain. My father was also a student at Dhaka University, two years junior to Buddhadeva, and they also had common friends. Formally, my father's subject was economics, but his life's passion was languages and literatures, and he read widely not only in English literature, but also in French and German, and knew many of the contemporary Bengali writers. His friendship with Buddhadeva continued in Calcutta, which is where I met the poet. In the forties and fifties I enjoyed the privilege of visiting the famous apartment home of the Boses in 202 Rashbehari Avenue. It was in their book-packed front room that as a teenager, I first met many well-known contemporary writers and editors, and even the scientist Satyendranath Bose, the Bose of bosons.

Buddhadeva saw the poetry I wrote in childhood and encouraged me to carry on writing, and occasionally gave me some advice. I was brought up on the back issues of *Kavita* and was influenced by his ideas on, and practice of, poetry translation. My translations of Anglo-Saxon poetry into alliterative Bengali half-lines were done under that kind of influence. Without even being aware of it, I possibly learnt from him a trick or two on how to describe foreign landscapes in the medium of Bengali, and above all, how to be internationally minded and at the same time keep writing in my mother tongue from abroad. I learnt from him that no matter how many other languages we learnt, it would be good for us as creative writers to keep writing in our mother tongues, even in difficult circumstances. When I settled in England after my marriage, he feared that I would not be able to continue writing in Bengali, but luckily, I was able to prove him wrong. My survival as a diasporic writer in Bengali for half a century owes him a great spiritual debt.

Without even being aware of it, I possibly learnt from him a trick or two in how to describe foreign landscapes in the medium of Bengali, and above all, how to be internationally minded and at the same time keep writing in my mother tongue from abroad.

Buddhadeva believed that in order to write with authenticity and to develop their potentials fully, creative writers really had to engage with their mother tongues and write in them, not in a language that was a colonial legacy. This belief earned him some hostility from the 'Indo-Anglian' lobby that was emerging in his time. It is curious how he has been buffeted by different winds of cultural politics: the anti-modernist Bengali Old Guard have ridiculed him and even brought the charge of obscenity against him, the left have found him leaning too much to the West, lacking in sufficient commitment to 'the people', while the 'Indo-Anglians' have disapproved of his view that writers should write in their mother tongues, which are of course the languages close to 'the people'. Now that 'Indian English writing' has achieved wide acclaim, nationally and internationally, both that event and Bose's own commitment to the mother tongue need to be looked at with new eyes. I have made some comments in the section entitled 'Translator's Testament' in my *Selected Poems of Buddhadeva Bose*, and here are some further thoughts.

The high noon of 'Indian English writing' is a complex phenomenon with many ambiguities embedded in it. English has indeed penetrated India far more than in Bose's time, but unevenly, and at certain levels only. Most of rural India is still unaffected by it, and vast swathes of the lower middle classes and the urban working classes relate to the English language only at superficial levels. Its hold is greatest in the metropolises, and amongst those who receive their education in the medium of English. It is from this class that 'Indian English' writers are

The high noon of 'Indian English writing' is a complex phenomenon with many ambiguities embedded in it. English has indeed penetrated India far more than in Bose's time, but unevenly, and at certain levels only.

recruited, and those who write exclusively in English, their only viable literary language, constitute a powerful group.

The literary scene in India is in reality heterogeneous and variegated. There are large numbers of people everywhere, from the big cities to the country towns, who, though able to read English-language material and handle the language for official purposes, would not choose English as their medium of creative self-expression. They would choose their first languages for that purpose. Some writers in India also write bilingually.

Buddhadeva's passionate commitment to the mother tongue has a deep relevance not only in the multilingual subcontinent, but also in the world at large. I see it as his loyalty to the long-term interests of his native language.

Buddhadeva's passionate commitment to the mother tongue has a deep relevance not only in the multilingual subcontinent, but also in the world at large. I see it as his loyalty to the long-term interests of his native language. Languages are the cultural equivalents of the rainforests, storehouses preserving intellectual diversity. We have to see to it that this living diversity does not shrink. How do we do it? The point is that unless we actually write in a language, we cannot augment and enrich its treasury of concepts. It is only when we write in a language in an active, sustained, and committed manner over a long period that we can seed it with new ideas and see those ideas grow, flourish, and bear fruit. 'Now more than ever seems it'[12] needful for us to grasp this, now that 'Indian English' has been conceptualized as an

Indian language and is being consciously developed as the lingua franca of the pan-Indian urban elite. Powerful forces of cultural entrepreneurship and patronage, as well as commercial interests within the educational establishments, the media, the academia, and the publishing industry are at work in this project. India has now become a major publisher of English-language books. A large section of the English-educated urban middle classes in India now read only English-language material. Books written in English receive instant pan-Indian publicity and media coverage, while books written in the native Indian languages are reviewed only in the papers and magazines of those particular languages. There is the obvious issue of sales. A book written in English can potentially reach not only the pan-Indian elite, but also a large international audience and be translated from English into many other languages. Western readers like to read books with an Indian connection but written in English. All in all, it is a question of the location of power: there has been an immense escalation in the 'post-colonial' power and prestige of 'Indian English writing', within the country and abroad. The genre developed by a narrow apex of the society has become a powerhouse, because the social apex of a subcontinent is nevertheless a sizeable affair, with plenty of talented, educated people to make good use of the available opportunities. English

India has now become a major publisher of English-language books. A large section of the English-educated urban middle classes in India now reads only English-language material. Books written in English receive instant pan-Indian publicity and media coverage...

departments in India and abroad have gladly taken over books from this sector and expanded their syllabi, while teachers and postgraduate students have contributed to research in the field.

Inevitably, there is a fallout from this process for those who wish to write seriously in the native Indian languages and nourish and vitalize them. We are under pressure. As contemporary writers in the Indian languages, we do not enter the ongoing literary discourse at the pan-Indian level, but are kept at the 'regional' level by the overarching, hegemonic presence of English. Abroad, it sometimes seems that scholars have almost forgotten that Indian writers may write in languages other than English. I sometimes wonder what Bose would have made of this situation. For those of us writing in our original languages while in diaspora, our work necessarily entails additional struggles at many levels that are not discussed or even understood by others. It is in sustaining these critical struggles that Buddhadeva's inspiration has been extremely important in my life, operating at a very deep level. Though I was not able to interact with him directly as an adult, he has always been there, a profound influence at the very centre of my literary life and a presence in the subterranean layers of the psyche.

For those of us writing in our original languages while in diaspora, our work necessarily entails additional struggles at many levels that are not discussed or even understood by others. It is in sustaining these critical struggles that Buddhadeva's inspiration has been extremely important in my life, operating at a very deep level.

A writer of Bose's stature deserves to be translated into the major modern languages of India. It is our duty to promote and disseminate his works at a pan-Indian and an international level. Our writers need to be translated both for the internal Indian market and for the international market, even if it means some use of a link language. I know that my translations of his poetry into English did find Bose some new readers in Europe, and not only among speakers of English. The book also found a Hungarian, a Slovenian, and a Finnish reader. The Finnish reader, Hannele Pohjanmies, herself a noted translator, was so deeply affected by the poem 'Calcutta' that she re-translated it into Finnish and published it in a magazine. She told me that she was reading it every night and that it was affecting her almost physically. Since then she has studied more of the poems carefully, has translated a few more for her creative pleasure, and is always asking me relevant questions by email. When we organized an event to commemorate Bose in London in May 2008, Hannele sent us a short message. She would like me to read it out in Delhi also. So here is her message:

> Ladies and gentlemen! Greetings from Finland, far away in the North!
>
> Poems are like migratory birds—they fly across seas and borders, following no tracks, just a mysterious instinct.
>
> I am so glad that some exotic poems have found their way from the Tropic

Our writers need to be translated both for the internal Indian market and for the international market, even if it means some use of a link language. I know that my translations of his poetry into English did find Bose some new readers in Europe, and not only among speakers of English.

of Cancer to the Arctic Circle, which goes across Finland. Thanks to Ketaki Kushari Dyson: her English translations have opened the possibility and shown the way. When I acquired the *Selected Poems of Buddhadeva Bose*, I was not planning to translate any of them; my hands were full of the poems of Rabindranath Tagore. But those poems started 'climbing up my body like a shrub', as Bose writes in his poem 'Nostalgia'.

When I acquired the *Selected Poems of Buddhadeva Bose*, I was not planning to translate any of them; my hands were full of the poems of Rabindranath Tagore. But those poems started 'climbing up my body like a shrub', as Bose writes in his poem 'Nostalgia'.

I am happy to announce that the first of my translations, the magnificent poem 'Calcutta', will be published in a Finnish poetry magazine very soon, in a few weeks.

The poems of Buddhadeva Bose are full of strange enchantment and they touch my heart in a special way. I send my greetings to your festival, where you are celebrating him! I cannot send flowers through the air, but I send my love with the first stanza of the Finnish 'Calcutta'—'Kalkutta':

Kerran kauan sitten Kalkutta oli
  silmissäni vailla vertaa,
  ihmeellisen kaunis,
kuin unen alku, tai outo kukka jonka
  mielikuvitus on luonut.

Sen pölyssä, sen tuulessa, kuumassa
  metalisessa hengityksessä
    intohimoni huusivat äänen.

Thank you!
[Hannele Pohjanmies[13]]

I should mention that since she sent this message, her translation has indeed been published. To bring this distant reader of Bose into the loop, I would like to read you my translation of this poem, 'Calcutta', which affected her so profoundly.[14] We might call this poem, written in 1953, Bose's love-poem to the city where he had made it as a writer in the thirties and forties, a poem which encapsulates chapters of our history—World War II, 1943, 1946, 1947 are all implicitly mentioned—and which blends powerful emotions with a terrific capacity for writing long lines and sustaining sinewy syntax over the length of a poem. The poem has a historical value now, for we know that in some ways the city has changed, but the text still connects us to its essence. As I read this poem, I feel reconnected to the city in which I grew up.

We might call this poem, written in 1953, Bose's love-poem to the city where he had made it as a writer in the thirties and forties, a poem which encapsulates chapters of our history—World War II, 1943, 1946, 1947 are all implicitly mentioned...

Notes

1. *The Selected Poems of Buddhadeva Bose*, Translated and Introduced by Ketaki Kushari Dyson, Oxford University Press, New Delhi, 2003. Henceforth referred to as SPBB.
2. Dyson, Ketaki K., *Tisidore*, Ananda Publishers Private Ltd., Calcutta, 2008.
3. *Buddhadeb Basur Chithi: Kanishtha Kanya Rumike*, ed. by Damayanti Basu Singh, Vikalp, Calcutta, 2006.
4. SPBB, pp. 72–3.
5. See SPBB, p. xv and p. lxi. The fragment is translated from Bose's autobiographical *Amar Jauban*, M.C. Sarkar & Sons, Calcutta, 1989 reprint, p. 25. The biographical outline in my Introduction to SPBB does, of course, draw many details from the three volumes of memoirs penned by Bose: *Amar Chhelebela*, *Amar Jauban*, and *Amader Kavitabhavan*. The last volume was left unfinished at the time of his death. All three can now be found conveniently in the first volume of his *Prabandha-samagra*, published by Paschimbanga Bangla Akademi in 2005.
6. See SPBB, p. xv and p. lxi. The fragment is quoted from Ray's *Introduction to Ray* and *Maddern* (editors), I have seen *Bengal's face: A Selection of modern Bengali poetry in English translation*, Editions Indian, Calcutta, 1974, p. 15.
7. See, for instance, Jeet Thayil or Bruce King, in *Fulcrum*, an annual of poetry and aesthetics, published from Cambridge MA, Number Four, 2005, pp. 232–37 and pp. 366–81. Thayil seems to date 'modern Indian poetry' from the publication of Nissim Ezekiel's first book in 1952 and says that 'Tagore was the last important poet before Ezekiel' (pp. 234–36). Discussing the bilingual poet Arun Kolatkar, King does acknowledge, en passant, the existence of 'a Marathi modernist tradition' (p. 378).
8. SPBB, p. 3.
9. SPBB, pp. 17–18.
10. SPBB, pp. xxv–xxvi.
11. See note no. 3 above.
12. I am echoing Keats's line 'Now more than ever seems it rich to die', from his 'Ode to a Nightingale'.
13. Thanks to an audiotape sent by Hannele, I was able to train myself to read out the Finnish fragment in both London and

Delhi; there was no speaker of Finnish among the audiences to detect any mistakes! Now, in 2013, I should add that Hannele has re-translated many more poems of Bose from my English versions, creating a circle of admirers for his poetry in her native land.

14. See SPBB, pp. 62–6. I did indeed read out this poem at my Delhi lecture, but it is a long poem, spanning five pages, and so I request readers to kindly look it up in my SPBB. Published in 2009 in the web magazine *Parabaas* (www.parabaas.com) and reprinted with the editor's permission.

Arunava Sinha in conversation with Damayanti Basu Singh

AS: *Black Rose—Golap Keno Kalo*—was one of Buddhadeva Bose's last novels. Would you call it the epitome of his fiction?

DBS: Among his last novels—*Black Rose* (1967); *Ayenar Modhye Eka* (Alone in the Mirror, 1968); *Bipanno Bishmoy* (Distressed Wonder, 1969); and his last novel *Rukmi* (written in 1971 and published in 1972)—*Black Rose* could be considered an ideal example of the narrative style of Bose's fiction. Many of his earlier novels and stories were written following a style that many reviewers labelled 'stream of consciousness'.

...*Black Rose* could be considered an ideal example of the narrative style of Bose's fiction. Many of his earlier novels and stories were written following a style that many reviewers labelled 'stream of consciousness'.

AS: Where would you place *Black Rose* in the context of Buddhadeva Bose's oeuvre of fiction in terms of content, theme and style—especially compared to his poetic epic *Tithidore* (When the Time Is Right) or his searingly uncompromising *Raat Bhor Brishti* (It Rained All Night)?

DBS: Well, as I have already said, *Black Rose* does represent Buddhadeva Bose's writing style, but it would be incorrect to say this is restricted to his fiction. His prose was poetic, at times magical, no matter what he wrote. You can go through his essays, travelogues, plays, literary reviews or analytical academic writings—*Mahabharater Katha* (Stories from the Mahabharata), for instance, and you will see that the narrative style is always poetic. As a writer of fiction, he would always weave the story in with beautiful language and style, without losing its masculinity, clarity and force. *Black Rose* is a great example of this characteristic.

Much like Rabindranath Tagore, Buddhadeva Bose was first and foremost a poet, a master of his language, moulding it in any way he liked. Like Tagore, he is considered a complete writer. At the same time, he was a highly cerebral writer and usually not a simple storyteller. In that sense, he wasn't what you might call a 'popular novelist'.

Much like Rabindranath Tagore, Buddhadeva Bose was first and foremost a poet, a master of his language, moulding it in any way he liked. Like Tagore, he is considered a complete writer. At the same time, he was a highly cerebral writer and usually not a simple storyteller.

His novels and short stories dealt with various aspects of life, including politics, religion and society, but I think what intrigued him most was the human mind—the psychological aspects of human behaviour and thought. He himself was the protagonist in many of his novels, he spoke through them. As a result, his own thoughts on art, literature, music, poetry and sociopolitical issues were often reflected in his fiction. And as he moved from one genre to another, his style remained the same, but obviously not the theme or content. That's why the same author who wrote *Tithidore*—the happy family drama in the 1940s—could later write *Raat Bhor Brishti*, depicting the hollowness of marital bliss, or *Black Rose*, a fascinatingly long monologue of a lonely man delving deep into his past as he is overcome by a feeling of nostalgia. The themes and contents of these stories are very different, but the style of writing and the poetic language remained unmistakably Buddhadeva Bose's.

Yet, the stories and novels he wrote to fulfil the demands of publishers of the Puja issues of magazines were critically acclaimed. However, it was *Black Rose*, with the slow unfolding of its story and unusual narration style, that was especially admired.

AS: What sort of response did *Black Rose* receive, especially in the context of the charges of obscenity against *Raat Bhor Brishti*?

DBS: It was a time when he was immersed in the Mahabharata and repeatedly expressed his unwillingness to write fiction. Yet, the stories and novels he wrote to fulfil the demands of publishers of the Puja issues of magazines were critically acclaimed. However, it was *Black Rose*, with the slow unfolding of its story and unusual narration style, that was especially admired. In any case, no intelligent reader took the obscenity charge against *Raat Bhor Brishti* seriously—it was another faceless attack on Bose, which, if anything, doubled the sales of the book overnight. Discerning readers had no trouble appreciating the merits of this slim book, which dealt with the complexities of a marital relationship.

AS: Did Buddhadeva Bose write more than one book simultaneously? What else was he writing at the time of *Black Rose*?

DBS: Oh, yes! Always. There was not a single day in the year that he did not write. The last decade of his life was particularly productive and arguably the best phase of his creativity. Consider a list of books published in the same year as *Black Rose*.

Fiction: *Ayenar Modhye Eka*;

Poetry: 'Ekdin Chirodin' (One Day, Always), 'Swagato Biday' (Hello Goodbye);

Drama: *Kolkatar Electra* (Calcutta's Electra), *Satyasandho* (Believer of Truth);

Children's Literature: *Hashir Galpo* (Funny Tales).

Ongoing body of works:

Translating Rilke's poems; Finishing the novel, *Bipanno Bishmoy*;

First drafts of Mahabharata-based plays like *Prothom Partho* (The First Partha) and *Kalsandhya* (Evening of Time).

There was not a single day in the year that he did not write. The last decade of his life was particularly productive and arguably the best phase of his creativity.

AS: What was the secret of Buddhadeva Bose's incredible prolificness without compromising on quality?

DBS: He was born prolific and versatile. He grew up with an unfaltering devotion to literature and never wavered from it even when he was under the enormous pressure to make both ends meet. He couldn't live his life any other way.

Scan QR code to access the
Penguin Random House India website